"I AM THE GUARDIAN, AND I HAVE COME TO HELP YOU OVERTHROW THIS TYRANT AND LIVE LIKE FREE MEN ONCE MORE. LOOK, AND I SHALL DEMONSTRATE MY POWERS!"

Wayne raised his right arm, and a crackling bolt of lightning descended from heaven, striking his arm and making his whole body glow so brightly with electricity that the men around him had to shield their eyes to keep from being blinded.

When he could see they'd had enough, Wayne lowered his arm and the lightning stopped. "The Guardian has powers to challenge this false prophet," he declared. "I will use them in your name, to keep you safe from his tyranny."

But Wayne knew things they did not know. Things about himself . . .

And Not Make
Dreams Your Master

by

Stephen Goldin

FAWCETT GOLD MEDAL • NEW YORK

AND NOT MAKE DREAMS YOUR MASTER

Published by Fawcett Gold Medal Books, a unit of CBS Publications, the Consumer Publishing Division of CBS Inc.

ISBN: 0-449-14410-0

Printed in the United States of America

First Fawcett Gold Medal printing: June 1981

10 9 8 7 6 5 4 3 2 1

this book is dedicated explicitly (as all my books are, at least implicitly) to ROBERT A. HEINLEIN, who Dreamed the Dreams for all of us. . . .
and to Virginia Heinlein, for helping to make him the person he is.

CHAPTER 1

THE CORRIDOR STRETCHED to infinity. Bright tubes of fluorescence above shone down on the smooth white walls and floor. A man and a woman ran down the empty hallway; their shoes should have clattered on the shiny linoleum, but there was no sound in the eerie passage—just the blank walls rushing past. Time was against them, time was the enemy. If they didn't reach their target soon, the terrorists would destroy Los Angeles with their homemade atomic bomb. But the corridor went on and on, and the man and woman ran and ran, never pausing for breath, never stopping to rest. They faced an eternity of running through the silent hall, while around them the world held its breath. They never looked at each other, and their feet glided silently over the smooth floor. They ran.

The end of the hall came suddenly. As they turned the corner a man appeared holding a rifle. He was dressed all in black, with the terrorists' insignia of a red cobra sewn on the left shoulder. He raised his rifle slowly, ever so slowly, to shoot at the pair approaching him.

The running man quickened his pace to deal with this menace, pulling ahead of his female companion. As he did so, the guard . . . changed. His outline wavered and became blurry. He separated into two images of the same guard, Siamese twins holding identical rifles in menacing postures. He/they barred the way, refusing further access.

The running man stopped with impossible quickness to fight this bifurcated threat, but actually the guard seemed to be more of a threat to him/themselves than to anyone else. His/their outline blurred still further, and jumped around the floor, literally trying to pull him/themselves together. The lights dimmed and the walls of the corridor flickered in and out of existence. The fragile thread of reality was on the verge of crumbling.

Then suddenly everything was right again. The walls steadied, the lights brightened. There was only the one guard with one rifle, determined to keep these two intruders away—and totally unaware of his personality split just moments ago.

The running man swung a fist at the guard, his arm drifting in a lazy arc toward the terrorist's face. The punch connected solidly, and the impact was like hitting a pillow. The guard's face exploded in a shower of sparks that rained like fairy dust to the ground. His headless body sagged slowly to the floor, melting into a flesh-colored puddle and then evaporating altogether.

There was a slight ringing sound that only the man and woman could hear. "Come on," the man said to his companion. "There's not much time left. The bomb'll go off in five minutes."

The woman nodded silently and turned into the cross-corridor from which the guard had come. She began running again, and the man joined her, just as the world was fading out around them. . . .

Wayne Corrigan lay in his dimly lit cubicle, panting from the exertion. There was the moment of disorientation he always experienced when switching from Dream to reality, that instant of not knowing what was true and what was pretense; then the world solidified again, and he was "home."

Funny how I think of this place as home, he thought. *I'm only here a few hours every three days, playing make-believe.* And yet, there were times when all that mattered, all that was real to him, was in this small booth, and the outside world faded to insignificance.

He opened his eyes slowly to stare up at the dim

whiteness of the ceiling. His scalp tingled from two dozen fiery prickings, and the sensation reminded him that there was still work to do. This was only an intermission—the last intermission of the evening. Then he'd be trapped in reality again until his next performance.

Wayne ran quickly through his posttransition routine. He flexed his fingers and his toes, letting the flavor of reality seep back into them. As they came to life once more he pulled the feeling upward through his body, into the muscles of his legs and arms, lighting the warmth in his torso, finally reaching into his head and neck. Then the brief isometrics, to tell his body he was back in command and banish the stiffness that had stolen it while he was away in Dreamland.

It never failed to amaze him how tired his body could get while it was actually lying still and peaceful on a couch. But he had seen the studies, read the technical reports. In dreams, the brain still sent commands to the muscles, but inhibiting factors usually kept the body from following through. Since he had to project more of his Dreams than ordinary people did, it was only natural that his body suffered.

Ernie White, the engineer on duty tonight, poked his head into the cubicle. "Is Sleeping Beauty awake yet?" he asked.

Wayne smiled, and the effort made him wince; his facial muscles were stiff, too. "I think you want the lady next door."

"If I do, it's impolite of you to notice." White's face, black as an ebony carving, vanished from the doorway.

Groaning from the effort, Wayne rose slowly on his couch into a sitting position. His head just missed scraping the ceiling of the cubicle—which had not, after all, been built for sitting or standing in. He gingerly lifted his own private crown of thorns, the Dreamcap, off his head and set it down on the couch beside him, then edged his way over to the door.

The bright lights in the room outside made his eyes water after the dimness of the cubicle. Wayne blinked back the tears as he slid out of his cocoon and looked over to his left, where White was helping Janet Meyers out of her own chamber. Janet was blinking against the light as badly as Wayne was, but Wayne recovered first. He took advantage of her moment of blindness to observe her in detail.

From a purely technical viewpoint, Janet Meyers was not a classic beauty. She was a little too tall and her bones were a little too thick. Her face was round, and there were some barely noticeable freckles on her cheeks. Her brown hair was dry and never perfectly in place; a few strands always managed to fly away somewhere, usually across her forehead. She was well-proportioned; any man with reasonable taste would give her a long, lingering glance, although he might not turn around as she passed to give her a second one.

There was nothing special about her that couldn't be found in hundreds of other women. *So why do I act like some goddamn teenage virgin when I'm around her?* Wayne wondered angrily.

She became accustomed to the light and looked over at him. Wayne quickly shifted his gaze to the clock over the door to the engineering booth, then got angry with himself for feeling guilty because he was looking at her. *Silly schoolboy games*, he thought. *I should have outgrown those years ago.*

"Any problems in there?" White asked them. "I thought I saw the dials jumping there for a second."

That reminded Wayne of the horrible screw-up with the guard in the hallway. "Just a little trouble coordinating an image," he said. "We were positioning a character differently, and he got fuzzy and jumped around a little before I finally took control of him."

"It was my fault," Janet said. "He was your character, you were supposed to handle him; I should have given you full control from the moment he appeared. I just didn't think; sorry."

"It's not your fault," Wayne insisted, feeling very protective. "How can they expect perfection when they change scripts on us at the last moment? We hardly had time to look it over, not much chance to re-hearse. . . ."

"It was only a little jumpiness, just for a second or two," Janet continued. "Probably made for good comic relief, if anyone in the audience even noticed. Or if there *is* an audience, for that matter."

"Twenty-two thousand of them, according to the computer," White said.

Wayne scowled. Mort Schulberg wouldn't be happy with so low a rating—but then, he was seldom happy with anything. "And Janet just worked two days ago," he continued in her defense. "She's got to be worn-out. It's the sort of thing that could happen to anyone."

"Hey, you don't got to apologize to me," the engineer grinned. "I just twiddle the dials, remember?"

"We've got ten minutes," Janet interrupted, glancing at the clock herself. "That mistake is history, but if we want to avoid any more of them we'd better coordinate."

She and Wayne walked into the Ready Room, where a sketch of their set had been quickly drawn up for them to study before they started. "Corridor is twenty meters long," she said almost mechanically. "Men stationed here, here and here. A metal grill gate, like the kind shops use to lock up at night, right across here, raised by a button over here. Two men past the gate. Think you can dismantle the bomb yourself?"

The question made Wayne feel suddenly insecure. Even though he was the newest Dreamer on the staff here, he did have previous experience elsewhere. He tried to cover his feelings with some lighthearted banter.

"I'll have to, won't I? Too late to change the script now. Besides, you'll have your hands full with all those guards."

"That's for sure. I'll have to ask Bill how come there's always more each time. He's turning me into a damned Amazon!"

"Maybe if you smile nicely at him he'll give you a love story next time."

"God, I hope not!" The vehemence in her voice sur-

11

prised Wayne. "If there's anything I *don't* want it's a pile of sappy garbage for frustrated housewives. I'd rather fight the Mongol hordes single-handed."

She looked up and saw the strange expression on Wayne's face. "What's the matter with you?" she asked.

Wayne quickly looked away. "Nothing," he said. Her reaction let him know all too plainly how she was feeling about romance at the moment. "We'd better decide who's going to handle which parts of the scene so we don't have any more confusion. I'd hate to ruin the ending."

They spent the next few minutes going over the scene step-by-step, discussing which of them would be responsible for visualizing which parts and which characters. Ernie White finally came in to break the discussion up, telling them they had to get back into their cubicles now if they were going to start on time. As they climbed back into their separate chambers, Janet suddenly flashed Wayne a smile and a quick V-for-Victory sign. It relieved somewhat the depression that had been overtaking him, and he eased himself into his cubicle.

Sitting upright on the couch, he picked up the Dreamcap from where he'd left it and held it for a moment in his lap, turning it over and looking at it from all sides. It wasn't much to see: two crossing arcs of plastic with a circular rim to form the framework of a skullcap, with wires leading from the back down to the floor. The quadrants of the cap were filled with an almost invisible wire mesh that came together at twenty-four node points corresponding to areas of the brain. And yet this simple device had created whole new industries, and a revolution in personal entertainment.

The first real explorations into the workings of the brain had begun decades ago. Electroencephalograms charted the course of brain waves so they could be catalogued and identified. Researchers found that different areas within the brain were responsible for different bodily functions. It was learned that portions

12

of the brain could be stimulated externally to modify behavior—the best example being the classic experiment with rats who'd had electrodes planted in the so-called pleasure centers of their brains. These rats were willing to cross over an area of severe electrical shock just so they could press a bar that would stimulate these pleasure centers. Starving rats would not willingly cross that barrier to get food, yet otherwise healthy rats would risk almost anything for a jolt to the pleasure center.

Experiments to map the areas of the brain became evermore finely tuned, until eventually psychologists and neurologists could pinpoint with complete accuracy where most of the common functions of the brain were stored. This in itself was an enormous advance for medical science. Many crippling illnesses could be shown to be caused by dysfunctions within the relevant brain tissue; in many cases, microsurgery could correct or alleviate the condition, rescuing millions of people from debilitation.

The areas that interested psychologists the most, though, were those controlling the higher brain functions: learning, retention, recall, thought processes, imagination, and so forth. Many neurologists had already suspected that some forms of schizophrenia were caused, not by emotional childhood traumas, but by simple chemical imbalances within the brain. Using the accumulating body of knowledge about the brain's mechanisms, they proved that these imbalances literally caused patients to perceive the world differently from other people, thus accounting for their different behavior. As a sidelight to this research, they also discovered how "normal" people perceived the universe.

To the great surprise of many, this turned out to be remarkably simple to chart. Except for those people with physical disorders—which were now easily identifiable—everyone stored the same kinds of images in the same places within their brains. By stimulating the exact same spot in two different people, it was possible to conjure identical images within their minds. At first, these experiments could only be done by the old-fashioned method of surgically implanting electrodes within the brain itself—but shortly thereafter, a method was found to stimulate these areas using electromagnetic waves instead of electrodes. The new method had several obvious advantages: it could be applied externally, so there was no need of surgery, and it could be guided by computer with pinpoint accuracy to the desired location within the brain, leaving all the areas around that site unaffected. A helmet—the direct forebear of the Dreamcap—was designed for the subject to wear. By stimulating the correct sites within the subject's brain, it was possible to produce an exact series of images in his mind, controlled by an outside influence.

At first, knowledge of the new techniques was limited to neurological specialists, and the applications were primarily in the field of psychotherapy. By scanning the output of a brain, analysts could visualize what their patients were actually seeing. For those patients suffering from delusions and physical misperceptions, the therapist could then substitute more correct images for the false ones. It was literally possible to change the way a person thought by altering the way he perceived reality.

But the implications of this discovery were too broad to be left in the laboratory. In totalitarian countries around the world, the Dreamcap quickly became the primary instrument of brainwashing and thought-control. If a dissident wouldn't cooperate with his government, the ruling powers could imprison him in a mental institution—a cover the Russians had already been using for many years—and impress their own thoughts into his mind. If the dissident's mind accepted the new perceptions as its own, the person was pronounced "cured" and released into society. If the dissident's mind refused to accept the new perceptions, his tormentors would keep at him, continually bombarding his brain with new images until his mind could no longer determine what was an outside influence and what was its own thought. The prisoner was then quite certifiably crazy, which justified his continued imprisonment. In either case, his ability to stand against the government's power was effectively crushed.

Such uses of the technique were banned as utterly abhorrent throughout the free world, although there were persistent rumors that the CIA and other intelligence organizations did maintain their own brainwashing "clinics." But free enterprise was not about to let such a powerful tool go undeveloped—not when there were potentially billions of dollars to be made.

It was frequently pointed out that the average person spent roughly a third of his life asleep. Aside from the fact that sleep allowed the body to rid itself of the day's accumulation of poisons, and that the normal mind had a definite need to dream, sleep had little to recommend it. It was a colossal time-waster. People's sleeping hours were a vast untapped resource waiting to be developed and exploited. The Dreamcap offered an ideal way to do this.

One way was through education. Although nothing could supplant the traditional teacher-student learning experience in school, the Dreamcaps were a godsend to the field of adult education. People who worked hard at a job all day could still find time, while they slept, to learn a second language or catch up on the latest theories of organic gardening. "News magazines" of sleep could keep the citizenry informed through articles dealing with world conditions. The most popular use by far, though, was in the entertainment industry. After dealing with mundane problems during the day, most people were happy to put such cares behind them and lose themselves in a world of fantasy. The Dream broadcast industry provided the ultimate in escapist entertainment.

In all previous entertainment media, the medium itself came between the storyteller and the audience—the printed page in the case of books, or a screen in the case of movies and TV. The audience had to rely on the artificial images the storyteller provided and translate those images into personal symbols within the mind.

In Dreams, all that had radically changed. The images were supplied directly into the viewer's brain, and the viewer felt as though he were actually undergoing the experiences conveyed. He could spend his night actually *being* a spy, or a detective, or the greatest swordsman in seventeenth-century France, then wake up in the morning with full memory of what had happened. He could go out and face the new day with a feeling of having been greater than he was, of having lived through an adventure without any personal risk at all.

Wayne Corrigan was an important part of the new entertainment industry, one of the select few people with imaginations vivid enough to be Dreamers. He and Janet Meyers and the other Dreamers projected the images that sleepers at home picked up on their own Dreamcaps. He created a role and broadcast it through his headset. His images were amplified and transmitted across wires to homes throughout Los Angeles, where they were impressed by Dreamcaps into the minds of his audience, allowing them to live the adventure along with him. In turn, each home Dreamcap sent a signal back to the studio when it was tuned in, allowing the studio to monitor its precise ratings and bill its customers accordingly.

One of the earliest problems discovered was one of sex role identification. Most men wanted to identify with male roles in Dreams, and most women wanted female roles. (There was an aberrant minority that seemed to prefer "cross-gender identification," but the major broadcasters ignored them.) In some cases, it was possible for a given adventure to star a genderless protagonist that could appeal to both sexes, but those stories were more limited in scope, and not nearly as popular as the ones with full identification.

One solution to the problem was the "Masterdream." In this sort, the Dreamer created not one, but a number of different roles for various members of the audience to identify with, as they chose. The Masterdreamer would then move these characters through his Dream world to fit the story he was telling. Since he could create both male and female roles simultaneously, anyone could tune in to such a Dream without upset.

The Masterdreamers were a rare breed, though. They had to be able to visualize an entire world all at once, and to keep individual characters moving through it simultaneously without confusion. The Masterdreamer ran his entire stage, and moved people through it like puppets. It was a difficult art to master, and the staff here at Dramatic Dreams had only one Masterdreamer— a genius named Vince Rondel.

The more common solution was to have separate Dreams for men and women. Usually such Dreams would be totally separated from one another, although in an emergency—such as frequently happened at a small company like Dramatic Dreams with a tiny staff of writers and performers—the two roles could work together within the same Dream world. That was what was happening tonight: Wayne and Janet were portraying a team of government agents working together on the same case. The men in the audience received Wayne's impressions, identified with him, and thought of Janet merely as another important character; for the women in the audience, it was the other way around.

For most Dreamers, this kind of Dream was easier to maintain than a Masterdream, because there was a straight one-to-one relationship between Dreamer and viewer. The viewer saw only what the Dreamer saw, and the Dreamer needn't worry about maintaining portions of the world that were not in the present scene.

The disadvantage was that when two Dreamers were operating in the same Dream, accidents could occur— such as the guard in the corridor. Wayne and Janet had each been visualizing him differently, and as a result the image became fuzzy and jumped around until Janet had relinquished complete control of him to Wayne. Since both Dreamers had an equal ability to affect the action within the Dream, coordination between them was essential.

Wayne was very grateful that Dreams did not run

straight through. Research had shown that Dreams were most effective when broken into fourteen-minute acts, with fourteen-minute breaks between them. Dreaming was such an intense experience that the body needed time to relax from one session before entering another. The scenario writers had learned to gauge the length of their scenes accordingly, and Dreamers universally considered the intermissions a blessing. It gave them time to recover from the previous scene, stretch their muscles, remind themselves what they were doing, discuss technical problems with the engineer on duty, and—in the case of two or more auxiliary Dreamers working in tandem—it gave them the chance to go over their mistakes and improve their coordination.

Wayne took a deep breath and let it out slowly as he settled the Dreamcap on his head. Twenty-two thousand people were tuned in to this Dream, from what Ernie White had said. That wasn't very many, not in a city the size of Los Angeles. Granted he was a new talent on a small local station, and it took time to build up a decent following. But Janet was a better Dreamer than he was, he knew that; she was one of the established artists at Dramatic Dreams, with a following of her own. Her presence in this one should have brought in a lot of women to bolster his ratings, maybe introduced a few new people to his style. Instead, he seemed to be dragging her down to his level.

Damn it, I know I'm good! he thought resentfully. *I may not be another Vince Rondel, but I know I can do better than this. How in hell can I break out of this slump?*

A blue light flashed in the ceiling, his thirty-second cue. Wayne lay back on his couch, wriggled himself into a comfortable position, and began the self-hypnosis routine all Dreamers learned to help them get into a trance state for better projection. He forced his mind to shed all extraneous thoughts. Above all else, he was a professional. He had a story to tell. He did not take his own problems and prejudices into the Dream with him;

18

that was the surest way he knew to get himself fired. As long as he was Dreaming, it didn't matter to him whether there was one person or a million on the other end of the line. Ratings were only a problem in real life; to any dedicated Dreamer, the Dreams themselves were all that mattered.

CHAPTER 2

THE CUBICLE FADED out in his mind, to be slowly replaced by the corridor he had left at the end of the last act. Janet was at his side again, and both were running a desperate race against time. He reminded himself—and the viewers—that he and Janet were a team of skilled government agents on the trail of urban terrorists. The terrorists' philosophy was deliberately vague—Dramatic Dreams didn't want itself left open to charges of using Dreams to propagandize against anyone's cherished beliefs—but they were generally in favor of killing innocent people and tearing down all the established values that everyone held dear.

Wayne and Janet had learned, from a terrorist they'd captured and questioned, that the gang had built a homemade atomic bomb, and were prepared to detonate it here in Los Angeles unless their impossible demands were met. There was no time to call the police or the bomb squad; this job had to be done *now,* and Wayne and Janet were the only people in a position to save millions of lives.

The terrorists, though, were not going to give up without a fight. They had stationed a suicide squad of their own people here in the corridor to guard their engine of destruction. These men knew they would die if the bomb went off, and they were prepared to sacrifice their lives for their cause. They would be demons in the struggle to protect their bomb; they had nothing else to live for, and would hold nothing back.

As Wayne and Janet burst into the cross-corridor where the bomb had been placed, they quickly eyed the situation. Twenty meters of danger separated them from their target at the other end of the hall. The moment they came into view, the three men who'd been guarding the corridor came instantly alert. Their guns had already been drawn and held at the ready for just such a contingency; in a reflex gesture they fired quickly at the government agents.

Wayne could feel the heated air as the laser beam from one guard's gun sizzled scant millimeters by his cheek and burned a small hole in the plaster of the wall. Using the momentum of his run as a push-off, he dove forward onto his stomach. His own gun was out in his hands, and as he slid to a halt on the smooth floor he braced his elbows on the ground, took quick but careful aim and fired. The guard who had shot at him screamed in pain as the searing blast from Wayne's pistol vaporized tissue in his right shoulder.

Behind Wayne, Janet was also in action. She had been one pace behind him as they entered the hall; the shot at him had given her enough warning. She rolled sideways, ending up in a kneeling position with her left side firmly against the wall. Her gun, too, was in her hand and burning down the enemy. Janet, of course, was a fully trained agent and knew how to use all manner of firearms.

Taking advantage of her covering fire, Wayne slithered snakelike on his belly twelve meters down the corridor to the button controlling the metal gate that barred his way to the end of the passage. Laser blasts were hitting all around him, but he ignored them; his sole concentration was on that button.

For dramatic effect, Wayne slowed down his time sense just a little bit. Like everything else in this Dream, the flow of time was controlled by the Dreamers. Wayne could stretch a moment out to eternity to make everything happen in slow motion, or compress any number of events into a single instant. Elongating the time flow here was an artistic effect to build up the suspense in the audience by making his progress seem slower and by increasing the threat from the guards' lasers. Every man out there identifying with him in this Dream would be straining to reach that fateful button, yet fighting through the molasses Wayne had imposed. He had, of course, discussed the time-flow variation with Janet, and she was slowing down her own time sense, too; otherwise her motions would be a quick blur to Wayne, and to all the men seeing things through his eyes.

Finally Wayne reached the button. He pressed it and, obediently, the metal gate slowly rolled up into the ceiling. As it did so, Wayne returned the time flow to its normal speed. The way now seemed clear for him to get at the bomb. But just as the wave of triumph washed through him, he was struck in the right calf by a laser beam from one guard's pistol.

This was a very tricky effect, and Wayne had been flattered when the station management agreed to let him do it. Throughout the industry there were very strict regulations against inflicting pain through Dreams. A sensation like that could have traumatic effects on someone lying peacefully at home in bed. There had been several successful lawsuits against Dreamers when the industry was just starting up, with the plaintiffs claiming mental and physical impairments because of such traumas. The result was that Dreamers walked around on eggshells, approaching the subject of stress in Dreams with extreme caution.

When Wayne ran in a Dream, he never got winded; when he performed strenuous feats, he never got tired, never strained a muscle; and now, when the script called for him to be wounded, he could not suffer any real pain. He'd be fired immediately if he let anything like that go across the wires.

Instead, he had to handle the wound on an intellectual level. Instead of transmitting the searing agony that a real laser burn would cause, he had to send the cool, rational thought that his leg had been hit by enemy fire and that he was experiencing pain. His leg would not bear his full weight and he would show all the aftereffects of the wound. The only ingredient missing

22

would be the pain itself. To carry off the maneuver successfully was one mark of an expert, and Wayne was glad to have a chance to show off his abilities.

He screamed out in his "pain" just as Janet's laser snuffed out that one remaining guard. But Wayne could not let himself be slowed down. There were only minutes left before that bomb was due to explode—and he, not Janet, was the demolitions expert. With the gate now up, there seemed nothing to stop him from reaching his goal. He couldn't stand up with his leg in this condition but, with the strength born of desperation, he began pulling himself along the ground by his elbows to reach the end of the corridor.

Two more guards seemed to appear out of nowhere on the other side of the gate. They had remained hidden until now, hoping that their comrades outside would be able to handle this threat without giving away their own position. They were the last line of defense, and they were undoubtedly the best men the terrorists had.

Wayne could hear Janet behind him muttering muffled curses as her laser ran out of charge, but she refused to give up. With an accuracy that would make a major league pitcher jealous, she hurled her weapon straight at the gun hand of one of the remaining terrorists. Now it was her turn to slow down the time sense; the gun wafted in slow motion through the air toward its target. Would the guard have time to fire before it hit? No—for at the last possible moment Janet accelerated time once more. Her pistol hit the guard's gun with sufficient force to knock it out of his hand and across the room.

The other guard had his gun out too, but so did Wayne. Janet's diversionary throw had given him enough time to get a bead on the second guard. He fired, but at that same instant the guard moved slightly, so that Wayne's shot only grazed the man's hand. Although the guard was not taken out of the fight, the pain was enough to make him drop his weapon and shake his hand to rid it of the stinging sensation. It was all right for the guard to feel pain in this Dream; he was only a shadow figure created by Wayne and Janet, and there would be no viewers at home identifying with his feelings.

Wayne readied his pistol for another shot, only to discover that it, too, was out-of-charge. Disgusted, he chucked it aside and resumed his crawl down the hallway. Eight meters and two suicide-bent guards stood between him and the bomb. All he could do was crawl and hope that Janet could take care of his antagonists.

The guard who'd had his gun knocked away by Janet's accurate throw looked around to try to retrieve his weapon, but could not spot it in his first hasty scan of the hall. Realizing that it was more important to stop Wayne on his mission, the terrorist abandoned his search and moved toward the crawling agent. At this point, Janet came to the rescue once more. Her exquisite body—modified in this Dream to make it more sensual than it was in reality, and propelled by legs that were ever so slightly stronger than could be expected of a human being in real life—leaped through the air, tackling the husky guard and knocking him to the ground. As she hit, she swung her legs sideways to trip up the other guard, who had also started to move toward Wayne.

Wayne didn't have much opportunity to watch the fight that went on to his right; he was too busy concentrating on reaching the bomb before it could explode. Having read the script, he knew exactly what was happening: Janet was having a fight on her hands, though the outcome was inescapable. The women identifying with her would have an exciting time before she finally subdued her two opponents. In the meantime, he had an atomic bomb to disarm.

He kept the time sense nice and easy; there was no point to rushing the matter, and a little added suspense shouldn't hurt anybody. He kept careful tabs on Janet's progress out of the corner of one eye; this was her big scene, and he had no right to ruin it by arriving at the bomb too early, before she'd finished beating up her terrorists.

His timing was perfect; he reached his goal just as the last guard slumped to the floor unconscious. Janet was not even breathing hard. Looking over at him, she asked, "How much time?"

Wayne looked at the timer on the side of the casing. "Three minutes," he replied. With exaggerated caution he leaned himself against the wall, pulled his miniaturized tool kit out of his pocket and began his work.

Calmly, refusing to allow himself to hurry, he unscrewed the four bolts that held the timer in place. Then slowly, ever so slowly, he pulled the timing device itself out of the bomb casing and set it gently down on the floor beside him. He let a few beads of perspiration gather on his forehead as an artistic touch, and he wiped his sweaty hands on his pants. The timer said two minutes.

There was a multicolored tangle of wires connecting the timer to the bomb itself—such a maze of them that it would surely confuse a layman, although Wayne instilled in his viewers the confidence that he knew what he was doing. "I have to disconnect these in a particular sequence," he told Janet—thereby informing the audience as well. "If I make any mistake, the bomb will go off immediately." He made a big point to study the order of the wires for several long seconds. "Here goes nothing," he said at last.

Pulling an electrodriver out of his small kit, he set about unfastening certain of the wires from the body of the timer. As he looked down at his hands, his fingers became longer and nimbler—another artistic effect, to make the hands seem more skilled. He separated the last of the wires from the timer with a minute to go, yet the bomb was still armed. He looked at it for a disbelieving moment, then said, "They must have put an auxiliary on it."

Time was precious now. He made the ticking sounds from the bomb louder, so loud that they nearly echoed in the narrow hallway. Quickly he scanned the surface

25

of the bomb, looking for the second fusing device. "They would have had to put it somewhere within easy reach," he told his partner. "They'd want to turn it off themselves if we'd met their demands. It's just a question of . . . ah, there it is." He pointed to a small nodule on one side of the bomb.

Forty seconds. The timer was attached by only one screw. Taking his electrodriver once more in hand, he undid the fastening. Twenty seconds. Carefully he used his long, narrow fingers to pry the timer off its mooring and examine it. There was only one set of wires.

Ten seconds. There was no time to be dainty. Wayne put down his electrodriver and took out his wire cutters. With two deft motions, the pair of wires was severed. The loud ticking came to a crashing stop with five seconds before detonation.

He slumped against the wall, breathing a deep sigh of relief. Janet sat down beside him, her own relief evident on her face. Reaching her arms around him, she kissed him lightly on the lips; the look in her eyes promised richer rewards to follow.

Then she stood up and helped him to his feet. He put his arm around her shoulders and leaned on her so he wouldn't have to put a strain on his "wounded" leg. The position forced his body into close proximity to hers, and he allowed his viewers—and himself—to enjoy that feeling.

"Let's see what the Chief says *now* about our being able to handle an explosive situation," Janet smiled, referring back to a line at the beginning of the Dream. Wayne smiled along with her as they hobbled together down the corridor.

Around them, the walls began fading to blackness. The Dream was over; it was time to return to real life.

CHAPTER 3

THE DREAMCAP WAS a burning itch around his skull as the dull whiteness of his cubicle faded back into existence. Wayne had to fight the impulse to rip it off; instead, he lifted it gently off his head and placed it on the couch beside him as he sat up following his isometrics. *Sometimes I wonder how I can stand that thing,* he thought, knowing at the same time that he'd hate to try living without it. As a Dreamer, he was as addicted to that Dreamcap—emotionally, if not physically—as any junkie was to his heroin. There was a special feeling that all Dreamers knew. Dreaming was a part of them; that's why they became Dreamers in the first place.

His stomach was rumbling, too, telling him how hungry he was. He'd eaten before starting his Dream, but not heavily; it distracted him from his performance if his belly was too full. And Dreaming itself took a lot out of him; even though the station amplified his signals so they could reach the thousands of viewers tuned in, he was still having to project a large part of himself into his role. Any good actor knew the sensation of throwing himself so totally into his work that he came out of the experience as drained as though he'd spent a hard day at manual labor. Wayne was usually famished by the time he finished a Dream, and he never ceased to wonder how someone like Vince Rondel could make it seem so effortless.

Ernie White knocked on the doorframe of the cubicle and called in, "It's a wrap, Wayne." The Dream was officially over, with no technical problems to worry about. If this were one of the networks, they'd be all set to start another Dream after the required fourteen-minute intermission, simply moving in a fresh Dreamer to start a new story. But Dramatic Dreams was just a small local L.A. station; they didn't have the manpower to run continuously all night. Sometimes they were lucky to stretch their resources just to do something every night. They could have used Wayne and Janet back-to-back instead of together in the same Dream, but that would have cut down on the audience in each case because of the gender identification factor. Bill DeLong, the program coordinator, had gambled on bolstering the ratings by using the two Dreamers together. It was a gamble he'd apparently lost.

The viewers at home did not have to wake up and readjust the settings on their Dreamcaps in order to change stations during the night. Each station published synopses and running times of its Dreams for the evening, both in the daily paper and on TV; the viewer could plan the selection he wanted and program the schedule into his home set, which would then change stations automatically without waking the viewer up. Right now, twenty-two thousand Dreamcaps in L.A. were doing just that. Some of them would be turning off completely, though most would probably switch to a broadcast from another station.

As Wayne edged himself out of his cubicle, he found himself facing a short, balding man with worry creases permanently engraved on his high forehead. "Did everything go all right?" asked Mort Schulberg, the station manager. "Ernie said there was a little blooper in the next-to-last act."

" 'Little' is the word for it," Wayne said irritably. He looked over at White, but the engineer was pretending to fiddle with his control board and didn't notice. "You don't have to get so upset."

"Sure, sure, that's easy for you to say." Schulberg paced around the office like a windup toy. "To you it's just a job. You don't have the FCC breathing down your neck. Their guy Forsch will be here day after tomorrow to check out the Spiegelman thing. When will you start to worry? *After* they've pulled our license?"

"There was only that one tiny mistake," Wayne repeated. It seemed that once again he was being compared, however implicitly, to the perfection of Vince Rondel. Rondel was a Masterdreamer. Rondel's timing was perfect. Rondel never made mistakes. Sure— Rondel was good, and Wayne was just a newcomer to the station, with a tainted background to boot. But that didn't give them the right to criticize every slight goof he made.

"I know I'm not Vince Rondel, but I do a damn good job of Dreaming," he went on, his voice getting louder as he continued. "Janet and I are getting our coordination down—and we'd do even better if we had our scripts a day or two ahead of time so we could go over them first."

"We *are* working well together, Mort," Janet said as she emerged from her own cubicle. She'd been listening to the discussion, and her cool tones interrupted Wayne in mid-rant. He realized she was trying to calm the situation down, and he was grateful to her for it. "That last act went like clockwork."

Schulberg had been prepared to answer Wayne with some yelling of his own, but he softened as he turned to face her. Janet knew how to play dainty and feminine, and could draw out Schulberg's fatherly instincts. "You're sure?"

"You want maybe I should have stopped everything and asked the audience?" Janet said, mimicking Schulberg's accent.

Wayne could see Ernie White laughing in the engineering booth, even though he had his back turned and was supposedly not hearing this conversation. Red-faced, but without rancor, Schulberg said, "Sure, go ahead, laugh at me, all of you. What am I, just the funny little man who signs your paychecks. I'd like to see how hard you laugh when the FCC shuts us down and you don't get any more paychecks. Then you'll see how hysterical unemployment is."

He left the room shaking his head, and walked down the hall to his office muttering just loudly enough for them to hear, "If I weren't around to run this place, they'd laugh themselves right out of a job. . . ."

Wayne gave Janet a weak smile. "Thanks for defusing me back there. I was starting to get a little carried away."

"Happens to all of us," Janet shrugged. "Especially coming out of a Dream—we're all a bit sensitive then. But you really shouldn't let Mort get to you. He didn't mean anything personal, he's just a professional worrier."

"I know. I just feel like the new kid on the block."

"So stay out of Mort's way until this FCC thing is finished. That's really turning him inside out, and I don't blame him for worrying. He'll be better when it's all over."

Wayne nodded. The so-called Spiegelman affair, and the FCC investigation that followed, were still the central topics of conversation around the offices, even a month after the event. In a way, Wayne had to be grateful; it was because of Spiegelman that he was hired here in the first place. But perhaps because of that, too, his every gesture was watched with suspicion by everyone around him.

Eliott Spiegelman had been a Dreamer on the staff here; worse yet, he was Mort Schulberg's son-in-law. About a month ago, Spiegelman had done a Dream, one that was supposed to be a routine detective story set in the 1930s, a la Raymond Chandler. The script was innocuous enough, and had been passed both by Bill DeLong and by the legal department—but every Dreamer knew that no matter how tight the script was, the Dreamer himself had enormous leeway to extrapolate on it.

Apparently Spiegelman had done just that. Beginning the next day, calls and letters started coming in to the station accusing Spiegelman of using the Dream to espouse his own economic and political theories, which were evidently somewhat to the left of center. Spiegelman only added fuel to the controversy by stating to a reporter that socialist movements were very popular in the 1930s, and that all he was doing was accurately reflecting the period of the story. That brought even more letters and phone calls.

There was no objective way to determine what had happened, because it was impossible to record a Dream for subsequent viewing. Every Dream was performed live, and vanished into memory when it was done. It came down to a question of Spiegelman's word against that of the complainants. At that point, the Federal Communications Commission, always sensitive to the issue of political manipulation by the media, stepped into the picture.

Spiegelman was immediately suspended pending a review of the case. For a while it looked as though Schulberg, Bill DeLong and the writer who wrote the script might be suspended, too; some of the angrier citizens were demanding that the whole studio's license be revoked. The FCC decided not to go that far, but they did appoint a man named Gerald Forsch, a long-time critic of the Dream industry, to investigate the incident.

The studio was really buzzing when Wayne had first been hired to fill in for Eliott Spiegelman. The industry in general, and Dramatic Dreams in particular, were concerned that this case could have serious repercussions. To allay their worst fears, Forsch's investigation had moved with deliberate slowness. Forsch himself was due here in two days to hear the studio's side of the matter. On the advice of his attorney, Spiegelman was not making any public statements. The consensus of opinion within the Dream broadcast industry was that Spiegelman would be thrown to the wolves as a sacrificial victim. All the blame would be placed on his shoulders; he would be barred forever from Dreaming, and Dramatic Dreams would get off with no worse than a stern reprimand. But poor Mort Schulberg couldn't win either way; even if he saved his company, he'd have to settle for seeing his son-in-law disgraced and kicked out of his profession forever. Yes, it was little wonder Schulberg was upset about the Spiegelman affair.

But the person Wayne really felt sorry for was Eliott Spiegelman. Dreamers turned to their profession because of inner visions they had to convey. In earlier days they might have been priests, or writers, or artists, or actors, or malcontents—those who saw things differently and tried to imbue others with their insights. Dreaming at long last was a way to accomplish that communication perfectly; once having tasted that perfection, how could any Dreamer settle for less? Spiegelman's life was not over by any means; there were other ways he could express his feelings and emotions. But none of them would have the power and the glory that Dreaming carried with it. A Dreamer who was no longer able to Dream was less than whole, and the rest of his life would ring hollow.

Wayne shivered, and the involuntary action brought his thoughts back to the present. Janet had started out of the room, probably to go to her own office. "Hey," Wayne called after her. "I don't know about you, but I'm famished. Why don't we go downstairs and see if they've got anything left in the machines?"

Janet paused and turned to look back at him. She gave him the strangest look, as though she were trying to read some secret meaning into his words. "Uh, thanks, Wayne," she said at last, "but I'm not really all that hungry right now. Maybe some other time."

"That's what you always say." The words slipped out before he could stop them.

Janet sighed. "I know. I'm sorry. I appreciate the offer, really I do, but . . . but. . . ."

She looked down at her feet, refusing to meet his gaze. "I really don't think I'm fit company for anyone these days. I've got a lot of things to sort out for myself, and it wouldn't be fair to inflict them on you."

Wayne stood there, uncertain how to reply. He wanted

more than anything to say, "Please, I'd love you to cry on my shoulder, I'd love you to trust me with your problems"—but he didn't know her well enough to breach that gap of privacy. And if he tried to say that her problems wouldn't bother him, it would sound as though he didn't think they were serious enough to worry about, and she'd think he was callous.

While he stood frozen with indecision, Bill DeLong ambled into the room. The program coordinator was a tall, lanky man in his middle fifties. Any signs of age in his graying crew cut were countered by the twinkle of youth in his eyes. He dressed casually in sweater and slacks most of the time, but his easygoing friendliness could not conceal the sharp mind that lurked within him.

"Program coordinator" was a catchall title that covered a multitude of sins. DeLong was the head writer, chief censor, program scheduler and all-around consultant in the studio. While Schulberg handled the financial end of the business, DeLong masterminded the creative side. DeLong was not a Dreamer himself, but he was a friend to all the Dreamers on the staff. He also functioned, when the occasion arose, as father-confessor to anyone who needed a friendly ear. If Schulberg was the head of Dramatic Dreams, DeLong was its soul.

"Janet, glad I caught you," DeLong drawled. He had an accent with traces of Texas and Oklahoma. "I've got your next script ready for you." He handed her a clipped sheaf of papers.

Relieved at being taken off the hook, she returned quickly to her normal bantering self. "I don't believe it. A script on time for once? I know it's not a birthday present, because my birthday was three months ago. Whatever did I do to deserve this?"

"Damned if I know. Helen turned it in this afternoon and said it was just inspiration that made her turn it out so fast. It's even good. Someone should inspire that lady more often; she's a good writer when she sets her mind to it."

"Great. I'll get right on it. Thanks." Janet smiled at DeLong, then turned and left the room, ducking out of the awkwardness that had been hanging in the air between herself and Wayne.

"Jack promised he'd have yours ready by tomorrow afternoon," DeLong said, turning to Wayne. "It's a Western, as I recall."

"Not another one," Wayne groaned.

"Well, we can't do *Hamlet* every time out. At least Westerns are quick and apolitical."

"I know. It's just that I feel I'm marking time. I'd like a chance to stretch myself, show you what I can do instead of spending all my energy on hackwork."

"Take it from someone who knows," DeLong said gently. "In any creative profession, the best people are the ones who started out doing hackwork and then moved on. Shakespeare, Dumas, Dickens, Michelangelo and da Vinci were all hacks. You need a solid foundation before you can build larger things on it. I've seen plenty of superstars flash in from nowhere and dazzle everyone for a while; they usually end up flashing out again just as quickly. This way may be slow, but its a surer bet."

"But in the meantime, it's damned frustrating," Wayne said.

"Yeah, I know. Say, didn't I hear you say something about getting some food as I was coming in? I'm not as pretty as Janet, but I could use a bite about now if you'd like the company."

Wayne grinned. "Sure, why not? Let's go."

The two men left the studio and went out into the hall. The building in which Dramatic Dreams was located was neither new nor particularly old. The luster had worn off the floor's brown and white linoleum tiles, but they weren't yet so bad that they needed replacing. The bare white walls were scuffed and scratched, but it was damage that one quickly got used to and then never noticed. The plastic light panels overhead were cracked in a few places, and the fluorescent bulb two-thirds of the way to the elevator had a slight flicker to it. These details hardly registered in Wayne's mind anymore after being here nearly a month. This was simply a place to work, and better than some he'd been in.

The only thing that really affected him was the silence. Most of the companies with offices in this building kept normal hours, and their employees had all gone home by now. Dramatic Dreams, on the sixth floor, was the exception. Since there was no method to record Dreams for later broadcast, they had to be done live. People who made their living in the Dream industry—except the writers, who could make their own hours—found themselves chained to an inverted life-style. Any Dreamer who couldn't accommodate himself to night work and empty buildings found some other occupation in a hurry.

Still, Wayne hated the stifling silence. It was a curtain between himself and the rest of humanity. He provided Dreams to pass the sleeping hours of the multitudes in the city, yet he had less and less contact with them as time went by.

As the footsteps of the two men echoed down the corridor, DeLong said, "Would you mind a piece of unsolicited advice?"

"Huh? About what?"

"Janet. She's coming out of a really bad time right now. Don't push. You're both young, you've got plenty of time to let things develop." They reached the elevator and DeLong pushed the down button.

Wayne blushed. "I didn't realize I was that obvious."

The elevator came quickly, and they stepped inside. "Maybe not so's a blind man would notice," DeLong said, "but I've got to keep track of everything around here. I can't have one of my Dreamers—and one of the most promising, at that—mooning hopelessly after one of my other ones. It's bad for morale, and it takes your mind off your job. Not to mention the fact that if it blows up in your face, I'd end up losing one or the other of you, which is something I don't want; you're both too good."

"I don't think I'd call it 'mooning,' " Wayne objected.

"Well, call it what you like, the effect's the same. When my son was fifteen, trying to get his first date, he showed more *savoir faire* than you do. You're not some teenage kid trying to score; what's the matter?"

Wayne shrugged. "I don't know. She's a better Dreamer than I am; maybe I'm afraid she'll think I'm beneath her notice. Or maybe I'm afraid she looks down on me because of what I did before I came here."

DeLong gave a mild snort. "Janet's a professional, son. She knows what you have to do to survive when you're starting out. I really don't think she'd hold that porno against you."

"There's sure something keeping her away."

"Yes," DeLong admitted, "but it has nothing to do with you."

The elevator deposited them on the ground floor, and they walked through the darkened hall to the food dispensers. The commissary consisted mainly of a bank of food machines in a large room, lit with only one row of lights at this hour. Plastic tables sprouted from the floor like ghostly mushrooms, their stools attached around them like fairy rings. The men's footsteps clacked even more hollowly here as they walked over to study the selections in the machines.

"What *is* the problem, then?" Wayne asked.

DeLong pretended for a moment not to have heard, and inspected the dispensers critically. "Damn! You'd think those people who fill the machines would realize by now they could get some real business overnight if they left any decent choices in there. All we get is stuff the day shifts won't eat—and it's stale at that!"

The program coordinator finally settled on a pathetic ham and cheese sandwich and a cup of black coffee, but Wayne was hungrier than that, even though the selection was far from appetizing. He ended up with a heated can of tomato soup, a wilted salad, a root beer and a dish of spongy pudding to go with his own ham and cheese sandwich. Balancing the load gingerly on a tray, he walked over to the table where DeLong had already sat down.

DeLong picked up his sandwich and stared at it a long time before venturing it near his mouth. "You know, don't you," he said casually, "that Janet had an affair with Vince Rondel?"

Wayne paused with his soup spoon halfway up to his mouth. "I'd, uh, heard a rumor."

DeLong shook his head. "This isn't a rumor. Not only was it common knowledge around the station, but I got the whole story spilled firsthand on my lap over a tearful dinner with Janet. The relationship lasted about a year and a half, and it broke up just before the Spiegelman thing. Maybe if I hadn't been so busy trying to patch Janet up I might have paid more attention to what Eliott was doing—although I don't think I could have stopped him. . . ."

"Why are you telling me about this?" Wayne asked. "Aren't you sort of betraying her confidence?"

"Probably," DeLong agreed, unconcerned. "But I think you can be trusted not to use this against her, and I definitely think you need to know about it."

"Why?"

"Because it'll show you what can happen when two Dreamers at the same station let their emotions get out of hand. Janet was a mixed-up young lady when she came to work here a few years ago—why aren't there ever any *sane* Dreamers?—but she had a lot of potential. Vince worked with her and built her into a major talent; he was great for her professionally, but I'm not sure how much he did for her as a person.

"She finally came to me in tears a month ago, saying she couldn't take it anymore and she had to get away from Vince. I'll admit to some pretty selfish motivations; she's a damn fine Dreamer and I didn't want to lose her. Then the Spiegelman thing came up, and we couldn't *afford* to lose her. So I coaxed her and wheedled her and persuaded her to stay around here, even though it means she still has to see and talk to Vince almost every day. That isn't easy for her; I think a large part of her still loves him."

"What broke up the affair, then?" Wayne asked.

DeLong finally took a bite of his sandwich, and leaned back in his seat to chew pensively. "Vince's mother," he said at last. "Mrs. Rondel is the cause of a great many unhappy things, not the least of which is Vince himself. But that's neither here nor there, and I probably shouldn't even have brought it up. This food really is disgusting, you know that? I rediscover that fact every time I come here. You'd think I'd have learned by now."

He put the sandwich back down on the paper plate and looked Wayne squarely in the eye. "But after helping hold Janet together after one unfortunate relationship, you can see why I don't want to do it again. If anything went wrong, one or both of you would leave—and as I said, you're both too good. I don't want to lose either of you. You should feel flattered."

"I do, but. . . ."

"I'm not one of those bosses who doesn't want his employees socializing after-hours. I'm not saying you can't see Janet, or get friendly with her, or even marry her and have seventeen kids. All I'm saying is: don't push. Let it happen. There are still a few shards she hasn't glued back in place; however well-intentioned you may be, if you topple her over she may never recover. You're both very attractive people, and you may very well end up together in the fullness of time. . . ."

"There you go again," Wayne said. "First you tell me to be patient with my career, now I've got to be patient with Janet. . . ."

"It does start to sound like a broken record, doesn't it?" DeLong smiled. "But it's all true. There are people who've been known to climb the highest Himalayas, at great personal risk and expense, to consult the great yogis and receive the exact same advice I've given you. You're getting the wisdom of the Ancients for free, son. Show a little gratitude."

CHAPTER 4

AS WAYNE WAS trying to decide how to reply to DeLong's half-serious remarks, Vince Rondel walked into the commissary. Rondel was of medium height and blocky, like a former college football player not big enough to make the pros and subsequently gone to seed. Most Dreamers dressed casually—Wayne was in jeans, a tee shirt and sneakers—but Rondel always wore a suit. He only had a wardrobe of two that Wayne had ever seen; the material on both was cheap, but they were always neatly pressed. The cut of the jacket only emphasized Rondel's blocky body, and made his head appear half a size too small. His face was clean-shaven and his blond hair was neatly combed, thinning slightly toward the front but not yet bald. His finger-nails were always manicured, and his hands were always clean.

Rondel spied DeLong and said, "There you are, Bill. I need a favor."

Wayne saw DeLong's fingers tighten on the Styrofoam coffee cup, but otherwise his demeanor was unchanged. "What's the matter, Vince?"

"It's my mother. She called—something's wrong. I've got to get back to her."

"That's the third time this week, Vince," DeLong said calmly.

"She's old, she's sick. I can't help that. She refuses to let me hire a nurse for her, she refuses to go to a nursing home where they'll take proper care of her. Can't you just drive me home?"

"You know I live the other way. Why don't you call a cab?"

Rondel ignored the suggestion and looked to Wayne for the first time. "Corrigan, you've got a car, haven't you? Where do you live?"

"Van Nuys," Wayne said reluctantly.

Rondel smiled. "There you are. I'm North Hollywood, right along the way. You can drop me off, can't you?"

"Well. . . ."

"Great. I'll go get my stuff and be right back." Rondel ran out of the room, back to the elevator.

"You've got to learn to say no a little faster," DeLong advised.

Wayne looked at the other, amazed. "You mean he doesn't have a car? How does he get around?"

"Buses, mostly—when he's not sponging rides off someone else."

"But he must make more than I do."

"Nearly twice," DeLong agreed.

"What does he do with it all?"

"Whatever doesn't go toward the mortgage, utilities or food goes to his mother's doctor bills. The rest goes to the church. Mama insists on that."

Wayne shook his head in disbelief. He could live quite comfortably on twice his present income—yet here was Vince Rondel, the star of the station, reduced to cadging rides where he could. "Is it all right with you if I take off now?" he asked. "I was through for the night anyway—and you said my next script won't be ready till tomorrow. . . ."

"Sure, go ahead," DeLong sighed. "We've got to keep our star happy."

Rondel was back in a couple of minutes with his briefcase, but there was further delay as Wayne had to go back up to his tiny office to get his jacket. Wayne found himself moving with deliberate slowness, and wondered why. Was it because Rondel had had an affair with the woman Wayne wanted? The idea seemed childish to him, and he forced himself to quicken his pace.

Finally they were set. Wayne led Rondel out to the parking lot, and to his battered, four-year-old car. "It's not much," he excused, "but it gets me where I'm going."

"Looks fine," Rondel said. "I hate imposing like this, but the buses don't run too often this time of night and cabs are so expensive."

"As you said, it's right along my way," Wayne shrugged. He started the car, and they surged out into the night.

At first they rode in silence. Although Wayne had been working at Dramatic Dreams for about a month, he and Rondel hardly knew each other. Rondel had made a halfhearted attempt to talk religion to him once, but Wayne had squirmed out of it. All he really knew was what DeLong had said. Rondel was the star of the station; not only was he the only Masterdreamer on the staff, but he was an all-around talent, writing his own scripts as well as performing them. Wayne had sampled some of Rondel's work before coming to the station, and he had to admit it was impressive.

"Do you mind a personal question?" he ventured after a couple of minutes.

"That depends on what it is."

"Well, I was just wondering why you're wasting your time here at a small, local station. You could be at one of the networks, doing really big things."

Rondel looked out the side window. "Yeah, I had some offers. Good ones. But I'd have had to move back East, and I can't do that."

"Why not?"

"My mother couldn't take the climate. She's in frail health."

"What's the matter with her?"

"Seems like everything. She's crippled with arthritis, one kidney's failed, her heart's bad, her digestive system, her lungs—you name it, something's wrong with it."

"I'm sorry to hear that."

Rondel shrugged. "It's God's will—nothing to be done.

41

All I can do is try to make her as comfortable as possible."

Silence descended on the car again as it drove the empty freeway. Wayne took his eyes off the road several times to steal glances at the man sitting beside him. There was only the dim profile to be seen, but Wayne, with his Dreamer's imagination, filled in the details he remembered from seeing Rondel in the light. He tried to imagine Janet in this man's arms, Janet kissing his lips, his cheek, his neck, Janet naked and moaning with passion beneath Rondel's body. . . .

The tires rattled sharply over the reflector bumps as his car veered gradually into the next lane. Wayne pulled himself out of the reverie and turned the wheel quickly the other way, straightening them out. *Keep your mind on your driving,* he warned himself sternly.

Beside him, Rondel also reacted. "Hey, don't fall asleep on me, there. It won't do my mother any good if I'm killed in an accident."

"Sorry," Wayne apologized. "I just got lost in thought. You know how that happens."

"Sure, that's our business. What are you going to be doing next?"

"Bill says it's a Western. I'll get the script tomorrow."

"Hey, Westerns are always great. The classic confrontation of good versus evil. I've lost track of how many Westerns I did when I was starting out. It's a good proving ground for sharpening your skills."

What makes you think my skills need sharpening? Wayne thought bitterly, but said aloud, "Yeah, that's what Bill says, too. But it's all so simplistic. I'd like a little more of a challenge."

"It's only as simplistic as you choose to make it. Do you have a copy of Ronson's *Way of the West?*"

"No. What is it?"

"It's the best reference I've ever found on the period. It cost eighty-five dollars, but it's worth it. Thousands of illustrations and even lots of the old photos of those days. It's the best thing going to help you visualize the

42

costumes, the buildings, the whole ambiance of the Old West. Just read it through a couple of times and your Westerns will be so real you'll have people waking up with a drawl." He paused for a moment. "I've got my copy at home. You can come in with me and I'll loan it to you."

"I don't want to intrude. . . ."

"No bother. It'll just take a second."

Wayne did not want to like this man. He was being so pathetically friendly, though, that there was little Wayne could do but accept the overtures on their own terms. "Uh, okay, Vince. Thanks."

More silence. Rondel cleared his throat a couple of times as though to speak, then thought better of it. Finally he gathered enough courage to pull himself over the edge of action. "Since you asked me a personal question, would you mind if I returned the honor?"

"I guess not." Wayne was trying to react as little as possible. This forced proximity to Rondel was making him increasingly uncomfortable.

"Did you . . . that is, I heard that you—before you came to Dramatic Dreams—that you worked in the porno field. Is that true?"

Wayne's hands tightened on the steering wheel. "Yeah. What about it?" The last thing he needed right now was a morality lecture, and Rondel was noted for his outspoken religious views. "I did it because it was the only job I could find open as a beginner. As you said, it's a great proving ground for sharpening the skills."

"I, uh, I'm sure it is. I'm not criticizing you for it. We all have to start out where we can, I realize that. At least God saw fit to raise you out of the muck. I only . . . I just wanted to know what it was like."

"Huh?" Wayne looked over in surprise to see Rondel staring rigidly ahead, wiping his palms nervously on his slacks. "What do you mean?"

"Well, all that sex. It must have been exciting."

So there it was, out in the open. Little mister perfect, the man who donated large chunks of his salary to the church, was a closet hypocrite. Wayne was almost blinded by the sudden flash of insight into Rondel's soul, and somehow this knowledge of the other man's weaknesses lit a warm glow inside him. He was careful not to let the feeling show, however, in his reply. "No. Actually it was kind of boring."

The announcement had the desired effect; Rondel looked at him, startled. "Boring? I really don't see. . . ."

"Sure, just think about it for a minute. When you get right down to it, the physical act of sex is just a repetitive action. When you're actually doing it, of course, you get lost in the feelings of your own body, but recreating the sights, sounds and smells becomes very clinical. Most of the great erotic literature in the world has been about foreplay, with the actual sex being only a small part. Besides, all we can do is tease; we're never allowed to consummate anything."

"Why not?"

"Same reason we're not allowed to hurt or kill any-one, I suppose. Even in regular dreams, nobody ever completes the act. You can get close a lot of times, but something always happens to prevent you from going all the way."

He shook his head. "Maybe it's the body's way of getting rid of tension—but the FCC laid down very strict rules for us. Absolutely no consummation, as they put it. If we'd even tried something like that, they'd have been down on us so hard it'd make the Spiegelman thing look like a tea party."

"What sort of things did you do, then?"

"Routine stuff, mostly. One-on-one, harem fantasies, orgies. I stayed away from the really kinky stuff, the S&M trips, discipline, scatology and so on. I tried a gay male Dream once, but it was terrible; I just couldn't relate to it, and the boss told me to stick with the straight stuff. I did some lesbian scenes every once in awhile, but that was different. Lesbian fantasies are almost exclusively for men; from what I've been able to tell, most gay women aren't interested in them. Funny how . . ."

Rondel interrupted him. "We get off here at Laurel Canyon."

For the next few minutes Rondel was busy directing Wayne along the surface streets to his house, and the conversation lagged. By the time Wayne's car pulled up in front of their destination, it was too late to resume talking about Wayne's former occupation— which was just as well with him.

"Come on in and I'll get that book for you," Rondel invited.

"You can give it to me at the staff meeting tomorrow."

"It'll only take a minute. Come on."

Reluctantly, Wayne got out of the car and followed Rondel to the house.

The house was spectacularly unimpressive, a modest one-story building crouched shyly away from the street. The front lawn was surrounded by a waist-high chain link fence, twisted and bent over many years by neighborhood children at play. The grass was ankle deep in many places, with bare patches in others. Whatever other talents Rondel might possess, gardening was not among them.

A dim light bulb glowed over the front door. Even in the feeble light, Wayne noticed as he climbed the stairs onto the small porch that the paint was peeling from the wood slat walls and the screen in the front window was torn and patched in several places. *Shabby,* he thought distastefully. *This man is one of the stars of our profession, and he lives like this. Why?*

But if he was dismayed by the outside of the house, the interior literally appalled him. As Rondel opened the door, Wayne's nose was assaulted by the acrid odor of a catbox that hadn't been changed in weeks. The floor was littered with old newspapers and magazines; the bookshelves that lined the walls were crammed, not only with books, but with dirty plates, glasses and assorted other objects placed there in a hurried moment and never removed; the furniture was old, and its

45

brocade upholstery was torn and leaking stuffing in numerous places.

"Excuse the mess," Rondel said self-consciously as he stepped carefully through the litter on the floor. "I don't have that much time for cleaning, and my mother can't really do it, so it just piles up. . . ."

Wayne made no comment as he followed Rondel inside. His discomfort was growing more acute by the second, and he wished he'd never accepted the other's invitation. As DeLong had said, he'd have to learn to say "no" a little faster.

"Vince, is that you?" called a shrill voice from the back. "Praise the Lord you made it. I thought you'd never get here."

"Yes, Mama. I'll be right with you."

"Is there someone else with you? I heard you talking to someone."

"Yes, Mama. It's Wayne Corrigan from work. I told you about him. He drove me home." He turned to Wayne. "Excuse me for a second, I've got to see how she is. I'll be right back." He went through the far hallway and vanished, leaving Wayne alone.

Something brushed by his leg, and he nearly jumped out of his skin; in a house like this, who knew what kinds of creatures roamed free? But it was only a cat, a short-haired gray-and-white, looking thin and scraggly. It was carrying something in its mouth, but it darted off again before Wayne could see what it was. Looking around, Wayne found himself the center of attention for several other pairs of feline eyes hiding in dark corners of the cluttered room.

Rondel and his mother were talking in the next room. Arguing might have been a better term; Wayne couldn't make out many of the words—Mrs. Rondel was saying something about "strangers in the house"— but the rising and falling speech patterns were very apparent. It always made Wayne uncomfortable to be an intruder in some family dispute, and he was tempted to turn and go—but there was no polite way of walking out after he'd accepted Rondel's invitation to come in.

He had to wait at least until Rondel came back so he could formally excuse himself.

The squalor of the room felt worse the longer he stood inside it. Wayne could see wadded up balls of tissue among the papers on the floor, and he thought he saw a large cockroach scamper across one corner and vanish under the baseboards. The dishes, which reminded him of his mother's cherished Limoges china, had been stacked haphazardly on the bookcases and still had bits of food on them, some of which were starting to grow mold. Beside one plate was a small piece of Steuben, a crystal whale with its tail arched up in the air—but the tail was cracked, and one flipper was broken off. There were lace curtains across the window, but they showed the evidence of years of cats' claws. There was a row of dead and shriveled plants along the windowsill, so dried out now that it was impossible to tell what they once had been. By the door that must have led to the kitchen stood a brown grocery bag filled with trash, among which Wayne could see the glitter of used aluminum trays from frozen dinners. From the kitchen came the slight whiff of an odor midway between a sewer and an open grave.

If I have to stay here much longer, Wayne thought, *I'm going to be sick. How can anyone live this way?*

Rondel poked his head into the room. "Corrigan, got a minute? I'd like you to meet my mother."

"Well, I really should be going. . . ."

"It'll just take a minute, and I've got to find that book for you anyway. Come on."

Wondering why he allowed himself to be trapped into these predicaments, Wayne walked through the mess gingerly, not wanting to step on a cat or anything else unpleasant amid the detritus of the living room floor. The hallway was actually free of papers, but that only allowed Wayne to see where cigarettes had been stamped out on the hardwood flooring. The butts had been kicked into one corner, where they formed a small pyramid of filter tips.

One door leading off the hallway was slightly ajar.

The room beyond was stark in its simplicity: bare wood floors; a twin-size wrought iron bed, neatly made; a religious sampler on the wall, proclaiming "The Lord is my shepherd." The room was an island of cleanliness in this dungheap of a house. Wayne guessed it was Rondel's room, in keeping with the man's personal neatness. But the room was empty, so Wayne continued on.

He could tell which was the mother's bedroom before he even entered it; the stench announced it quite forcefully. The air was heavy with the smell of cheap Devon violet perfume interwoven with the scent of stale cigarette smoke and urine. Any of the odors would have been sickening, but somehow the combination more than tripled the unpleasant effect. Wayne had to stop just before entering and gag back the quick meal he'd had at the station. He did not want to vomit here, in front of Rondel, even though he doubted it would be noticed among the general decor.

Mrs. Rondel's bedroom was no disappointment. The marble-topped walnut dresser was stained with coffee cup rings and cigarette stains, and the sides had provided ample sharpening ground for cat claws. A Coromandel screen stood in one corner; it must once have been very valuable, but now most of the inlay work had long since disappeared. Clothing, none of it very clean, was draped randomly over chairs and on the floor. On the walls were pictures of a very attractive woman—but any resemblance between her and the Mrs. Rondel of today was tentative at best.

In the center of the room, against the far wall, was Mrs. Rondel's bed. It was king-size, with carved wooden posts at the corners supporting the remains of a canopy; the tatters of lace hung down as wistful reminders of the glory the bed must once have been. The Oriental brocade bedspread, too, bespoke better days long past; now it was only faded, torn and covered with large, ugly stains. Around the bed, piles of cigarette butts lay unheeded.

Mrs. Rondel was in a half-sitting posture, lying back

against a mound of pillows. She was a large woman with a fat face and dark, piggy eyes. Her skin was mottled with liver spots, her white hair was up in rollers and her face was covered in thick, almost clownlike, makeup. There was a dingy gray shape at her throat that Wayne first thought was another cat; then he realized it was the dirty marabou collar of a dressing gown that must have had some color at one time—but he wouldn't have tried to guess what that color was.

"This is my mother," Rondel said anticlimactically.

Mrs. Rondel made a disgusting noise in her throat and coughed up some phlegm into a tissue, which she then tossed casually into a corner. She looked at Wayne with an analytical stare and said, "Corrigan, huh? You Irish?"

"I'm an American. Fourth generation."

"Catholic?"

"Not very." Wayne was bristling under this rude cross-examination.

Mrs. Rondel looked to her son. "Have you showed him the way of the Lord yet?"

Rondel was clearly embarrassed. "Mama, I hardly know him."

"That doesn't matter. All men are brothers under God." She turned back to Wayne. "Do you want to be saved?"

Looking at her, Wayne was not so sure—not if she was any example. "It's not something I worry much about—and frankly, Mrs. Rondel, I don't think it's any of your business."

The woman *humphed* and turned to her son. "Some friends you have at this job. Is this the sinner you told me did the filthy Dreams?"

"Mama!"

"Godless heathen!" Mrs. Rondel's eyes were flaring as they locked onto Wayne. "Slave of Satan, luring men from the path of righteousness with your filth and your lust. But the Day of Judgment will come, and it will be a day of retribution. The bowels of the earth will open and swallow the sinners like you. How will you enjoy your lust then, when you're wallowing in fire and choking on the smell of brimstone? Beware the verdict of the Lord, beware the punishment of the sinners. Jesus forgives, but you must come to Him and confess your sins. You must plead on your knees. . . ."

"Mama," Rondel pleaded, "this is our guest."

Mrs. Rondel paid no attention. "Pray for your soul, or be swallowed up in eternal damnation."

Wayne stood speechless in the face of the unbridled hostility, not knowing how to react. He was shocked and mad and embarrassed and even a little frightened, all at the same time. As the old woman ranted on, Rondel took Wayne by the arm and led him out into the hallway. Mrs. Rondel barely knew they'd gone; she was in full rant, and the mere absence of a target was not going to stop her.

"I'm sorry, really," Rondel said. "Sometimes these things come over her. Her mind isn't what it used to be."

Wayne took a few deep breaths to regain his composure. "I thought you said you had to come home because something was wrong with her."

Rondel shrugged. "False alarm, I guess. It happens sometimes. At her age and with her condition, I don't like to take any chances. Look, can I get you a cup of coffee?"

A brief memory of the smell from the kitchen tickled his mind, and Wayne's stomach did a quick flip-flop. "Uh, no, thanks. I really do have to be getting home."

"Let me at least find that book for you."

"No!" he said, a bit too sharply, then forced more calmness into his voice. "Tomorrow is fine, really. You can bring it to the staff meeting. I'll be there."

"It'll only take me a couple of minutes. . . ."

"Sorry, I . . . I've just got to go." Without further hesitation, Wayne picked his way back through the living room and out the front door. He stumbled down the porch steps in his haste to be away from the Rondel house.

He made it to his car and leaned against it for several minutes, content to breathe in great gulps of the cool night air. It took a few moments for his hand to stop shaking long enough to fish in his pocket for the keys. Even as he drove off, he could still hear Mrs. Rondel's shrill voice expounding her sermon to the uncaring night.

CHAPTER 5

WAYNE HAD NEVER thought of his apartment as any kind of showplace, but it was straight from the pages of *House Beautiful* after a visit to Rondel's home. Wayne's was a furnished one-bedroom flat decorated in California stark, and its prime recommendation was a bleak and cheerless efficiency. The walls were all clean and white, the furniture cheap but serviceable. The thing that struck him the most about it, though, as he entered and switched on the light was that it was neat and odor-free. Wayne was not a conscientious house-keeper, and there was dust on the shelves, but at least everything was in its proper place and the gold shag carpeting was not littered with refuse.

Sometimes it takes a really bad experience to make you appreciate what you've got, Wayne thought as he looked around.

Nevertheless, the sterile quality of his apartment bothered him. As long as he was being critical, he might as well extend the criticism to his own life-style. Aside from the TV set and a couple of prints he'd hung to brighten up the stark walls, there was little here he could really call his own. He took an inventory, and became more depressed. In the kitchenette he had his dishes and utensils, a toaster-oven and a typewriter on the table that belonged to him; in the bedroom was his Dreamcap and a closetful of clothes. Those things and his ever-growing library of reference books—many of which he kept at the studio, anyway—were the only items that had not come with the furnished apartment.

When he thought about it, he realized that most of

the Dreamers he knew were neither worldly nor materialistic people. The best that could be said of them was that they endured reality; their real lives lay in Dreams. The world was just an address where they satisfied their bodily needs. Everything that mattered to them was lived inside their own heads, to spill out through the Dreamcaps to other people. Wayne wondered whether this was how the fastidious Rondel managed to survive living with his mother in that house—by treating it as a temporary phenomenon, to be suffered with quiet dignity until he could escape again into Dreams.

He felt a wave of self-pity building, and tried to stop it. After all, were Dreamers worse off than anyone else? The others, those faceless masses who served as the nightly audience, didn't even have the imagination to create their own Dreams. They lived out their lives in jobs most of them hated, and their only outlet was to tune in to the vicarious Dreams created by others. Dreamers at least had an independence to their existence that freed them from the shackles of mundane life.

It was a familiar rationalization. He heard those same elitist arguments, or variations of them, every time Dreamers got together to talk about their lives. Was it the truth, or was everybody saying it as loudly as they could to mask their own insecurities? It sounded brave at parties and in the halls of Dream studios—but Wayne wondered whether those same Dreamers ever had the quiet moments of despair alone at night that he suffered from—the knowledge that they faced an empty life ahead and that their sharpest realities were firmly grounded in make-believe.

It had all been different when Marsha was here. Life had a purpose then, or at least it seemed to; if Wayne had any doubts about the validity of his life and occupation, it was easier to bury them below the surface of an emotional relationship. If nothing else, being involved with Marsha had shielded him from the harsher truths about himself.

But Marsha had sold insurance for a living. There was no one in the world more firmly entrenched in reality than Marsha Framingham. Their initial attraction had seemed to prove the old saw about opposites, but their year of living together had shown them that a couple needs *some* common ground to keep a relationship growing. Marsha had little understanding of, or sympathy for, his artistic needs, and his inverted working hours as a Dreamer had given them less and less time together.

Six months ago, in a desperate attempt to keep a grip on the relationship, Wayne had committed an unpardonable act: he asked Marsha to marry him.

She stared at him a long time before replying. "No," she said, "under these circumstances it'll never work— and you'll never agree to the circumstances where it might."

"Try me."

"You'd have to give up Dreaming."

They split up a week later. It was an amicable parting, as such things went. They vowed to remain friends—but with few common interests, their paths seldom crossed. The last Wayne had heard, Marsha was involved with a stockbroker and had never been happier.

Wayne wondered if that was one of the things that drew him so strongly to Janet Meyers. Physically, she and Marsha were quite similar—neither was staggeringly beautiful, but each of them radiated a sense of warmth and intelligence that he admired in a woman. The difference between them was that Janet, unlike Marsha, was a Dreamer herself. She would recognize the special needs, the moods, the doubts, because they would be mirrors to her own feelings. She and Wayne could share the unique world of Dreaming and its peculiar problems. The two of them could brace each other in times of trouble; together, they'd make a team that could weather the emotional storms. If only he could make her see that. . . .

The apartment was suddenly cold and very lonely.

The world around him was still, and he felt cut off, isolated, from the flow of humanity. Most decent people would be asleep right now, many of them wearing Dreamcaps and living through someone else's predigested fantasies. Wayne was overwhelmed by the urge to dive in and swim with the pack, to lose himself in the mass identity and surrender his problems until tomorrow.

Without even thinking, he went over to the TV and turned it on to the informational channel. Lines of print filled the screen, and for several minutes his eyes scanned them without absorbing any of the data. When he finally became aware of what he was doing, he instructed the set to show him the Dream listings for the night. If Dreaming was his problem, he would make it part of the solution as well.

He read carefully through the offerings from the major stations. There were a couple of entries that sounded interesting, being done by Dreamers whose work he respected, but they'd already started. Coming into the middle of a Dream was worse, in some ways, than coming into the middle of a movie; it left the viewer feeling terribly disoriented and unsure of himself. Wayne definitely did not need anything like that tonight.

He continued on in the listings until he came to the smaller, specialized stations. There were a couple of studios in L.A. that offered inspirational religious experiences, and advertised themselves that way explicitly, so no one could complain to the FCC that they'd been propagandized against their will. After Mrs. Rondel's fanatic harangue, though, the last thing Wayne needed was another dose of religion.

That left the porno stations. As he came to those listings, Wayne realized they were what he'd been seeking all along. The feelings of frustrated love for Janet, of loneliness, of a hollowness in his soul—these feelings were building past the point of endurance. They had to be relieved somehow. Even though he knew entirely too much about the porno Dream industry, even though he knew it wasn't anything more than a gigantic tease, he needed some way to release the tension in his body. It might as well be this.

He skimmed quickly through the listings. There was eroticism pandering to every conceivable taste, be it straight, gay or fetish. Wayne had always been considered the "square" at the station because of his failure to get into any of the kinkier fantasies; he'd done a good job on regular eroticism, but left the esoteric stuff to the others. That was just the way his own taste ran, yet he'd found himself apologizing for it time after time. It was one of the reasons behind his dissatisfaction there, and his jumping at the offer from Dramatic Dreams, even though it meant a slight drop in salary. At least he was no longer ashamed of what he was doing—and there was always the chance of moving on to better things.

There was a heavy diet of B&D going over the wires tonight. "Slave Mistress," "Leather Lady," "Whips in the Night"—he didn't even have to read the synopses, he could tell just from the titles what they'd be about. It had never failed to amaze him precisely how many submissives there were in the audience. He would have guessed that sadists, the people wanting to give pain, would far outnumber the masochists who were willing to receive it. Instead, the situation was the exact opposite. Masochistic fantasies always rated very highly, while sadistic ones went begging for an audience. It was upbringing, he supposed; people were conditioned to feeling guilty for things they did and knew they ought to be punished. Living through a Dream wherein they *were* punished expunged the feeling of guilt and allowed them to face the world again. He knew Dreamers who honestly felt they were helping keep their audience on a sane course by allowing them this safety valve—and perhaps they were right. But it still was not the sort of thing Wayne needed tonight.

Similarly, he passed up the two listings obviously for gay men, "Muscle Boys" and "Backdoor Blues." The choice of Dreams for heterosexual males was surprisingly slim tonight—and at this hour there turned out to be only one still on the agenda: "Harem Hopping," offered by Panegyric Productions, his former studio.

He looked to see who the Dreamer was, and frowned. The name listed was "Richard Long," which was a house pseudonym. He'd been hoping it would be one of his friends with a proven talent, but he'd be taking a chance here. "Richard Long" could be anyone who was working at the studio tonight, good or bad. Wayne would have no way of knowing until he actually began the Dream—and then it would be too late to back out.

This was one of the points which critics of Dreaming loved to harp on, the fact that a sleeping person was a helpless subject for anything the Dreamer did to him. Safety regulations ensured that all home caps contain a smoke detector hookup, to waken the subject in case of fire. But other than for such emergencies, the person on the receiving end could not wake himself up if he didn't like a given Dream; he was literally a prisoner until the broadcaster faded the Dream out in his mind. That was why the FCC was so touchy about the entire matter, and why the Spiegelman affair was so important: the public had to know that their minds were being protected from unwarranted interference. If that fragile confidence ever evaporated, the Dream broadcast industry could vanish overnight. The members of the industry knew this, too, and normally policed themselves far more vigorously than the government did.

The only other way out of a Dream was to set a timer on the Dreamcap to turn off at a specified time, but few people ever did this unless they needed a substitute alarm clock. What was the point of getting into a Dream at all, possibly one that was very enjoyable, if you were going to cut it off before it was over? That way lay frustration. Once again, there was the old bugaboo that Dreams could not be recorded for later play; everything was live, and people had to take their chances. A good Dreamer built up a following of people who tuned him in regularly; a bad Dreamer took the leavings.

Wayne stood for several minutes staring at the display screen, debating with himself whether it would be worth it. He definitely needed a strong erotic Dream to release his tensions—but there was no way to tell in advance who the Dreamer was. A bad Dreamer would be almost worse than none at all, leaving Wayne more frustrated afterward than he'd been before. Did he want to risk it?

He turned off the TV, went into the bedroom and got undressed. As he slid under the covers, he picked up the Dreamcap from its hook on the wall above the bed. From what he'd learned in his classes while studying for his Dreamer's license, there was absolutely no difference between one of the home caps and the cap he used at work. Either was capable of impressing sensations into the brain or of taking images out of it. There were just two factors making the crucial difference. A Dreamer in a studio knew what he was doing, and was consciously forming and projecting his images outward for the audience. A Dreamer also had the broadcast power of his station behind him, amplifying his own thoughts so that they'd be strong enough to reach into the viewer's mind and override whatever was happening there. Theoretically, the home viewer could send his own dreams back into the broadcast studio—but the signals would be so weak when they got there that they could have no effect at all.

Wayne turned out the bedroom light, slipped the cap onto his head and settled down into bed. He tried to clear his mind of the day's clutter and fall asleep quickly; the Dreamcap wouldn't work on a waking mind. Theoretically it was possible to build a cap powerful enough to override the impressions of a conscious mind—but again, such things were prohibited under U.S. law. The Dreamcaps commercially available could only make their suggestions when the subject was asleep; if Wayne was still awake when the Dream began, he might as well not bother.

As a Dreamer, he had to be able to put himself into a trance state at will, and had trained in self-hypnosis to do so. He used his training now, focusing all his mind within himself, and gradually—without his being aware of it—reality faded into grayness around him.

He was in a large, airy room, open to the blue afternoon sky through the skylight in the center. The room was rectangular, with shadowed, covered walkways all around the central court. Vaguely Arabic designs—he couldn't see them too clearly—covered the walls. In the center was a rectangular bathing pool. The air smelled sweetly of dates and pomegranates.

His friend at his side nudged him. "Let's go," he whispered urgently. "We've been here long enough. It's instant death for any man who isn't a eunuch to be caught here."

"If I've risked my life for this much, I might as well see a little more," Wayne replied calmly. "I made up my mind I was going to see the royal harem chambers, and I haven't seen enough yet."

"You'll have seen the sun rise for the last time," his friend warned him. "I'm leaving now. Your fate is upon your own head." He slinked off into the shadows and disappeared, and Wayne never gave him another thought.

Walking quietly over to the pool, Wayne dipped his hand in and found the water warm and slick with scented bath oils. He looked around at the comfortable couches that the sultan's wives could lounge upon, and regretted that he could not be here while they were—but that would be pressing his luck a little too far. At least he could now go home knowing how lavishly the harem women lived.

There was a noise to the left, and he looked around, startled. Someone was coming, and it meant his life to be discovered here. He spotted a small alcove behind an ivory screen, and dashed quickly into it just as the doors at the far side of the room opened. Into the room came some of the most beautiful women Wayne had ever seen, accompanied by just a single eunuch—a muscular man who carried a gleaming scimitar at his waist.

The women were mostly brunettes, with just a couple of blondes and a redhead mixed in for variety. There were at least twenty of them—Wayne never got an accurate count—and all were young and slender, with clear skin and elegantly curved bodies. They were dressed in a pastel rainbow of gauzy fabrics that did little to hide the details underneath; none of them wore veils here in the privacy of their own chambers.

One woman in particular captured his attention, a tawny tigress who stretched herself out on the divan at the head of the pool. This, Wayne knew, must be the Wife of Wives to the sultan. She obviously feared no one and nothing as she lounged languorously on her couch, and the other wives deferred to her.

The regal woman yawned, then said in a bored tone, "Here must we rest and amuse ourselves while our noble and generous lord spends the week hunting in the mountains. I never cease to marvel at his subtle tortures, that he can imprison us here with no company but a lone eunuch, when he knows that each of us is a passionate woman fully capable of satisfying the needs of any mortal man. The cruelty of his jests at times is hard to bear."

She looked over to the eunuch. "Come here," she ordered.

The man obeyed, standing beside her couch, his bulky body towering over her. She took his meaty hands and placed them on her breasts, making him caress her in a grotesque parody of passion. "Tell me," she said in a husky voice, "don't you ever regret being less than a man? Wouldn't you like to take me now and consume me with passion?"

"If ever I did regret it, I would lose far more than I already have," the eunuch replied. He took his hands away from her and folded them across his chest. "I am as content as any man may be in this realm."

The woman pushed him away and stood up. "Bah. There is not a real man in this entire kingdom. My lord

60

rules a *nation* of eunuchs, I fear. If only a real man would come to quench the fires burning in my loins."

She stretched, and as she did so her diaphanous clothing dropped away to leave her standing naked by the edge of the pool. Wayne's field of vision narrowed to contain just her; his gaze wandered up and down her magnificent body, inspecting its beauty in intimate detail. Time stood still for a while as he completed his inspection, then began slowly again. The woman waded briefly in the pool, dunking her entire body from the shoulders down in the scented water. She stood up again and climbed out of the pool. The water beaded in delicious droplets all over her skin. One of the other women came up to her with a towel and sensuously began the process of drying off the moisture.

"You're lucky," one of the other women complained. "At least our husband visits you several times a month. Most of us are fortunate if we see him five times in a year. Just imagine the passions we have stored up for him."

"And what about me?" asked a girl at the far end of the room. She had the sweetest, most innocent face Wayne had ever seen, and he doubted she could be more than sixteen. "I've been married to him for two months now, and not once has he called me to his bed. I'm beginning to fear I may die a virgin. Perhaps our lord feels I know not the ways of pleasing a man and of being pleased by him. But that is wrong. I've studied, I *do* know."

"*What* do you know, my little mouse?" sneered the Wife of Wives. "Come here and show me what you've learned." She lay back on her divan again as the young girl approached and knelt beside her. "Demonstrate on me," the woman commanded.

The girl nodded her head in obeisance and began to gently caress the older woman's body. Her fingertips made but the lightest touch on the woman's skin, wandering up and down the length of the body from shoulders to knees, with particular emphasis on breasts and loins. The Wife of Wives moaned softly and stretched

61

her body in feline undulations to appreciate the experience to its fullest extent.

As the young girl progressed, she gained more confidence in herself, and her ministrations increased in their passion. Her deft fingers began a detailed exploration of the tight black curls in the woman's pubic triangle. The Wife of Wives spread her legs and raised her buttocks, encouraging the young girl's fingers to penetrate her. The woman's breathing became more rapid until, with a passionate gasp, she reached up and pulled the virgin down on top of her.

The two bodies writhed on the couch, the women's hands caressing one another's skin with passionate tenderness. They kissed with the full fervor of their charged emotions, and they rubbed their bodies together, the full breasts of the older woman rubbing against the small, immature bosom of the younger.

Then the Wife of Wives rolled over on top and began kissing the girl's body, starting at the lips and working downward. Her tongue played teasingly over the nipples for some time before continuing lower to the navel and beyond. Finally the older woman buried her face between the virgin's thighs and continued her ministrations until the girl cried out and her whole body shook with unbearable pleasure.

At last the two women lay exhausted on the couch. The Wife of Wives lifted her head to look at the younger girl. "You've learned your lessons well," she panted. "I'll make sure to tell our husband that you will easily be able to please him." Her mouth spread in a wide grin. "Just make sure you continue pleasing me as well."

"Certainly, my lady," the young girl smiled.

The other women in the harem had begun removing their scanty clothing and waded into the pool in the center of the room. They splashed about playfully and began oiling each other down with loving care. Wayne's gaze roamed the room, noting the beautiful features of each lady in turn, until the Dream faded into intermission.

As the Dream faded back in again, Wayne leaned forward to get a better look at the bathing beauties, and accidentally bumped the screen that covered his hiding place.

"What was that?" one of the women cried.

"What was what?"

"Over there," replied the first, pointing in Wayne's direction. "I saw the screen move. I think someone's there."

There were some squeals from some of the more nervous women, and someone yelled, "Send for the eunuch!"

The Wife of Wives sat up and looked thoughtful. "Let's not be too hasty. Let's see what the trouble is, first." She sauntered over to Wayne's alcove, swaying her hips broadly, and pulled the screen aside, revealing Wayne to the others. One of the women fainted, and most of the others turned away modestly to hide their nakedness. Only the Wife of Wives flagrantly stood her ground and stared Wayne straight in the face. "Who are you, who dares invade the sultan's harem?" she asked haughtily.

"My name is Ali," Wayne said with calm precision.

"Do you know the penalty, Ali, for a man who beholds the sultan's harem?"

"Death."

"And yet you are here anyway. Are you known as Ali the Fool?"

Wayne knew he was a dead man anyway, so he might as well go for broke. "I am called Ali the Fortunate," he told her, "for never have human eyes beheld so much beauty in one place at one time. How could any man be more blessed?"

"If the eunuchs find you here, they will bless you with their scimitars."

"Then it is up to you not to let them find me."

"Up to me?" The Wife of Wives arched an eyebrow; clearly Wayne's impertinence intrigued her.

"Don't you see, lovely lady of my heart, it is kismet that brings me here. Some benevolent *djin* passing by heard your heartfelt sighs for a man to satisfy your needs, and plucked me from my tent in the desert to be with you. But even I, as great a lover as ever the desert brought forth, can do little to please you if the eunuchs skewer me with their swords."

"Allah certainly does work in mysterious ways," said the Wife of Wives with a mischievous smile on her face.

The other women in the room had now gotten over their initial shock at Wayne's presence and were gathering around him. Curiosity mingled with naked lust in their beautiful faces. "He is indeed most fair of body and countenance," one of them remarked, looking Wayne over approvingly from top to bottom.

"We wouldn't want to offend whatever *djin* it was who brought him," another said.

"Only a fool rejects a gift from Allah," commented a third.

One of the women stepped brazenly forward until she was directly in front of Wayne. She had just come out of the pool, and her body was dripping with beads of water, delicious droplets inviting him to lick them off her smooth, warm skin. She placed her hands on his shoulders and ran them sensuously down his arms. "The wise men tell us to embrace our fate happily," she said. "I have always tried to do so."

She took another step closer, so that her body was now pressed up against Wayne's. Her hips pressed against his own, and the tips of her nipples brushed against his chest as she swayed slightly back and forth. Wayne put an arm around her to draw her closer to him, and leaned over to kiss her eager lips.

Suddenly she was pulled away from him by another of the women. "No you don't," the newcomer shrieked. "He's mine! I saw him first."

"All you did was cry and turn away," said the woman who'd been pulled from Wayne's embrace. "If that's the only way you react to a man, you don't deserve to have one."

"I can please him ten times better than you can. I'm skilled in forty-three different techniques."

"But *men* do it differently than the camels you've practiced with."

The two women grabbed at each other and started to fight while the rest of the harem looked on, taking sides with one or another of the combatants. The fighters wrestled themselves to the ground and tore at one another's hair as their naked bodies writhed about. They were very evenly matched, and neither could hold the other down for very long before being tossed over and pinned herself. The other ladies thought this was grand amusement, and screamed encouragement to their friends, occasionally kicking the backside of whoever was on top and knocking her over.

"What's going on here?" bellowed a loud voice. Turning, Wayne could see the imposing, half-naked figure of the eunuch standing in the doorway, his massive arms folded imperiously across his chest. The slave glared at the ladies, willing them into silence, until his gaze came abruptly to Wayne standing among them.

"Who are you, swine, and how did you get here?" the eunuch roared, his hand already reaching for the hilt of his scimitar.

"Abou doesn't believe in *djinni*," the Wife of Wives whispered to Wayne. "Do you have any other fables for him?"

Wayne broke away and started running as the big eunuch came after him, scimitar in hand. Time slowed down for Wayne, and it seemed he could barely make any headway as the giant slave closed in on him. The shiny steel blade gleamed in the sunlight that came through the open roof in the center of the room, and the other man's battle cry echoed through the room like a thunderclap. Wayne's feet were leaden and the air like molasses as he tried to move through it. The eunuch came closer and closer, bearing down on him like Death personified, and there was no way to avoid the sweep of that razor sharp blade.

Then, just as the scimitar came slicing toward Wayne's throat, the eunuch slipped on a wet spot on the ground. He lost his balance and fell, hitting his head on the side

65

of the pool and slipping down under the water, where he lay unconscious and drowning.

Wayne and the women gathered around the rim of the pool to observe the drowning man. "Whatever will we tell the sultan?" one of the ladies asked, her eyes wide with terror.

The Wife of Wives smiled. "Why, the truth, of course."

Wayne caught her gaze and locked it on his own. "And what have you determined the truth to be, lovely lady of my heart?" he asked.

"That Abou was fetching a pillow for me when he accidentally slipped, hit his head and drowned," she answered coolly. "And since there was no one but us ladies here, we had not the strength to lift him out of the water in time."

"I like that truth," Wayne smiled. "Its light covers some shady areas quite nicely. But it does leave me in your debt. Do you have any suggestions for how I may go about repaying your kindness?"

"I do indeed." The sultry lady came up to him and put her arms around him, holding him just tightly enough against her that he could feel the warm smoothness of her naked body. "But you must face the fact that you can never leave this harem again, for to do so would mean your instant death. The other ladies and I will hide you, bring you food and clothing and whatever else you need—but in return for these things, you must do us the service that our lord so often neglects."

Her hands began slowly working at the fastenings of his clothing, her long delicate fingernails tickling his skin. "I warn you," she continued, "that you will grow old quickly in our company. We are a demanding group, and we will see that you are constantly performing at your best. Between us we know all the ways there are to bring out the passion in a man."

Her body pressed closer to his, her hips grinding against his own in a sensual pattern. Wayne looked deep into her eyes and gave a light shrug. "Well," he said, "if that is to be my fate then, as was already said, I can do no more than embrace it."

He put his arms more tightly around the woman who held him, and the other ladies in the harem closed in around the two of them. Gentle feminine fingers stroked his body all over, easily removing his clothing and caressing the most intimate parts of his person. He and the Wife of Wives seemed to float down to the ground, surrounded by the adoring throng of women who were all eager for their own turns with the "prisoner." Wayne realized that a man could indeed age prematurely under such strenuous conditions, but he no longer feared such death. After all, wasn't he in Paradise already?

On that thought, the Dream faded to blackness once more.

Wayne awoke shortly after the Dream finished. He lay for a moment on his back, panting heavily as he stared up at the darkened ceiling. He'd known all along that the Dream would leave him unsatisfied, but despite his better sense he'd tried it anyway. Now here he was, lying alone in bed, sweating at the sultry heat the Dream had produced, but with nothing further to show for it.

The Dream may have seemed all right to a layman, but as someone who'd spent four years in the porno field Wayne could spot altogether too many flaws in it. The "friend" who had accompanied him into the harem and then disappeared had served only to give some clumsy exposition to the piece. The Dreamer had never specified the exact number of women in the harem; they fluctuated according to his abilities to visualize them at any given moment. His research on the period was probably shaky, which meant that the room itself and the clothing were nondescript, mere props instead of an integral part of the Dream. The eunuch who was in the first act abruptly disappeared at the beginning of the second, only to reappear when needed. The whole incident with the scimitar was much too bloodthirsty, and detracted from the titillation of the rest of the Dream. Worst of all, the deus ex machina of having the eunuch slip and drown was the mark of a rank amateur; Wayne would have found some way for the viewer to defeat the eunuch on his own, thus increasing his feeling of confidence and positive attitude toward the Dream.

Of course, these sorts of things happened in normal dreams all the time—backgrounds were imperfect, characters drifted in and out, things happened for no discernible reason. There was a growing clique of Dreamers who strove for this more "naturalistic" feeling, claiming they were being truer to life—but to Wayne, that just seemed like an excuse for sloppy craftsmanship. If Dreaming was an art—and he thoroughly believed it was—then it behaved the same way all the other arts did. Art imposed its own order on reality, and Dreaming should be no exception. Wayne believed his duty as an artist demanded he keep tighter control of his Dream than had the Dreamer whose work he'd just experienced.

He lay in bed for an hour while thoughts drifted through his mind in total turmoil. His growing infatuation for Janet, his feelings of frustration at not being able to work to the best of his abilities, his revulsion at Rondel's homelife, his loneliness, and above all his need to make Dreaming into the great art he knew it could be—all these were eddies in the sea of his mind. Not until the sun began to rise and light the sky outside his window did he mercifully slip into a na ral, if belated, sleep.

CHAPTER 6

THE SCHEDULING OF staff meetings was always a delicate compromise at a Dream broadcasting studio. The "talent," the Dreamers, were of necessity late-night people. Even when they weren't working that particular night, they tried to keep to a nocturnal schedule; working during the day some of the time and at night the rest of the time could have dire consequences for body and mind. The Dreamers had to be pampered; it was upon their shoulders that the whole enterprise rested.

The administrative staff, on the other hand, preferred the normal business hours of eight to five. The day-to-day operations of a business had to be in tune with all the other businesses in the city, or nothing would ever get accomplished. Further complicating the matter were the writers, who fell into a gray area somewhere in between. Management preferred having the writers work in offices during regular business hours—but that was a system honored more in the breach than in the observance. Writers were always over deadline and working late or coming in early, or they'd take a script home with them to work on it there; as a result, they frequently worked staggered hours that never coincided with anyone else's.

Staff meetings at Dramatic Dreams were usually held at about four in the afternoon. The Dreamers didn't like that because it meant coming in to work "early"; the staff didn't like it because most of the day before the meeting was considered a waste, as everyone looked forward to what would be said and done at the meeting. The writers didn't much care; any excuse to take them away from their typewriters was a welcome one. But four o'clock was the only time Bill DeLong could guarantee any kind of reasonable attendance from every branch concerned.

Wayne arrived at the studio just a couple of minutes before four. He had just enough time to dump his jacket in his tiny office, grab a notepad and pen and rush off to the meeting. It was, as usual, held in Mort Schulberg's office, which was the largest on the floor. That didn't mean much; if everyone on the staff showed up at the same time, they still crowded it to the walls and most people had to sit on the floor. It was one way of assuring that everyone got physically close, if not actually friendly.

Today, though, was not quite that bad; Wayne would still have to sit on the floor for coming late, but he'd at least have a choice of places. Looking around, he noticed that Rondel had managed to grab a seat on the long couch next to Janet, who was leaning against the arm on the other side, not happy about Rondel's proximity. When Rondel spotted Wayne, he held up a book to show that he'd remembered to bring it. Wayne nodded acknowledgment and turned back to the front of the room. There he saw that DeLong was already passing over to him a copy of his new script. Wayne barely had time to glance at it and see that it was indeed a Western before two more people came in and DeLong stood up.

"I guess that's everybody we were expecting," the program coordinator began. "Not a terribly great attendance, but we've got a lot of people out. Can't say I blame them, considering what's on the agenda for tomorrow; I wish I could get out of it myself. We'll talk a little more about that later. Right now, let's start off with the routine stuff. Ratings. They're not good, but when were they ever? The Spiegelman thing has hurt us there, too, I think, and on top of that there's the normal seasonal slump. Nobody's job's in danger just yet—you can all breathe easier for a while—but if this continues we might have to try something to shake up the numbers. You all keep track of your own scores pretty well; I'll be going around individually in the next week or so to see if you have any suggestions for improvements. In the meantime, think about it; any and all ideas are welcome."

DeLong checked the piece of paper on which he'd written his agenda. "Let's see, we get into scheduling. Vince is up again tonight, and I for one think we all owe him a small ovation. This is his fourth Dream in a week, which is really above and beyond the call of duty. I'm not sure how else we could have managed with Dory on her honeymoon and Fred in the hospital. Vince, what are you doing tonight?"

Rondel cleared his throat. "It's a Masterdream, a quick little sci-fi story I whipped up. It's set in the far future, when Mankind has reverted to savagery except for a small group of wizards who know how to work the old machines. The main story line follows a hero from the outlying areas who challenges the power of the wizards and brings technology to the masses."

DeLong nodded. "Sounds promising, especially on such short notice." He then went on to summarize the rest of the scheduling. To Wayne's dismay, he and Janet wouldn't be working together again for at least another week; Janet had the second Dream tomorrow night—a police procedural mystery—and Wayne had the first Dream the night after that. With any luck, DeLong told them, their manpower problems would soon be over and they could get back into a more relaxed schedule. Wayne hoped that meant more doubling up; he was looking forward to another chance at working with Janet.

DeLong spent a bit of time talking to the writers, suggesting new directions and asking them to emphasize character a little more than plot. He was toying with the notion of introducing series characters as a means of building viewer identification, but wanted some more input before taking the plunge.

Then there were some routine administrative details

to be discussed. Group health insurance premiums were going up again, so the new paychecks would have a bigger bite taken out of them. Charity time was also coming up, and several withholding plans were offered to make giving as painless a procedure as possible.

With all the petty details out of the way, Mort Schulberg stepped forward to discuss the subject that was on everyone's mind. "As you know," he began, "Gerald Forsch from the FCC will be here tomorrow to conduct his inquiry into Eliott's *alleged* misconduct. He'll probably be questioning everyone individually, except for Wayne over there, since he wasn't with us when it happened. Wayne gets off the hook this time."

There was a mild nervous laugh in the room, and Wayne grinned sheepishly.

"I don't know exactly what Forsch is going to ask," Schulberg went on. "He's sure to ask you questions about Eliott—how well you knew him, what his political beliefs were, whether he ever expressed any interest in converting people to his way of thinking, that sort of thing. He might even start asking you some questions about yourself—but remember, there hasn't been the faintest suggestion that anyone else is guilty of anything. I hope to God you don't give him any reason to dig deeper. Don't hide anything—if he thinks you're covering up, he'll only probe deeper. But don't volunteer much, either."

Schulberg hesitated, and ran a hand nervously over his balding scalp. "Look, you all know I'm in a bind. Eliott's my son-in-law, and I want to protect him as much as I can. At the same time, my first obligation is to this station, and to make sure that it keeps going so that you all have jobs. I don't want to risk that, either. The FCC puts enough restrictions on us already; I don't want to give them the excuse to shut us down."

There was a consensus of nods and muttered comments. The FCC was not popular within the Dream industry. It prohibited broadcasters from projecting ads over the wires, a potentially lucrative field, because of the possible propaganda abuses; it restricted

Dreaming to nighttime hours in an attempt to keep it from becoming too addictive, thereby eliminating people who worked at night as potential daytime customers; it prohibited minors from using Dreamcaps, on the theory that children's minds were far too impressionable; and it kept a constant eye on the contents of Dreams, to prevent even the appearance of misconduct. Hardly a month went by without some complaint surfacing, though the Spiegelman case was by far the most serious to date.

Schulberg looked around the room and sighed. "I know what conventional wisdom says: throw Eliott to the wolves and protect our own asses. Well, I don't intend to do that. I'll back him within the limits of my ability to do so. As for yourselves, that's a matter between you and your consciences. I'm not asking you to lie; if Eliott is guilty of this, he deserves to be punished. But remember when Forsch is questioning you that it could just as easily be your head on the chopping block. Think about how much you'd want your friends to back you, and how disappointed you'd be if they sold you out to save their own skins. Whatever happened with Eliott is over, and we've got the future to think of—but let's not walk callously over his body."

He shrugged. "That's about all I've got to say. Good luck tomorrow with Forsch."

The meeting broke up, and everyone left the office and poured out into the hall. People broke into small groups of twos, threes and fours, with the main topic being the impending investigation. Wayne talked to Jack Silverstein, the writer who'd done the new Western for him, and got a feel for what the story was about. They didn't talk long, though. Jack had other things on his mind; he had written the Dream Spiegelman projected on that controversial night, and he was bound to field some pretty tough questions tomorrow.

Wayne took his script and started up the hall back to his own tiny cubicle of an office when he saw Rondel and Janet. The Masterdreamer had backed Janet into a corner, and was insistent on talking to her. Janet looked even more uncomfortable than she had during the staff meeting. Wayne hesitated to butt in, remembering DeLong's advice of last night, then decided it couldn't hurt matters any if he just went over to talk to them.

"Please, Vince," Janet was saying as Wayne approached. "Don't stir things up again. It would only be too painful for both of us. Just let it die."

"I'm not trying to start anything," Rondel insisted. "But if your car's in the shop, you'll need a ride home with *somebody*. I was just offering. . . ."

"And I said no. Why not leave it at that?"

"Vince, do you have that book for me?" Wayne interrupted. He tried to keep his tone neutral, so that all three of them could pretend he hadn't heard any of the fight.

"What? Oh, sure, here it is. Take good care of it—I went without lunch for five weeks to pay for it." Rondel handed the volume to Wayne, who just glanced at it and made no move to leave.

"What seems to be the trouble?" Wayne asked casually.

Janet started to say something, but Rondel cut her off. "Janet took her car in for repairs, and she just learned it won't be ready until tomorrow. I was offering to take her home. . . ."

"How could you?" Wayne asked. "You don't have a car."

"I could call a cab," Rondel said.

Wayne felt a surge of cold fury rip through him. Rondel had pleaded poverty last night to get Wayne to drive him home, subjecting him to that horrible ordeal—and yet now he was perfectly willing to pay cabfare to take Janet home. The cold-blooded selfishness of the man was beyond words; what was worse, Wayne could tell from his face that Rondel saw nothing wrong with this hypocritical behavior.

"Don't be silly, Vince," Wayne said with feigned affability. "You were just telling me last night how unaffordable cabs were—and besides, you've got a Dream to do tonight. You can't spare the time to go back and forth. Don't worry—I'll take her home."

"It's not really along your way," Rondel protested.

Wayne's voice was firmer now. "It's not along yours, either."

Rondel looked from Wayne to Janet, and decided the best course lay in tactical retreat. "Well, I just thought I'd offer," he said. "But I do have to polish my script for tonight. If you'll excuse me." He turned and walked off down the hall.

Janet waited until he was out of earshot, then turned to Wayne. "Thank you," she said quietly. "That was getting embarrassing."

"My pleasure. Always willing to help a lady in distress."

"You don't have to drive me home if you don't want to," she said. "I *do* have money for my own cabfare."

"It's no problem."

"Well, I'm up near Pasadena, and I know you're out in the Valley. . . ."

"Look, I don't want to replay that last scene with you. If you *want* to spend your money on cabfare, I won't arm-wrestle you out of it." Wayne paused. "But I really would like to drive you home, Janet."

Janet opened her mouth to say something, then shut it again. When she finally did speak, her voice was softer. "Sorry. I guess I was being too defensive. My nerves haven't been all that hot in the past month, ever since . . . well, never mind. Yes, all right, you can take me home if you don't mind going now."

Wayne was a little surprised, but he shrugged. "Why not? I've got my script, and I can study it just as well at home as I can here."

"Thanks. It'll just take me a minute to get set." She went off and disappeared into the ladies' room.

When she came out, he led her downstairs to the parking lot. She gave him directions and the two of them set off in his car. At first they talked about general topics—the Dream they'd done last night, the problems with Janet's own car—it needed a new starter, she explained—and the Forsch inquiry tomorrow. At last Wayne got around to asking her why she'd left the office so early.

"I've got a few things to do around the house," she said. "And I wanted to make sure I got them done early enough so I could catch Vince's Dream tonight."

"You mean you're going to tune him in?" Wayne couldn't keep the surprise from his voice.

"I know it sounds kind of funny," she replied, "but I do try to catch his Dreams every chance I get. In spite of our . . . our troubles, he's the best Dreamer I've ever seen. He's got so much power, so much depth, so much detail. I like to study him, like young playwrights study Shakespeare. I'm still learning this business, and there's so much he can show me. It might not hurt you to try him, too."

Wayne snorted. "I'll pass."

"You don't like him, do you?"

"I think he's an arrogant, self-righteous prig. He tried to convert me once. . . ."

"Only once?" Janet laughed.

"I've only been here a month. I was polite but distant. Thank God Bill came in and interrupted."

"Bill's good at that," Janet nodded. "But you're wrong about Vince. Well, you're right in a way, he's like that on the surface, but there's so much more underneath."

"I'm surprised to hear that coming from you, considering. . . ." Wayne stopped abruptly.

"Considering what?" Her eyes narrowed. "Do you know that we . . . that he and I. . . ."

"I'd heard rumors."

Janet sighed. "Yes, I guess you would. I broke it off. It's definitely over now—but every once in awhile there are these little echoes."

"And yet you're *defending* him."

"I didn't really break off with him—I broke off with that goddamn mother of his."

"Yes, I just had the, uh, pleasure of meeting her last night." Wayne shivered at the recollection.

"Then you have some idea of what I was up against. Vince has some marvelous qualities, really he does. He can be kind and gentle, and he's extremely honest. A little on the dull side, perhaps. . . ."

"All that religion, I suppose."

"He takes it very seriously," Janet nodded. "More than I ever could, I'm afraid. I was raised with a God who took care of things in Heaven and pretty much let people run their own lives here on Earth. Vince's relationship is much more personal. I got the feeling he even took God with him into the bathroom. That's something you never think about, you know, God being in there and looking over your shoulder while . . . anyway, the subject is a very personal one with Vince. That was the only time I ever saw him really excited and enthusiastic, when he was talking about religion. Even in bed there were . . . problems. Part of it was him, part of it was my own damn hang-ups. Maybe even most of it was my fault, it's hard to say. I can't pretend I don't have my own flaws. But things never really worked right in bed."

The thought of Janet having sex with Vince made Wayne distinctly uncomfortable, but he could think of no easy way to change the subject. He tried to let the words flow through him without letting their meaning register.

"His mother caused a lot of his problems, though," Janet went on, oblivious to Wayne's discomfort. "She had him for thirty-five years before I got to him, and I couldn't break that training. I tried to improve him, I tried to make him over into someone who was worth knowing, and sometimes I even got the feeling he really wanted to improve. He was like a pathetically eager puppy trying to be paper-trained and never quite getting the idea. But every time I got him one step forward, his goddamn mother pushed him two steps back.

"She can be so casually cruel. Do you know she once flushed a pet kitten down the toilet for scratching her? And she has all sorts of tricks at her disposal. She

77

knows when to baby him and when to boss him. If those tactics don't work, she switches to religious pressure. If that doesn't work, she's got all her various illnesses. She's fabulous at making him feel guilty for her hypochondria. 'Don't let me die knowing my son is a sinner.' Or, 'If you keep this up, I know I'll have a heart attack.' How could I fight something like that? Even when he and I were alone, I could always feel her there, glaring at me. No woman on Earth, of course, was good enough for her son. I got the feeling she was just like God, that he took her presence with him everywhere, too, even into the bathroom. It must get awfully crowded in there with all three of them."

"How could you . . . care for someone like that?" Wayne couldn't bring himself to use the word "love."

Janet shrugged. "As I said, he had good qualities, too, and even better potential. There were times, I know, when he wanted to break loose, get out of it all. I could feel it. I could see the storm building up behind his eyes when his mother was forcing him to do something he didn't want to do. But the rebellion never got any further than that. I kept waiting for him to break free, but he never quite had the courage."

"It's funny you should mention that," Wayne said. "Last night as I was driving him home, he was asking me what it was like to do porno Dreams. It was like some forbidden fruit dangling just outside his reach."

Janet nodded. "Exactly, yes. Time after time I'd get him to a point like that, and just when I thought I could break him through the barrier, something would happen—usually his mother—and he retreated again. It was so frustrating, there were times I went home after a date with him and I'd cry for hours. I made all sorts of plans to poison that old bitch, but I knew that would *really* send him off the deep end. Finally I couldn't take it anymore. I had to get out of it for my own sanity's sake. I still don't think he understands why it was necessary. And his mother's probably making the most of it, pointing out how she was right about me all

78

along, that she knew I'd betray him. I just couldn't win."

"Maybe he's hoping you'll reconsider. 'Hope springs eternal within the human breast,' and all that."

She shook her head. "Not a chance. Even after his mother is dead and gone—please God, let it be soon—it still wouldn't work. She'll always be with him, always be a part of him in the back of his mind, disapproving of everything he does and refusing to let him relax and be himself. That was what finally led me to the break, when I knew she'd always be there and he'd never have the courage to throw her out. I could never live that way."

They came to the address Janet had given, and Wayne's car pulled up in front of an apartment building that looked as nondescript as his own. "I guess we're here," he announced.

They sat in silence for a moment, each wondering what to do next. Finally Janet pulled up on the handle to open the door. "Yeah. Thanks for the ride, Wayne."

"Janet. . . ."

"Don't say it, Wayne," she interrupted.

"How do you know what. . . ?"

"Whatever it was, please don't say it." She looked him straight in the face and reached out to place her hand on top of his. "I know—that is, I can guess what's on your mind, and I do appreciate it. I really like you, Wayne, I think you're a nice guy. . . ."

"That's really the kiss of death," he laughed bitterly.

"Not necessarily." She gave his hand a slight squeeze to reassure him. "The truth is, Wayne, my life is all screwed around right now. When I broke off with Vince, it was like surrendering after a year-long war with his mother. It made me question everything about myself as a woman, and what I want from life, and . . . and just everything. I've never been all that secure, and this only made things worse. I need time to sort my head out. That's all. I enjoyed working with you last night, and I've asked Bill if we could do it again more often. Maybe something can grow from it. I hope so.

But right now I have to let the dust settle. I hope you won't be angry with me."

She slid halfway out the door, then turned back to him again. "I really do appreciate the ride, honest, even if I talked your ear off with my own personal problems."

"I enjoyed it," Wayne said. "And as for talking about problems, now you'll have to let me talk about mine sometime."

"Sounds fair," Janet smiled at him. "You're on. See you at work tomorrow."

Then she was gone, leaving only a trace of her perfume in the air to prove she'd been there. Wayne didn't remember too much about his own drive home; his mind was too much aboil with a mixture of hope and frustration. Janet did seem to like him, but she had the same message for him that DeLong did: wait. Her personal problems all seemed to stem from the one source, Vince Rondel, and that fact did nothing to increase Wayne's feeling of brotherly love for his colleague.

He arrived home and fixed himself a frozen dinner while watching the news on TV. His mind was still in a turmoil, and he needed time for it to settle. He glanced at his typewriter and thought about working a bit on the novel he'd been playing with, but decided against it. In his present mood, nothing good was likely to come out.

Instead, he leafed through the book Rondel had given him. Just as the other had described, it was a superb reference; it could almost have been written with Dreamers in mind. It was crammed with illustrations and old photographs depicting buildings, clothing and furniture as they existed in the Old West. Details were what a Dreamer always needed; the more accurately he could visualize a scene, the more real it would feel to the audience. Wayne had always relied previously on scenes from old Western movies and TV shows to get his images—but going back to original source material like this could only improve the flavor of what he did.

He became so absorbed in the book that he didn't notice the time until nearly midnight. Rondel's Dream was due to start very shortly. He thought about what Janet had said, that studying Rondel's work would improve his own abilities as a Dreamer. He'd sampled Rondel's Dreams before, and knew that was sensible advice—but Wayne was not in a very sensible mood tonight. Rondel had been nice enough to loan him this fabulous book, but Wayne was still mad at him for what he'd done to Janet, and for making Wayne go through that ordeal last night. *I'll skip it tonight,* Wayne thought. *I've got too much other work to do, anyway.*

He put the book aside for a while and turned to his script. He skimmed through it once to get the general feel, and was not impressed. It was a very routine shoot-em-up, and he felt the stirrings of dissatisfaction again. Why couldn't they give him something to challenge him, to let him stretch himself as a performer? He might not be a star of Rondel's magnitude, but he liked to think he was capable of better things than this.

Of course, he knew perfectly well why they weren't giving him challenging material. It was the Spiegelman affair again. Until that matter was resolved one way or another, Dramatic Dreams was taking things as easy as possible, deliberately avoiding anything that showed the faintest hint of controversy—even at the risk of being trite and boring. Wayne wondered whether he ought to suggest to DeLong that *that* could be a prime factor in their ratings slump. The audience wanted more originality than they were getting here.

Well, whether he liked it or not, this was the script he had to work with. Heaving a sigh, Wayne dug in and began studying the story in depth, making little notes to himself in the margin about scenery and costumes, and what the various characters should look like. He would have to memorize the script before performing it, of course—there were no cue cards in

Dreams—but writing the notes out reinforced the images in his mind. Slowly the Western town of Little Creek and all its inhabitants took on an air of reality that he would have to convey to his audience.

Then the phone rang, breaking his concentration. Muttering curses at anyone who would call him at this hour of the night, Wayne got up and walked over to the receiver. "Hello?"

It was Bill DeLong's voice on the other end. "Wayne? Thank God someone's answering their phone."

"Bill? What's that supposed to mean?"

"Look, can you come down to the station right away?"

Something in his tone made Wayne stiffen. "Why? What's happened? Is something wrong?"

"I . . . we think so, but we can't be sure. That's why we want you down here, to check it out."

"What's the matter?"

DeLong paused. "Well, from all we can tell, something's gone wrong with Vince's Dream. It's out of control, and it seems to be taking the audience along with it."

CHAPTER 7

WAYNE MADE IT down to the station in record time. Fortunately he was still dressed, his car had plenty of gas, the freeways were next to deserted at this hour of the night, and he encountered no Highway Patrol officers, so there were no hindrances to his speed. Even so, it took more than twenty-five minutes to reach the studio.

The broadcasting rooms were in chaos. Mort Schulberg was practically bouncing off the walls in frustrated rage, swearing Yiddish obscenities at the perversity of the universe. Bill DeLong was conferring with Ernie White in the brightly lit engineering booth against the back wall; DeLong was reading numbers off the dials while White had his shirt-sleeves rolled up and had taken half the wiring apart. The only spot of quiet was the cubicle where Rondel's body lay still. The Dreamcap was in place on his head, giving no indication that anything unpleasant was happening.

"What's going on?" Wayne asked as he entered the room.

"The whole world is crumbling beneath us," Schulberg moaned. "It's not bad enough I've got this *putz* Forsch coming tomorrow to stir up trouble. Now this has to happen on top of it. It's enough to give my ulcer an ulcer. Why didn't I stay in the meat-packing business like my father? You can make a nice living as a butcher. . . ."

DeLong, seeing Wayne come in, emerged from the engineering booth. Wrapping a friendly arm around the station manager's shoulders, he said, "Calm down,

Mort. We still don't know anything for certain." He looked over to Wayne. "As a matter of fact, the *only* thing we know for certain is that we don't know anything at all. Something is definitely wrong, but we don't know what it is."

"What exactly is happening?" Wayne asked. He hoped DeLong could give him a slightly more coherent explanation than Schulberg.

"Come on into the booth and I'll show you." DeLong released Schulberg, who promptly began fidgeting again. The program coordinator led Wayne into the engineer's booth, where Ernie White nodded a quick hello. The control board was a shambles, with plates taken off at intervals to reveal an intricate maze of wires and printed circuitry. In the bright lighting of the room, White's face glistened with the sheen of perspiration.

"Are you familiar with the board?" DeLong asked Wayne.

"Not very. I had the standard classes during training, but electronics wasn't my specialty. I didn't kill myself studying that end of the business. I didn't understand it too well then, and that was six years ago. I always thought that was someone else's job."

"That's what I thought before tonight, too, but necessity makes a great teacher. Okay, these dials over here on the right are measuring Vince's mental activity and output while he's under. Notice anything peculiar about them?"

Wayne studied the meters, trying hard to remember what his teacher had told him about output levels. The worst danger, he recalled the teacher saying, was a wildly fluctuating output level; that would indicate a potentially unstable mental process, or perhaps a Dreamer who wasn't in full control of what he was doing. Rondel's readings were nice and steady. "No," he admitted to DeLong.

"I'll give you a hint. This one over here should be reading somewhere between thirty and sixty."

Wayne looked more closely at the indicated dial, and his eyes widened. The needle was way over to the right, reading a steady two hundred and fifty. "Wow. That's a bit high then, isn't it?"

"That's like saying the ocean's moist. It's so high it's unheard of. The only reason the meter is even calibrated that high is because it's a multipurpose gauge, so they have to have a wide variety of readings on its face. Otherwise, these readings would just be off the scale. And that same phenomenon is registering on all the other dials as well—they're all reading at impossible levels."

"What does it mean?"

Ernie White looked up from his work and took up the explanation. "It means Vince is putting out mental energy at a rate nobody would have believed possible. He's exerting more control over his Dream than anyone's ever seen before. I couldn't say for certain, because nothing like this has ever happened, but I'm willing to bet he can't keep it up for long. His mind will burn out like an overloaded fuse if this continues for any length of time."

Wayne gave a low whistle, and DeLong nodded. "But that's only half the problem—and the simpler half, at that," the older man said. "Look at these meters over here."

They squeezed past the reclining White to get to the right-hand side of the panel. Wayne didn't need any training to see that something was wrong here. Four of the dials, labeled "Audience," had their needles plastered to the left hand edge of their faces. "Something's happening with these," he pointed, "though I couldn't begin to guess what."

"I can only *just* begin to guess," White spoke up. "Those dials are there to show gross audience reaction. When the home cap picks up our broadcast, it sends a signal back over the wires to us and to our computer. That's how we know who to bill. Normally the return signal is very weak, just enough to tell us who's tuned in. It should never even be a thousandth of what those dials are showing. By all rights, what you're seeing there is impossible. As far as I've been able to tell, that is feedback."

"Feedback?" Wayne blinked a couple of times uncomprehendingly. "What . . . how can that happen?"

White shrugged. "Damned if I know. The caps at home aren't really any different from the ones in the studio here, except that ours are hooked into a transmitter that boosts the power a few million times. If a home set, which is normally a receiver, had the power, there is nothing in theory to prevent its becoming a transmitter. The customer could theoretically send his own neural impulses back along the line. If they came back in far enough and Vince's cap picked them up, he could register the impressions and rebroadcast them, sending the individual actions out over the broadcast wires again. We'd hit an accelerating loop that might—just might—account for what we're seeing on those dials."

"But the home sets don't have that kind of power," Wayne protested.

"You weren't paying attention when Bill showed you the output dials. Vince is radiating power like nobody's business. Normally a Dreamer wouldn't be aware of any incoming signals, because his own outgoing signals drown them out—oh, like trying to hear a mouse crawling across a rug while at the same time you're shouting at the top of your lungs. But if Vince somehow reached out and started pulling in the signals from the audience, he could then use our transformers, hitched up to his cap, to amplify *everything*. He could be assimilating the audience reaction and broadcasting it back at them, loud enough to incorporate it into the Dream."

White shook his head. "Damnedest thing I ever saw in my life."

Wayne was now totally confused. "But what . . . how could that be? What would that do to the Dream?"

"We've been trying to figure that out ourselves while waiting for you to get here," DeLong said. "It's not a simple situation. As near as we can determine, it means the audience is somehow contributing to the Dream. Instead of being passive recipients, riding along with the story Vince was spinning for them and acting out the roles he dictated, they've now got 'free will' and can take an active part in whatever is going on."

Wayne stood for a moment, contemplating in shocked silence what DeLong had said. Such a thing was nearly impossible to comprehend. A Dreamer *had* to control what went on during the Dream, or chaos would result. The spectators couldn't be allowed to change things; it would ruin everything. It would be like trying to produce a play while the audience was permitted to wander onstage and influence the action.

Rondel would have a couple of advantages. He had the power of the station's transmitter behind him, making him stronger than any other individual in the Dream. Then too, he was in conscious control of himself; he *knew* he was Dreaming, and knew that he could alter the Dream by changing his visualization of it. If one member of the audience acted out of line, Rondel could surround him with a glass cage. If a mob of people rebelled, he could build a wall around them, or confront them with a sheet of flames, or have an earthquake shake them up, or resort to any number of other techniques to scare them back into submission.

Of course, with free will, they could also change things around—if they realized they had the power to do so. But they were asleep when they tuned in to the Dream. Their unconscious minds had accepted the world Rondel presented to them as truth. If they didn't know they could change things around, they wouldn't try. Still, Rondel would have his hands full keeping them all in line.

Wayne shivered. "No wonder Vince is burning up energy like that. It's probably taking every last bit of his resources just to keep things under control."

"He's certainly got enough of a crowd on his hands," White said. "Computer shows a rating of nearly seventy thousand."

Seventy thousand people. Wayne tried to visualize a

87

mob that size. They would more than overflow most baseball stadiums; that many people would fill up a sizeable proportion of the Los Angeles Coliseum. On that large a scale, it became impossible to think of them as individuals; they lost not only their names and individual identities, but even their faces as well. They became a throng.

He shook his head at the enormity of it. "That's an awfully big flock to shepherd. How did all this start, anyhow?"

"Your guess is as good as ours," White said, throwing up his hands in despair. "The first act seemed to go perfectly. Vince is so good that I never have to worry too closely about his work. We made it to the first break, and he came out smoothly. As soon as he went in again for the second act, I sneaked out to the bathroom and to get a cup of coffee. I wasn't gone more than five minutes. When I got back, my instruments were going crazy. The first thing I did was check Vince, but he looked okay in his cubicle, and since the readings were so impossible I just assumed something short-circuited in the board. I mean, there didn't seem to be any way I could get readings like those *naturally*. The transmitter itself seemed to be all right and since, as I said, Vince is so good, I didn't worry about him. I concentrated on trying to find the short circuit instead.

"Then Vince didn't come out at the scheduled break after the second act. I kept giving him the little buzz signal to let him know he was going on too long, but he didn't respond. By this time, Bill and Mort were getting worried, too, so we thought we ought to call in another Dreamer for his opinion."

"You were the only one I could reach," Delong added. "Nobody else answered their phone."

"That break seems to have been some kind of turning point, then," Wayne mused. "Did anything happen between the first and second act that might have affected Vince somehow?"

DeLong answered. "We thought of that ourselves. He got a phone call of some kind. He and I were talking about how the first act had gone, and what changes he wanted to do for the second act. Then Mort came in and said there was a call for Vince. Vince took it in Mort's office. It only lasted a minute or two, and then he came out white and shaken. There was a look on his face that . . . well, I'm a writer and I'm supposed to be good with words, but I'm damned if I can describe that expression. He walked right by me and into his cubicle, without saying a single word. As soon as Ernie gave him the signal to start act two, he put on the cap and started."

"And that's when all hell broke loose," Wayne mused. "I guess we're safe in assuming it was the phone call that triggered whatever happened."

DeLong nodded. "That's our supposition for the moment. The bitch is that we don't know who that call was from or what it was about. Mort says he never heard the voice before. Some stranger just called and asked to speak to Vince on a very urgent matter of personal business. That's all we know."

"We don't even know what's going on inside that Dream," said White. The engineer was shaking his head. "I only know it isn't supposed to happen that way."

Mort Schulberg, who'd been pacing around outside the control booth, chose this moment to enter. "That's why we called you. We need another Dreamer to go in there with an auxiliary cap and tell us what's happening, so we can maybe think of some way to straighten things out."

"Why don't you just turn it off?" Wayne suggested. "If we stopped broadcasting, we could wake Vince up and ask him."

"That was the first thing we thought of," White said. "We'd have done it by now except for that damn feedback. It complicates the picture something fierce. It's an unknown quantity, and we don't know what would happen if we tried it."

"Remember," DeLong elaborated, "to those seventy thousand people in the audience, the Dream seems like reality. They're part of it and, with the feedback, they're apparently even contributing to it. What would happen to you if suddenly your reality were cut off, or even just slowly faded out right in the middle of something? We're always careful to end stories at a crucial point where the audience feels fulfilled—but again, they're usually just passengers along for the ride."

"Normal dreams end without hurting people," Wayne said.

"Sure—but remember the old saying about how dangerous it is to wake a sleepwalker? I never understood *why* it was supposed to be dangerous—maybe the disorientation could be a psychological shock, I don't know. But multiply all that by seventy thousand and you'll see why we're worried.

"Maybe absolutely nothing would happen if we cut off this Dream—but can we afford to bet on that? I can see the possibility of serious traumata at least, to a number of people; perhaps a few of the less stable might go insane. It might even be enough of a shock to give some people out there a heart attack."

"There probably wouldn't be that many adverse effects," Wayne said.

"Oh?" Schulberg interrupted. "How many is enough for you? It only took six complaints to start the FCC investigation of Spiegelman. Could you guarantee there won't be six nut cases out of seventy thousand?"

"No," Wayne admitted. "But look, I just Dreamed last night. You know it's dangerous to do too much Dreaming in too short a time."

"If there were any other way, we'd do it," DeLong said. "We tried everyone else on the staff first; nobody else was home. And, for obvious reasons, we don't want to go outside our own staff."

Obvious reasons, indeed. It was the Spiegelman affair again. The investigator, Forsch, would be here in just a few hours to begin a probe into what by all rights should be just some minor irregularities. If he were to catch wind of a major catastrophe such as this, the results were totally unforeseeable. At the very least,

Wayne could imagine the entire station would be shut down. If things got bad enough, the entire Dream broadcast industry could be hobbled. DeLong and Schulberg were obviously hoping Wayne could keep the problem in-house and keep the outside world from learning anything about it. Looking at those dials again, Wayne wasn't sure that was possible.

"All right," Wayne said wearily. He was tired, and he didn't feel at all like Dreaming tonight, but he had little choice. "I'll go into the Dream. That won't be any problem—we have auxiliary caps and I'm used to working in tandem with another Dreamer. Usually, though, the other Dreamer is working *with* me; I don't know what kind of reception I'll get from Vince. And once I get inside, I'll be totally lost. I won't know what's going on at the moment."

"You were at the staff meeting when Vince described his story," Schulberg said.

"Sure—some sort of science fiction thing set in the far future when a few wizards who know how to use technology control the barbarian masses who don't. That wouldn't be much help in any case—and especially now. I doubt whether Vince has stuck to his script, with all this going on."

What Wayne didn't add was that Rondel had said this would be a Masterdream, where the Dreamer created a universe and peopled it with a number of characters for the audience to identify with. It took a mind of extraordinary breadth and imagination to create such a Dream successfully, and Wayne had never been very good at it.

"We know the first act went as planned," DeLong said. "Or at least, that's what Vince told me before he got the phone call, so he was probably telling the truth. We can assume *that* universe is still the basis at least—with all the troubles he'd have coping with the feedback, I don't think he'd want to change the background very much."

"Probably not," Wayne agreed. "He'd have too many other problems on his hands."

"Let's go to Vince's office," DeLong suggested. "He had his scenario and his plans written up there."

The two men left the broadcasting room and walked briskly down the hall to Rondel's office. Like Wayne's it was a small, windowless cubicle with overhead lighting, a desk, a typewriter, and a few shelves of reference books. Wayne had never been in here before and, after visiting Rondel's house, had been dreading the mess he might find here. But the office, like Vince's own bedroom, was immaculate, with all papers, books and files in neat and logical order. On the desk was a photo of Mrs. Rondel as a young, attractive woman. Wayne remembered DeLong's comment that Rondel's mother was responsible for a great many unhappy things, and wondered whether her responsibility extended to the condition of her domicile.

"Vince was going to be the leader of a primitive group, and the roles he created for the audience were other members of his tribe," DeLong explained. "The hunting has been bad, which led Vince to dare to enter the city of the Wizards, which is called Urba. The primitive people are usually scared of the Wizards, who periodically conduct raids for women or food. Technology looks like magic to them, so it takes a brave leader to risk going into the Wizards' home den, as it were. In the first act, Vince leads his people into the city, where they're confronted with things like elevators and cars. Just as the first act ended, they were surrounded by a group of the Wizards' robot guards, who were going to take them prisoner. In the second act, they were supposed to escape and wander down into the subterranean vaults below the city, where they meet up with a helpful old librarian robot who can plug into the city's main computer and tell them all sorts of useful information. As the story progresses, Vince and his people use this information to challenge and eventually beat the Wizards at their own game."

He reached over and handed Wayne a sketch. "Here's a brief map Vince did of the layout of Urba. These towers over here are the Citadels of Power, this large building is the Central Computer Complex, with the entrance to the subterranean library in its basement. It's not very detailed, I know; Vince drew it up more or less as a reminder to himself of what would be approximately where. He probably had a much better visualization of it in his own mind, which you'll see when you get inside."

Wayne studied the layout. The city was designed in a rectangular grid, precise and unimaginative—but then, even a genius like Rondel would have to take shortcuts somewhere. He also read through the script once. He had little hope that it was being followed, but at least it would give him an idea of the psychology within the Dream.

After about five minutes, Wayne announced he was as ready as could be expected. The two men went back to the main studio, where Schulberg and White were waiting nervously.

"Any change?" DeLong asked.

White shook his head. "Situation's as bad as ever. Vince's output gave a couple of minor flickers, but it's still impossibly high. He may be tiring just a bit, but he's still putting out an unbelievable amount of energy."

Wayne looked over to the cubicle where Rondel's body lay still, with its Dreamcap firmly in place. The Masterdreamer was sweating profusely, but otherwise the scene looked so peaceful it was hard to believe that things inside the Dream would be so chaotic. "Are you all set for me?" he asked.

White nodded. "Cubicle Three's plugged in and raring to go."

"How about a plan for getting *me* out of there if something goes wrong?"

"I'll ring the buzzer after ten minutes," White said. "If you don't come out voluntarily, I'll cut your power."

Wayne frowned. That plan wasn't very good, but it was better than nothing. The whole problem boiled down to the fact that they didn't know *what* he'd be facing inside.

"Will Vince be able to tell you've entered the Dream?" Schulberg asked. "Will he suddenly know you're there and try to block you out?"

Wayne hesitated. This had been a private fear of his own that he hadn't wanted to voice. "Under ordinary circumstances, yes. The Dreamer in a Masterdream is like a puppeteer with a million strings. Someone moving around independently can't help touching some of the strings and letting the Dreamer know he's there.

"But in this case," he added with a shrug, "I just can't be sure. If there's free will like Ernie says, then the strings have already been cut. There'll be so many independent people moving around—bumping into the furniture, you might say—that one more shouldn't be noticeable. I'll have more power than any other single person there, because I'm backed by our transmitter just like Vince is. There are some strings Vince has probably retained—control over the environment, control over the flow of time, et cetera; I'll have to be careful not to interfere with those until I know what I'm doing. But if I don't go moving the buildings around, he probably won't think of me as anything more than one of the other people in the Dream."

"Good," Schulberg sighed. "Just be careful at first. Don't try to be a hero. We only want to know what's happening in there. Think of yourself as an Indian scout or something, looking over the land. When you find out what's going on, come back out and tell us. Maybe if we all put our heads together we can decide what to do about this. Maybe—just maybe—there's a way to keep it from exploding in our faces. But *don't do anything*. I don't want us to get any deeper into trouble than we already are."

Wayne nodded. He certainly didn't feel like doing anything. He'd Dreamed last night, both as creator and as audience, and his mind felt drained of energy. He was mentally exhausted. Still, people were counting on him; perhaps if he proved himself in this emergency situation, he could convince them of his talents and he wouldn't have to feel so inferior all the time.

That thought bouyed his spirits considerably. Despite his fatigue he climbed briskly into the designated cubicle and lay down on the couch. The cap tingled as he settled it snugly on his head. Then, with a wave at White, he announced, "I'm ready."

He started his self-hypnosis, and the familiar feeling crept slowly over him. The dim reality of the cubicle faded out and he began his descent into an unknown world of fantasy.

CHAPTER 8

AS RONDEL'S DREAM formed around him, Wayne did not materialize at once. The sudden appearance of a new person in the Dream might startle a few people at first, although they'd get over it quickly; such things frequently happened in Dreams. He was more concerned that such an abrupt appearance might alert Rondel to Wayne's presence here—and that was something he wanted to avoid for the present.

Instead, he became an invisible, ethereal presence, floating in the sky above the Dream as an impartial observer. As such, he was free to admire the breadth of the mental canvas on which Rondel painted. The world was spread out below him in a vast plain extending to infinite horizons. There were forests and rivers, and even squares of farmland to give some variety. Off in the distance, at the far limits of visibility, there were hints of mountains.

But it was the city that captured his attention and held it captive. It stood out from the nearly flat surroundings, towering majestically into the air. The image was instantly familiar to Wayne: it was the Emerald City from the classic movie of *The Wizard of Oz*. The tall, cigar-tube citadels were chrome and glass rather than green, but the overall effect was the same. It was a magic place, shining in the sunlight, promising a crystaline perfection it could not hope to fulfill. Rondel had found an image that would instantly invoke awe and mystery in his audience, and Wayne had to admit it was a superb touch.

He hooked himself into the timeframe of the Dream,

and was nearly whisked away. Time was enormously accelerated here, which meant events would happen at a prodigious rate. The Dreamer, of course, had ultimate control of how rapidly things occured in his Dream—he could speed it up if he had a crowded plot, or slow it down to pad out a scene. Even so, Wayne had never seen a Dream moving this quickly; no wonder Rondel was burning up energy. Then too, considering how long the Dream had been going on, an awful lot of things could have happened in here already.

Satisfied at last with his overview, Wayne swooped lower for closer inspection. The city was surrounded by a high wall, and the gates were all guarded—a departure from the script, wherein the city had been largely uninhabited except for a handful of Wizards and a lot of robots. Wayne wondered why the change had been made; what was so special about the city that Rondel thought was worth guarding? More importantly, what would be the best way for Wayne to investigate it?

One solution appeared as he saw a group of travelers walking along a road toward the city. In a very short while they would encounter Rondel's guards at the gate, and that meeting would give him some information. If he joined the travelers, he would have a first-class view.

He materialized beside the road ahead of the party, just around the bend so they couldn't see him appear out of thin air. As an added precaution, he decided not to look like himself. Given the almost omnipotent power he had within this Dream, he could take any guise he chose—and he was dissatisfied enough with his own looks to want to improve on nature. He increased his height a little, trimmed off some excess flab, improved his facial features and generally molded himself into his own ideal of masculine good looks. It made him feel confident and, more important, made him unrecognizeable as Wayne Corrigan should he accidentally meet up with Vince Rondel.

He created a boulder beside the road and sat down on it, pretending to be taking a pebble out of his shoe while he waited for the approaching group. He had made his clothing similar to theirs—a simple cotton shirt and trousers—so that he wouldn't look too outlandish.

Wayne hailed the group as they came into view. "Where are you headed?" he asked.

"To the Holy City," said one older man, who seemed to be the leader. "We've decided to seek salvation before the Judgment Day."

Holy City? Salvation? Judgment Day? Wayne didn't like the sound of any of those terms. While there were some Dream broadcast stations specializing in religious experiences, federal requirements said they had to explicitly advertise themselves as such—which Dramatic Dreams did not. This could be considered blatant propagandizing, of the sort that had gotten Eliott Spiegelman into so much trouble.

"I'm going that way myself," Wayne said with a friendly smile. "Do you mind if I walk along the road with you?"

"The road is free to all," the man shrugged. "My name is John. Who are you?"

Wayne had hoped to avoid giving out his identity if at all possible. If he let anyone know his real name, word of it might somehow get back to Rondel and the Masterdreamer would realize his creation was being inspected. But if Wayne refused to identify himself, he might alienate these people whom he hoped to pump for information. After a bare instant's hesitation, he settled on using his brother's name. "You can call me Tim."

John nodded and continued walking along with the group. Wayne put his shoe back on and matched their stride. One of the other men looked at him and said, "Are you going to be saved, too?"

"I don't know. What does it involve?"

The man's eyes narrowed. "You must give your mind and soul completely over to the will of God, and to our blessed Lord Jesus Christ."

Wayne felt a cold chill go through him, though

outwardly he remained calm. "I see. And, uh, who determines what the will of God is?"

It was John who answered now. "Why, the Prophet, of course."

"Of course," Wayne muttered. "How stupid of me."

John, too, was suspicious. "Where do you come from, stranger?"

"From Munchkinland, just down the yellow brick road."

The reference went completely past the others, which was just as well. Wayne cautioned himself not to be too flip in this situation; things were serious, and laughing at them could be dangerous.

"I've never heard of Munchkinland," John said solemnly. "Haven't they heard of the Prophet there?"

"Just vague rumors," Wayne said. "That's why I've come here, to learn the truth for myself." That answer seemed to please them, so Wayne added, "Perhaps you would care to enlighten me along the way."

"What may I tell you?"

"How can I answer that? If I knew what it was I don't know, I wouldn't have to ask for help. Just start explaining anywhere. Where did the Prophet come from, and how does he offer salvation?"

John nodded and began to tell his story. It sounded almost like a village elder explaining the old myths. "In the Time Before, the Wizards controlled the Holy City of Urba. Legend has it that they were evil men, enslaving people and stealing their food. Then the Prophet came. Charged with the spirit of God, he invaded the Holy City, cast down the Wizards to the fiery pits of Hell and purified the Holy City of its wickedness. Now the Holy City is hallowed ground, and only those who accept the salvation of Jesus Christ may enter and escape the coming holocaust."

"Holocaust?" That word raised images too terrifying to contemplate.

"Yes. On Judgment Day, which is coming soon, the oceans will boil and the earth will shatter. All nonbelievers who are not within the protected boundaries of the Holy City will be cast down into the fiery pits of Hell, and will roast forever in eternal damnation."

"When is this Judgment Day going to be?" Wayne asked.

"No one knows precisely," John answered, "but the Prophet has said it will be soon enough that everyone now alive will see it come. There are some who refuse to believe, of course, but many of us hope to find salvation before it is too late."

"Can't argue with that," Wayne muttered.

He walked along with the group in silence for a while. There were seven of them, not including himself—five men and two women. One of the men looked to be in his twenties, but the rest were all between forty and sixty. Wayne reminded himself that each of these figures was a real person who was right now lying peacefully at home in his or her own bed, tuned in to this Dream that was rapidly becoming a nightmare. The number seventy thousand that Ernie White had been tossing around had no reality—but these people did. At the moment, this was the real world to them, and what happened here would affect their lives forever. That realization brought home to Wayne more forcefully than ever the exact nature of his responsibilities.

The members of the group questioned him about his mythical Munchkinland, and he tried to satisfy their curiosity while being as evasive as he could. While there was no way they could ever check the veracity of his story, he didn't want to become enmeshed in a series of inconsistencies. Then too, he could never be sure when Rondel might be around to overhear.

After an indeterminate period—it was hard to keep time straight within this accelerated Dream because the sun never moved in the sky—they approached the city. A high, smooth wall, gleaming mother-of-pearl, barred their progress. The road led up to a massive gate of glittering diamonds, before which stood two guards. The guards wore silver lamé uniforms with a large blue cross embroidered on each shoulder. Each guard had a holstered handgun and carried a futuristic rifle. From reading the script, Wayne knew these were weapons that emitted a beam of yellow energy, stunning their victims into unconsciousness for a short time. Rondel wouldn't have wanted to use more lethal weapons in a Masterdream. Wayne wondered whether the guards were real people or merely creations of Rondel's. Either way, he couldn't take a chance with them. He had to play this straight.

One guard pointed his stun-rifle at the approaching group. "Why do you come to the Holy City?" he asked.

"We seek the salvation of our souls through the blessing of our Lord, Jesus Christ," John replied.

"And are you prepared to dedicate your mind and your soul to God?"

"I am," John said.

The soldier looked at the next person in the group, who also made the response. The guard questioned each of them in turn and, when the question came to him, Wayne answered as sincerely as the rest. At the same time, he couldn't help wondering what sort of devotion Rondel was asking of people.

"It is required of all who enter the Holy City that first they pass a test, that they may see for themselves the fate awaiting them if they should spurn the benevolent mercy of our Lord," the soldier said when he'd finished interrogating the group. "Come with me if you would truly be saved."

Wayne went with the rest through the gate and into a large, empty room beyond. "Wait here," the guard said. He left the room again, closing the door behind him. The travelers were alone and confused, not knowing what came next.

Suddenly the air all around them erupted in flames. Pillars of fire sprang from the floor and licked at the ceiling. Between one second and the next, the chamber became a raging inferno, filling with thick clouds of choking, sulfurous fumes. The world went blood red, and the air became so intolerably hot that it wavered, making everything around them indistinct. The crackling roar of a blast furnace drowned out all lesser noises.

Wayne immediately withdrew most of his senses, refusing to allow the effect to touch him. The scene became no more real to him than an image on a TV screen. He could appreciate in an abstract way the strength and the passion in the imagery that had been conjured here, but he was not touched by it.

Not so his companions. To them, this was the real world and everything that happened in it was real. The fires, the fumes and the heat were real. So were their screams of agony, which Wayne fortunately couldn't hear over the roar of the fire. They were literally on a visit to Hell.

Without allowing any of the discomfort to affect him, he feigned the same reaction as his companions. He imagined the pain and torment they were suffering, and allowed the counterfeit feeling to take over his body. He screamed along with them in the agony of the fires. A couple of them fell to the ground in their anguish, rolling in the liquid flames that lapped at their feet, but this only increased their suffering. A distant part of Wayne's mind, a part that held back and observed the horror, noted that despite the intensity of the flames, nothing was consumed by them, not even the clothing the people wore.

As abruptly as it began, the torture ended. The pillars of flame vanished, leaving the room as stark as before. The sudden emptiness and silence was like a ringing in the ears. Both women and three of the men were sobbing hysterically; the other two men sank to their knees, trembling. After a moment's reflection, Wayne emulated them. He didn't want anything to make him stand out from the others, so he had to pretend he'd been as badly affected as they were.

Inwardly, though, he was seething. Rondel must have gone completely mad to do something like this to an unsuspecting audience. All Eliott Spiegelman had done was introduce a little political propaganda, and that caused shock waves that were still echoing through the industry. Not only could Rondel be accused of religious proselytizing, but an outburst like those flames could conceivably cause mental damage—even breakdowns—in some weaker minds. This could mean the end of the Dream broadcast industry, a thought that horrified Wayne more than he cared to think about.

Just as the people in the room were recovering from the shock of their visit to Hell, they heard a voice. It came as though from loudspeakers, set so high it hurt their ears. The voice might have been Rondel's, but it was hard to tell at that loud volume.

"Know ye," blared the voice, "that all people are born into the world as sinners. Know ye that most people remain sinners to their dying day, preferring the easy life of sin to the hard path of God, the path of virtue and self-denial. The easy road of the sinner leads straight to Hell. Come the Judgment Day, everyone who does not give himself over to the way of God and Christ will roast in everlasting torment.

"You are the lucky ones. You have been granted a taste of Hell while you still live. You have been given the divine choice: accept the ways of God and renounce all your blaspheming, or die and spend eternity in Hell as you have experienced. Only the pure in soul and spirit may enter the Holy City of Urba. Only those who give their souls over to the Prophet of Christ have hope of redemption and salvation. Swear now to uphold the Prophet's laws, or doom yourselves forever to exile in the outer lands, and death and damnation on the Day of Judgment."

The people around Wayne were babbling frantically, ready to swear to anything to avoid a fate like the one they'd sampled here. Wayne babbled with the rest of them, but inwardly he was observing all of this with a cold, analytical eye. This, then, was how Rondel managed to control his audience. He had somehow reached out to them and given them free will, and then just as quickly snatched it back again. They were capable of making their own choices, but he gave them no real choices to make. After a convincing demonstration like this, no sane person could refuse to accept Rondel's word as law.

It was all very clever, in a maniacal way, but Wayne still could not see beyond the outlines to the deeper question that lay inside: Why was Rondel doing this? Why give people free will in the first place only to take it back? Why torture seventy thousand people he'd never even met? What was the point of this entire charade?

The guard who'd originally brought them into this room now returned, bringing four more soldiers with him. Two of them grabbed the women briskly by the arms and yanked them to their feet. "You two must come with us," one soldier said.

"Where are we going?"

"You're going to the Temple to serve God."

The main guard sneered at her. "All women are sinful. The Prophet tells us that. You will have the evil chastised from you until you're worthy of redemption."

Both women looked stunned. "But surely that's not fair," one of them said.

"Do you question the orders of the Prophet?"

The woman was instantly submissive. "Oh no, I . . . I wouldn't think of doing that."

"The Prophet decides all matters of morality," the main guard lectured sternly. "It is by his order that women are taken to the Temple to be purified."

Is that what he calls it? Wayne thought, but voiced none of his cynicism aloud.

As the women were led away, John addressed the main guard. "What about us? What does the Prophet command us to do?"

"You are free to enter the Holy City," the soldier said. "There you may do as you wish, provided you break no laws of God or the Prophet. You are encouraged to attend the public exhortations and to visit the women at the Temple. Live well, pray well, and remember—God's retribution is fierce and powerful."

With that, the guard opened the inner door of the room and Wayne and his companions were allowed to enter the Holy City of Urba.

CHAPTER 9

WAYNE WAS NOT expecting what he saw. According to Rondel's notes, the city of Urba was supposed to be ultramechanized, spotlessly clean, a technological masterpiece running with clockwork precision. It had been created by the Wizards using all the engineering skills at their disposal, and was as glittery and artificial as a display in a toystore window at Christmas. The city of Urba ran from beginning to end as a masterpiece of silent efficiency.

Rondel had transformed the entire place. While keeping the same mechanistic foundation, he had changed its emphasis from temporal to spiritual. Crosses were everywhere—over doors, in windows, on streetlights, and displayed in the center of the broad streets which, not incidentally, were paved with gold. The people, hundreds of them, who walked along the streets were draped in white robes that reminded Wayne of nothing so much as Roman togas. Overhead, angels floated serenely, oblivious to the human activity below them. Those angels had to be Rondel's creations rather than any members of the audience; they were semitransparent and sexless, with wings, halos and long, diaphanous robes. All through the city, as though from invisible loudspeakers, came the sound of celestial music, as though some angelic chorus were trapped on an endlessly repeating record.

Wayne took in a deep breath, and almost gagged. There was a strong smell of . . . *something* in the air. He'd smelled that sickly sweet odor somewhere before and it filled him with revulsion, but he couldn't identify it immediately. It didn't seem to bother his companions, though, who sniffed at it as though it were orange blossoms. Wayne did what he could to ignore it, although the smell pervaded the entire city.

"What do we do now?" Wayne asked.

In reply, John fell upon his knees. "We give thanks to God and to the Prophet for delivering us from our sins," he intoned.

The other four men followed his example and knelt down on the sidewalk to begin their prayers. This was more than Wayne could accept right now.

"What about the women?" he asked. "Don't you wonder what's become of them?"

"They are in the Prophet's hands," John replied, not looking directly at Wayne. "No harm can befall them here as long as they obey the Prophet's wishes."

"Your faith is very touching," Wayne said. "I'm sure the Prophet will be pleased with you." He started off.

"Where are you going?" John asked him.

"To the Temple. The guard did say we were encouraged to go there."

John had a hurried conference with the other men in their group, and left them kneeling on the ground while he stood up and followed after Wayne. "I'll come with you, if you don't mind."

Actually, Wayne did mind. On his own, he could use his powers a bit more freely to aid his observations; with John at his side, he'd have to be more careful what he did, lest he give too much away. But there was no way he could brush the man off without arousing other suspicions, so he just nodded and continued on at a brisk pace.

"You look like a man heading for trouble," John said breathlessly after a few moments.

"Do I?"

"How can you act this way after the test we went through? I sense a lack of faith that. . . ."

Wayne stopped and looked the other man squarely in the eyes. "John, you may find this hard to believe, but I probably have more faith in the Prophet than you do. I have no doubts at all that he speaks with the voice of God, and that his will must be obeyed here in Urba." And that was perfectly true. No one knew better than Wayne that Rondel's powers here were limitless. Within this crazy Dream, Rondel *was* God—a mad, demented deity with some twisted purpose Wayne couldn't begin to guess.

John looked shaken. "Then why do you speak so harshly when you've only just arrived here?"

Wayne hesitated, pondering his words carefully. "Perhaps even gods and prophets need someone to question their morality at times. Forgive me, I have no right to drag you into this. Go back to your friends and live piously as the Prophet has commanded. Leave me to my inner quarrels."

John shook his head. "No. I brought you here, I'm responsible for you."

"You're responsible for no one but yourself. I'll be all right."

But John refused to take that for an answer, and insisted on going with Wayne. Reluctantly, the Dreamer accepted his companionship and walked more slowly through the streets of the Holy City.

As he walked, he continued to observe the elements of the Dream about him. That strange, disturbing smell continued through the air, tickling at the back of Wayne's memory—but each time he tried to identify it, it pulled away from him again. And there was something else about the city that bothered him, something about the men walking the streets. . . .

That was it. There were only men walking the streets. Everywhere he looked, there were men in robes. Occasionally they would kneel for spontaneous prayers, or gather together in choirs to sing hymns. A few even played small harps, which Wayne thought was both tacky and a lack of imagination on Rondel's part.

But nowhere did he see any women. They were not walking about in the streets, nor did they look down out of the windows of the buildings on either side. There obviously were some women in the audience of this Dream—he'd traveled with two of them for a short while. Had they all suffered the same fate? Had they all been taken to the Temple to be part of whatever sickness Rondel had in mind? The more he thought about it, the more crucial it became that he investigate exactly what *was* happening at this so-called Temple.

But first, he had to find it. He'd studied the rough sketch of the city that Rondel had made in his notes, but there'd been nothing in them to indicate a temple. Rondel had probably appropriated one of the other buildings for this purpose, but Wayne didn't know which one.

The simplest method seemed the best, so he stopped a man on the street and asked where the Temple was. The man gave a brief set of directions that allowed Wayne to orient himself properly. The building that now housed the Temple was the one that had been the Central Computer Complex in the old plans. That made sense, in a way, because the computer complex had been the center of activity in the old version of the city, and could easily continue to function that way in this newer incarnation.

Wayne thanked the man who'd given him the directions and started to walk off in the indicated direction. The pedestrian gave Wayne and John a nod and a knowing wink, and continued on his own way. Wayne found that wink disturbing, and quickened his pace.

The city was crowded. Even assuming that half the audience had been women, that still left thirty-five thousand men free to walk around in the Dream, most of whom had already accepted Rondel's brand of salvation. No one seemed to do much in the Holy City except walk aimlessly about the streets, occasionally praying or singing hymns. Again, Wayne wondered what the point of all this was—if, indeed, there was a point to it. Why was Rondel forcing all these people to convert to his twisted religious precepts and then not doing anything with it?

Then a worse thought occurred to him. Maybe Rondel *was* planning to do something with it. Wayne couldn't guess what it was, but the concept chilled him. "Judgment Day" had been mentioned several times. What if that wasn't just an abstract notion here, but a very real possibility to occur in the near future? What horrors would that hold for everyone?

His thoughts were interrupted by a commotion up ahead. There was a general shouting, and a crowd began to gather. Curious, Wayne and John joined the others to see what was happening.

One of the angels flying above the city had swooped down upon a robed figure who was trying to flee through one of the side streets. The winged cherubic figure sounded more like a banshee now; it wailed ferociously as it zeroed in on its prey. Its hands curved and became talons, extending downward to grip the runner and prevent escape.

Time suddenly slowed, and it caught Wayne unaware. Everything around him seemed to be moving through thick syrup as Rondel decelerated the time frame to add effect to the actions. The audience, caught up in Rondel's reference frame, slowed down with the rest of the world; but Wayne, who was here independent of Rondel's control, did not. He'd been moving quickly to catch up with the crowd, and had a hard time stopping himself; he must have looked like a blur to the others.

Fortunately, most people's attention was focused on the angel and the fugitive. The few who might have noticed Wayne's burst of speed probably would not believe it. Wayne forced his own timeframe to slow down until it once more matched that of the people around him. He made a mental note not to take such things for granted again, and hoped he hadn't given himself away to Rondel by his mistake.

The runner was moving ever so slowly, even in this decelerated timeframe, and the angel was closing in. Just before the talons reached out to make a grab, the runner stumbled and the cowl came off the head, revealing a long mane of shiny black hair. The crowd gasped in amazement. The fugitive was a woman!

The angel overshot its mark, but turned around

more quickly than it should have been able to and reached for the woman once more. Its clawlike hands grabbed the back of the robe and lifted the woman into the air, just high enough that the spectators had to look up to see it clearly.

The timeframe suddenly accelerated once more to its previous level, but Wayne was ready for it this time; he figured that, with the runner captured, there was no longer the dramatic need to stretch out the chase. Even through his madness, Rondel was still adhering to the principles of dramatic storytelling.

"Behold a sinner," the angel said to the growing crowd, and this time the voice was unmistakably Rondel's. "This woman has fled her proper service at the Temple and defied the laws of God and the Prophet. But she shall learn the harsh lesson of her disobedience. The laws of God are strict, and divine retribution is certain. Come, all of you, to the next public exhortation and you shall see the fate that awaits such a sinner."

With that, the angel lifted its prisoner quickly up into the sky and disappeared from view. Wayne would have liked to follow and see what happened to the woman, but with John and other people around, he didn't dare expose his own "superpowers."

With the excitement over, the crowd began to disperse. People were buzzing, though, as men turned to their neighbors to comment on what had just occurred. There was a great deal of agitation and discomfort, and probably also some relief that the angel had not come for any of them; everyone knew, deep in his heart, that he had at some time or other committed some indiscretion that he was afraid would be found out and punished. Many people decided that now was a good time to pray, thus showing their continued devotion to God and the Prophet—and not necessarily in that order.

Wayne, though, felt a renewed determination to go to the Temple and see for himself exactly what sort of "service" that sinner had been fleeing. Once again he was hindered by John's presence. On his own, he could have withdrawn into a corner, become an invisible presence, and traveled to the Temple instantly—but with the other man watching him, he had to travel in a more conventional manner. He walked at a pace that was as brisk as he could make it without attracting attention; after all, he had no worries about becoming tired or out of breath. Beside him, though, John was having some difficulty keeping up. *Serves him right for slowing me down,* Wayne thought.

The Temple, when they reached it, was unmistakable. It was an enormous marble building in a city of chrome and cement. It was three city blocks long and five stories high; Wayne could not see from this angle how far back it extended. The facade was a colonnade, with massive stone columns standing four stories tall, all atop a long series of white marble steps. Wayne thought irreverently that there were no pigeons here to stain the integrity of the building's design.

There was a wide expanse of open ground to set the Temple apart from the rest of the city, a large park with artificial grass and no trees. Wayne and John strode across it and climbed the long series of steps to the front door. There were other men around them coming and going all the time. The Temple was a busy place, obviously one of the few places in the Holy City that had any action going. Wayne took some small comfort in that. As powerful as Rondel's mind was to sustain this whole world, he still could only concentrate his main attention on a couple of things at a time.

Inside the door, the two men were stopped by a guard in the standard silver lamé uniform. "Have you come to pray or chastise?"

"Uh, I'm not sure," Wayne began in what he hoped was a properly meek voice. "We just entered the Holy City a little while ago. We were encouraged to come here, but we weren't told what sorts of things we could do. Could you give us some guidance?"

The guard beamed like a minister spotting a fifty-dollar bill on the collection plate. "Certainly, brothers, I'd be most happy to." He turned to another guard behind him. "George, watch the door while I show these newcomers around."

He stepped out from behind his small desk and led them to the center of the entrance hall. A large spiral ramp led upwards around a circular well leading to all the different levels. Although the floor of the ramp appeared solid, it moved at a slow, steady rate once the men stepped onto it. This, Wayne supposed, was a holdover from the earlier period when the city was run by the technological Wizards.

"The ground floor of the Temple contains rooms for silent prayer and meditation," the guard lectured as the ramp took them upwards. "There's nothing much to see there. I expect you'd prefer an explanation of the more involved sections."

"Yes, precisely," Wayne nodded.

"I thought as much. That's pretty standard for the newcomers." He stepped off as the ramp passed the second floor, and Wayne and John followed after him.

"This second level is for self-improvement and self-dedication. Men can come here to atone for their sins and prove their devotion to God. Would you care for a look inside?"

He took them to one door, opened it, and led them in. They were in a large, open room like a gymnasium, in which many men were scattered about, kneeling and praying. Every so often, a man would pick up a scourge that lay on the ground and start whipping himself, screaming out a confession of his sins and praising either God or the Prophet. Some of the men had obviously been here a long time; their skin was raw and bleeding from repeated lashings. Men would scourge themselves into unconsciousness, and be left there by their unheeding fellows until they came to, when they would repeat the cycle of prayer and scourging all over again.

"Who forces these men to undergo such punishment?" John asked. "Is it the Prophet's decree?"

"Oh no, they're all here voluntarily," the guard assured him. "They want to be certain of their salvation on Judgment Day by beating the sins out of their flesh while they live. As the Prophet says, 'Blessed is he who suffers in love of God, for he shall attain the kingdom of Heaven.' By punishing themselves for their own wicked misdeeds, they are showing God that they are worthy to join Him in Paradise."

Wayne looked over the scene, dozens of men scarred and bloody from beating themselves, and had to fight the urge to ball his fists in frustration. Everyone, he knew, carried around a load of guilt for the little things that were a part of normal, day-to-day living. Under the right conditions—which Rondel had certainly encouraged in this Dream—those guilts could easily turn into self-punishment. He knew from his own readings in psychology that most people punished themselves worse than other people would. The porno Dream business frequently catered to such masochists, though the Dreams there often had a little more sexual content to them. The end result, though, was much the same.

"I don't think this is what I had in mind," he told the guard quietly.

"Very well." The guard took them out of the room again. "There are other rooms further down the hall where men may make sacrifices to God if they wish."

"What sort of sacrifices?" Wayne asked.

"Mostly mutilation. Some men castrate themselves; others cut off an arm or a leg, sometimes an eye or an ear to prove their devotion to God. If you'd like to watch . . ."

"We'll pass for now," Wayne said quickly. The thought of what Rondel was doing to these people—or rather, what he was encouraging them to do to themselves—was disgusting. Even though this was only a Dream and the people weren't really mutilating themselves, it would seem real to them at the time. They would go through much the same psychological trauma as if they actually had been dismembered, and they would live with the memory of the experience for the rest of their lives. While self-mutilation had historically been one test of religious fervor, it was not a normal one in

114

modern American society, and most of these people would not have done anything like this without Rondel's specific encouragement.

"I understand you have women here," Wayne continued after a moment.

"Yes indeed," nodded the guard with a smile. "I suspected that was what interested you, but by duty I had to offer these alternatives first. Yes, the women are by far our most popular feature. Come this way."

He led them back to the moving ramp, which took them up the spiral to the next level. The guard got off here, and they followed him obediently. "Did you wish to observe or participate?" he asked them.

"That depends on what's involved," Wayne said. John, he noticed, had been very quiet since their visit to the previous floor. Evidently he was not as pious as he'd originally thought he was; Rondel's ideas on religious zeal were affecting him adversely.

"Well, you can take a look for yourself." Their guide took them into a gallery that overlooked a dimly lit room. Wayne glanced down and found himself gazing on a scene out of Hell.

The room was based on a medieval dungeon, its grimy stone walls lit by the flicker of torchlight and its floor damp with a mixture of bodily fluids. The air reeked of foul odors—excrement and urine mixed liberally with vomit, sweat and charred flesh. And above all were the deafening noises—moans of pain, screams of terror and repeated pleas for mercy that went totally unheeded.

There were women in there all right, thousands of them scattered about the floor of the enormous torture chamber. Some of them were strapped to posts, stripped naked, while automatic machinery flogged them repeatedly; the majority of these women were already in a state of semiconsciousness from the whippings, and hung limply by their wrists or clung desperately to the posts, as though hoping to gain strength from them. Other women were tied down in chairs while their feet, hands or hair were set afire. There was a series of racks on which were stretched a dozen women who were obviously pregnant. Beyond them, more women were strapped into chairs where they underwent repeated shocks, or where they had noxious liquids forced down their throats. Farther off in the large room, Wayne could see some women tied on top of tables, being repeatedly raped by mechanical dildos thrust savagely into their private parts. On closer inspection, he saw that it was mostly the older and less attractive women being tortured; the rape was reserved for the younger, prettier women.

As his eyes became accustomed to the darkness, he could see other men in this gallery, lots of them, seated in tiers as though they were attending some theater production. They stared avidly down at the women being tortured, paying no attention to the three newcomers who had entered the gallery. Many of them, Wayne noticed, had their hands discreetly in their laps; he wondered what Rondel would think if he knew his temple was being used to foster these men's masturbation fantasies.

John, who'd been chastising Wayne's lack of piety just a short while ago, was looking pale, even in the dim light. "My God," he whispered. "What crimes did these women commit to deserve such punishment?"

The guard looked at him sternly. "You must be careful not to take the name of the Lord in vain, brother."

"Uh, sorry, but. . . ."

"In answer to your question, they are women, which is crime enough."

"I don't understand," John said.

"All women are tools of Satan," the guard said as though reciting a prepared speech. "Ever since Eve, they have served to weaken men's devotion to God. They lead men into wickedness, away from the path of righteousness. Of all women, only the Holy Mother has been worthy of redemption; the rest are harlots and wantons who seduce men from the ways of God and lure them into Hell."

"Even so . . ." Wayne began.

The guard, who hadn't finished his soliloquy, cut him off. "But God is infinitely merciful, and is willing to forgive even the most hardened sinners. The more sinful a person is, the more atonement she must perform to receive God's grace. The Prophet has assigned these women to atone for their many sins this way so that, on Judgment Day, they will be deemed pure enough to enter Heaven and partake of the abounding joy with God's hosts."

"But surely this is too cruel, no matter how many sins they've committed," John protested.

The guard shook his head. Apparently he was used to this reaction from first-timers here, because his voice was calm as he replied, "Nay, brother, do not question the wisdom of the Prophet. To do so is to be cast out of the Holy City and doomed to eternal damnation on Judgment Day. These women suffer now only that they may be saved then. It is for their own good, I assure you. As you entered the city, you experienced a small taste of Hell. Would you want these women condemned to that for all eternity?"

"No, but . . ."

"Then think of *them*, think of saving their wicked souls. This is done not to be cruel, but to be kind. If we punish them now, they will sing our blessings forever after; but if we spare them through misguided mercy, they will curse our names in Hell for all eternity. The ways of God are harsh, I know, but if you will sit here and watch for a while, I'm sure your conscience will be eased."

"I don't know if I have the moral strength to watch," Wayne said. He was personally repelled by all he saw here and did not want to go any further, but he had a job to do: he must see as much as possible of what was going on in this Dream and report it to DeLong and Schulberg. He didn't think they'd be any happier with this than he was. "You mentioned participation," he continued to the guard. "What does that entail?"

"Yes, that is the most noble route of all, to take

117

personal responsibility for the saving of another person's soul. There are many men who find that gratifying. If you'll follow me up one more level, I'll show you what happens there."

They returned to the spiral escalator and rode up to the next floor. "Instead of just passively watching the women be redeemed," the guard lectured, "a lot of men choose to help the process. I'll show you first the public rooms."

They walked through a door into another dungeon similar to the one on the floor below. Here, too, women were being tortured—only here, their tormentors were men instead of machines. The torchlight, the stench, the screams were virtually the same, except that the men seemed to take a more vindictive attitude; while the machines downstairs doled out their cruelty in an impersonal manner, these men took a positive delight in abusing their women, no matter how loudly they cried for mercy.

As Wayne watched, a man dragged a woman into the room, ripped the clothes unceremoniously from her body, and began beating her with his fists. When she fell to the ground, sobbing, he grabbed a large blood-stained dildo from a rack on the wall and began jamming it into her while she cried out. Elsewhere in the room, another man was squeezing a woman's large breasts, twisting them until she screamed with pain. Whippings and beatings were commonplace, while one whole area seemed to be set aside for men who wanted to urinate on their victims.

It was a sorry fact, but one Wayne had learned well in his years as a porno Dreamer, that most men harbor strong subconscious antagonism toward women. He didn't know precisely what the cause was; perhaps it was the fact that, in normal sexual relationships, it was the woman who determined how far the man could carry his attentions, leaving the man to feel that his sexual desires were being controlled and manipulated by women. Porno fantasies generally emphasized the man being in control and made women into interchangeable objects. It was pure, blind hatred that made men want to treat women that way.

Rondel had found a way to tap that hatred with a vengeance. This outlet for sexually frustrated rage was having a cathartic effect on the men. Rondel had let loose a furious demon from the male psyche, all in the name of goodness and religion, and there was bound to be hell to pay.

As Wayne watched, one of the men took the woman he was beating over to an empty corner and removed his own robe. Not content with using a dildo to rape her, he was obviously going to try a more personal touch.

The guard spotted this, too, and acted quickly. He pressed an alarm button on the wall that set up an instant siren screech. Activity halted in the room, and even the man who'd been set on rape stopped in midaction, startled. They all became charged with a feeling of expectation. *Something* was going to happen.

A door at the far end of the room opened, and Vince Rondel strode into the chamber. He was taller than in real life, and his hair wasn't as thinning, but Wayne still recognized him instantly. Rondel walked with the assertive manner of a man who knew he couldn't be challenged. His features were as benign—and hard—as a plaster Jesus, and his robes were so brilliantly white they dazzled the eye, even in this dungeon. This was indeed a prophet to be reckoned with.

Rondel strode without hesitation toward the man who'd been about to commit rape. The man, seeing the Prophet coming toward him with a look of vengeance in his eyes, immediately knelt to the floor and began praying. His prayers were not going to be enough.

Rondel stopped beside him and looked scornfully down at the cowering figure. "This is not a whorehouse," he said, his voice rolling mellifluously throughout the room. "These women are not here for you to sate your sinful, animal lusts. Sex is evil, an invention of Satan himself. It is not to be practiced by anyone who hopes to enter the kingdom of Heaven."

The man cowered even lower, muttering a string of apologies that Wayne could barely make out. Rondel stood over the man sternly, unmoved by his pleas.

"You were supposed to scourge this woman, purify her so she could be made ready to meet God on Judgment Day. Instead, you gave way to your base lusts. you yourself want to avoid everlasting damnation, yo had better look to scourging your own soul."

The man muttered something and scurried off. Wayne presumed he would go downstairs and scourge himse for a while, or maybe even castrate himself to banis his sexual thoughts. Somehow, though, Wayne found hard to pity him—not after what he'd been about to d to that woman.

Rondel looked around the room, his eyes lighting o everyone in turn. Wayne shrank away, trying not to b seen, even though his face was unrecognizeable. Fon tunately, other people also avoided Rondel's glance and Wayne did not stand out.

At last the Prophet, having made sure the lesson wa relearned, strode masterfully across the room and dis appeared out the same door he'd come through. It too a short while, though, for activities to return to nor mal.

"Things seem to become more . . . interesting th higher we go," Wayne commented. "I hesitate to thin what's on the next floor up."

"The top floor is private," the guard told him. "Th High Priestess tends to the shrine of the Holy Mothe but only she and the Prophet are allowed in ther Don't concern yourself with it. There is plenty to on cupy yourself with down here."

"This is it, then?" Wayne asked.

"Well, for those who prefer more privacy," the guar said, "there are private chambers where a man can b alone with the woman he's chosen to save. If you' follow me, I'll show you to the Waiting Room, wher the women who have not been sufficiently redeeme wait to be chosen. Perhaps you will find someone ther you wish to save."

Wayne and John followed after him. Privately, Wayne was wondering how much more of this he could take, and how many more depths there were to the depravity of Rondel's soul. It took a twisted, perverted mind to conjure such living hell for these poor women.

Instead of leading them back to the main hall, their guide took them through a side door. The room they now entered was lit only with oddly flickering red light, giving everything a ghastly tinge of blood. The room was circular and large. A ring of stark wooden chairs was spread around the outer wall, and a smaller concentric ring of chairs was on the inside of the circle. Some of the chairs were empty, but there were plenty in which women sat, apparently waiting to be chosen for redemption.

Despite the horror of the situation, Wayne almost had to laugh at the ludicrous way Rondel had forced the women to dress. They were all wearing corsets of differing colors, covered with lace or embroidered ruffles; most had fishnet stockings, garter belts and spike-heeled shoes. Their hairdos were frizzed and dyed in bizarre colors, looking even more eerie under the red light. Their makeup looked to have been applied by a nearsighted house painter; piles of rouge adorned the women's cheeks, oceans of lipstick had been applied to their mouths and false eyelashes extended so far that Wayne wondered how the women could see anything through them.

At least there are some limits to the man's imagination, Wayne thought. *This is clearly a virgin's idea of a whorehouse.*

But the situation was far from comical. Each of these women was a candidate for torture. Even as he stood here taking in the situation, several men came in and began looking over the women seated here. Eventually they made their choices and took the women they picked out through a door on the far side where, the guide explained, there were private rooms available. Wayne tried not to dwell on what sort of degradation might be going on just beyond those walls.

"Feel free to browse and make your choice," the guard said expansively. "Each soul you see here is praying for redemption; each has given herself up to the Prophet's divine law. Never forget: the sterner you are to her now, the better her chances of reaching Paradise, and she will end up thanking you for all eternity."

Wayne looked again at the selection. On closer examination under this garish lighting, he could see that many of the women had already been through the process before; that thick makeup hid ugly bruises and scars. They sat quietly, disconsolately, apparently resigned to their horrible fate.

Just then, the door flew open with a loud bang. Wayne turned to see what was happening, and faced directly into the barrel of a gun.

CHAPTER 10

ABOUT TEN WOMEN, all armed with stun-rifles, burst through a door at the back of the room. They were wearing the loose white robes that were common garments in the Holy City, but they had hitched them up and tied them behind their backs so they wouldn't hinder rapid motion. Each woman had a determined scowl on her face that promised to brook no opposition.

The guard who'd been guiding Wayne and John reached for his own gun as soon as he saw them, but he was far too slow; the women with their rifles at the ready fired before he could draw his weapon. Rays of yellow energy blazed out of several rifle barrels, striking the guard squarely in the chest. He fell to the ground, temporarily paralyzed.

Wayne, John and the other men in the room choosing women to "redeem" were unarmed and unsure what to do about the invasion. A couple made a break for the door, and were gunned down as efficiently as the guard. The rest stood frozen, hoping to be spared.

But the attacking women were not inclined to be merciful. The leader, a striking black woman in her middle thirties, said, "Shoot the men."

Her team obeyed, and beams lashed out from the women's rifles, paralyzing all the men in the room. One of the beams hit Wayne. He was immune to its effect because he was not trapped into the fallacy that this was the real world; nevertheless he fell to the ground as the other men did, pretending to be paralyzed. He didn't want to betray his immunity just yet; and besides, this looked interesting. He wondered what role these women played in Rondel's scheme of things—or whether they were a wild factor that Rondel hadn't counted on.

With all the men incapacitated, the leader of the assault group stationed several of her women at the various doors to make sure they wouldn't be interrupted. Then she turned to face the women of the Temple, many of whom were frightened out of their wits by this sudden attack. "My name is Laura," said the leader, "and I'm here to free you from the tyranny and pain of the Prophet's rule. If you're tired of abuse, tired of degradation, tired of men's torture and depravity, then come with us. The Heretics welcome all who would be their own masters."

The women who'd been seated remained silent for a moment, not sure what to think. Finally one woman got up the courage to ask, "What about our souls? We're here to be punished for our sins so we'll be admitted to Heaven on Judgment Day. If we run away, we'll be doomed to Hell for all eternity."

"You're in Hell now, or can't you recognize it?" Laura countered. "These men will never set you free. Your only chance of salvation lies with us."

"Who are you, and what can you do for us?" another asked. "How can you protect us from the Prophet's harsh law?"

"We're all women like you. Each of us served here, being beaten and degraded until there was nothing left of our self-respect. We were all abused until we couldn't take it anymore. One by one, we ran away from the Temple and hid in the back streets and alleys of the city. Eventually we grouped ourselves together and formed the Heretics—and now we've come to rescue you, our sisters in suffering. We won't rest until we've liberated everyone who serves the Prophet against her will."

"But Judgment Day is coming," one woman said. "Aren't you afraid of being condemned to that . . . that. . . ."

"If God is as merciful as the Prophet claims," Laura answered, "then He would never permit this cruelty to exist. This God is a god of men only, not of women. He serves only to keep us enslaved. If He exists, and if He condemns me, then I welcome it. I wouldn't *want* His blessing."

"But . . ."

"We have no time to argue, sisters," the black woman interrupted impatiently. "The Temple guards will be here soon, and we must be away. Those of you who want freedom and an end to your pain must decide now to come with us. We don't know when we'll be able to make another raid like this. Anyone who gets left behind has no one to blame but herself."

Laura nodded at a couple of her women, who opened the door they'd come through and checked the hallway beyond to make sure it was safe. Some of the Temple women stood up hesitantly and looked around, hoping to get encouragement from their fellows. The air in the room tasted of indecision. A few more stood up when they saw that others were brave enough to do so, but in the end only about twenty of the women accompanied the Heretics out of the room. The rest sat nervously where they were, too frightened even to run away and save themselves.

As the attackers left, Wayne wanted to follow them, but he faced a problem. If he stood up and ran out of the room, he'd be seen by the women who stayed behind, who thought he'd been stunned along with the rest of the men. He decided to risk a minor interference with the Dream and caused the lights in this room to black out. There'd be so much confusion over the raid anyway that Rondel wasn't likely to think much about it—and by the time the lights came on again, the women wouldn't notice one less male body lying paralyzed on the floor.

He made himself into an invisible presence and floated out into the hallway, following the retreating women. They were not going out toward the front entrance, but instead were heading toward the rear of the building. Wayne could see evidence that they'd passed this way before: the paralyzed bodies of other

125

men who'd been stunned by the invaders' rifles. Leaving by the same route they'd come in was not good strategy, Wayne thought. He knew from his brief study of Rondel's maps that there should be other seldom-used corridors the women could take—but perhaps they didn't know about them.

Laura was in the lead with six of her other Heretics. The twenty or so women they had just liberated were in the middle of the group, and three more Heretics guarded the rear. That much, at least, made sense; even if any of the newly freed women had second thoughts and wanted to return, she would be unable to leave the group without being shot by one of the Heretics, and thus could not endanger the whole group.

They had almost reached ground level when they ran into an ambush. Rondel's forces, realizing something was wrong, had regrouped and were blocking the exit. As Laura and her people rounded a corner, they came into a field of heavy fire. Two of the Heretics fell, and Laura ordered her team back the way they'd come, getting off a few return shots of her own as they retreated.

Wayne faced a moral dilemma. When he came into this Dream he'd been given orders not to interfere or do anything that would bring attention to himself. But after experiencing the sample of Hell Rondel was dosing out to everyone, and after seeing the degradation and torture he was encouraging against women, Wayne could not remain neutral. These Heretics had chosen to rebel against the truly godlike authority Rondel had established, and that courage won him to their side. He couldn't stand by and let their daring raid be crushed by Rondel's forces.

He had little time, though, to think a plan through. Had this been a Dream of his own creation, he could have slowed down the time reference, making events happen at a more relaxed pace while he had time to devise a scheme. But he dared not do that here; tampering with Rondel's Dream on that scale would unquestionably alert him to Wayne's presence. Whatever action he took, he would have to disguise himself sufficiently so that Rondel would not suspect another Dreamer was at work.

He took on a material form again, this time cloaking himself in long gray robes with a cowl that covered most of his face. He appeared in a side corridor just off the path of the retreating women. As they came past him, he stepped into their view. "Quick, Laura, this way!"

One of the Heretics, startled by his sudden appearance, raised her rifle and fired at him. A beam of yellow energy hit him squarely in the chest, and Wayne cursed to himself. He didn't have time to play games and fake unconsciousness once more, so he would have to violate the reality of this Dream and not let the rifle's stun effect bother him. It would cause comment, but right now everyone was so confused and frightened that they might not notice it as much.

"Don't shoot," he said. "I'm a friend. I want to help. I know a way out."

There was an unreadable expression on Laura's face. The Heretics' leader had seen Wayne take the full force of the stun-rifle without effect, which in itself was pretty remarkable. He had come out of nowhere in her time of trouble and offered to help. He looked strange, and he had no reason to help her, so she had no reason to trust him. But the Prophet's soldiers were blocking the exit, and there were probably more closing in behind her. The question in her mind ultimately became not whether she could trust him, but whether she dared not to.

She was a leader, though, and she knew the importance of making a fast decision. "Lead on," she said to Wayne. "We'll be right behind you."

Wayne smiled. He could read the implication at the end of her sentence: *If this is a trick, you'll be the first to get it.*

While his manufactured body started leading the way, Wayne sent his mind ahead to scout the path. He remembered vaguely that there had been a series of back corridors planned in the computer building that was now the Temple; that was how Rondel—in the now-abandoned script—was to have gone into the basement and met the computer that helped him defeat the Wizards. His reconnaissance showed him a complicated route, going up and down several levels, that avoided all the patrols Rondel had scattered through the building.

Behind him, the women were confused and upset. The Heretics were angry that their plans had gone awry and, worse, that they had to depend so strongly on the goodwill of a total stranger for their safety. Several others had seen Wayne survive the rifle beam, too, and that made them doubly uneasy. What sort of help were they getting, and what would be the price of it?

But Laura was in charge, and if she said to follow the cloaked stranger, they would do it. The black woman herself was ominously silent, her glance constantly darting around, alert for the slightest signs of betrayal. Some of the route Wayne prescribed took her through territory she didn't know, but as they approached the outer wall she found herself in familiar surroundings once more.

"I know the way from here," she said, drawing even with Wayne.

Wayne looked ahead and saw no immediate obstacles to her escape. "Then you may lead now," he said. "May I accompany you?"

Laura hesitated. This stranger had helped her so far, but she still was not sure she could trust him. "Who are you?" she asked.

"A friend," Wayne said. "My name is Tim. That's all I can tell you, for now."

"You're a man." Laura spoke that simple sentence as a condemnation. She had every right to, Wayne realized, considering the treatment women received from men in this Dream.

"I can't help that," he said, though actually he could. He could change his bodily appearance to that of a

128

woman, but that would cause even more consternation at this stage. He had picked a masculine shape out of reflex, and now he was stuck with it.

"But I am no believer in this false prophet," he continued. "I'm as opposed to his regime as much as you are. I'd like to help you, if I can."

There was little time for debate; Laura knew she had to make a command decision. "I'll trust you for now," she said. "But at the slightest hint of betrayal, our alliance ends."

"Fair enough," Wayne said.

"Watch him," Laura instructed one of her followers. She then took her place at the head of the column and led the way out of the Temple. The Heretic who'd been told to keep an eye on Wayne was nervous about her assignment, because she had to guard this stranger as well as look out for signs of Rondel's forces. Wayne tried to give her little trouble, following obediently after Laura while keeping his own senses extended to watch for danger.

Outside the Temple, the fugitives found themselves in a back alley. Laura knew the path from here, as she led her group through the twisting paths between the buildings. She picked her route carefully, so that at no time did they ever have to cross a major street where they might be spotted by ordinary citizens.

Wayne spotted the danger with his extended senses while it was still a good distance away. "Laura!" he whispered. "One of the angels is coming this way."

Laura stopped and looked up into the sky. When she saw no flying menace, she looked suspiciously at Wayne. "How do you know?"

"I can sense these things. Trust me. Get everyone under cover."

Once again the woman hesitated. She could see her command being usurped by this stranger, and she was not at all happy about taking orders, or even suggestions, from him. But once again she realized that following his suggestions would probably not hurt them, and might save them if he was right. She had to put the success of the mission ahead of her own personal feelings.

She had them all take cover just inside the doorway of a deserted building, and they waited. Within thirty seconds, as Wayne had predicted, one of the angels drifted overhead. They couldn't see it from their hiding place—just as they hoped it couldn't see them—but its shadow moving across the ground was more than obvious. The angel circled back and forth across the valley, like an eagle who knew there was a rabbit hiding there somewhere and was reluctant to leave. As it finally floated down toward the far end of the alley, the fugitives started to breathe a sigh of relief. Then, without warning, the angel swooped and came to Earth right in front of their door.

Laura and two other Heretics fired their stun-rifles point-blank into the creature, but the angel showed no effect. It stepped toward them with a beatific smile that was particularly macabre under these circumstances. Wayne knew there would be nothing these women could use within the arsenal of Dream weaponry to free themselves from capture by this supernatural specter.

Once again, if he wanted something done he'd have to do it himself. He knew Schulberg and DeLong had given him orders not to interfere, but there was no way they could have known the hideous conditions existing for the people here. Even though none of this was real, the people here *thought* it was, and that was bad enough. Not to act would be criminal under these circumstances.

Since he'd already blown part of his cover, he might as well make a show of it. He extended his right arm and pointed directly at the advancing angel. A bolt of lightning leaped from his finger and hit the angel dead center. The angel exploded in a silent shower of sparks that rained down on the alley floor like spent fireworks.

The women were looking at Wayne now with renewed awe. He tried to get them moving again before they had too much time to dwell on his feat. "Let's go. There may be more of the angels around, and we can't hold them off forever."

If Laura had distrusted him before, she was doubly suspicious now, despite the fact that, so far, he'd been the ideal ally. Wayne could see a thousand questions darting behind her eyes, and there was no time to voice any of them. With a shrug to shake off the worst of her doubts, she motioned her party forward once again.

They encountered no further resistance as they moved through the back streets of the Holy City, and at length they came to a building near the west wall. Laura stopped before the main door and knocked once, then twice, then once again. The door slid open, and Laura ushered her party of Heretics and rescued Temple women inside. Wayne hung back to the end, and Laura hesitated. Wayne could see she harbored strong doubts about letting him into her sanctuary.

"I still don't know who you are or why you're helping us," she told him candidly.

"We have the same enemies," Wayne said. "Isn't that enough for now?"

Laura grimaced. "For now." She motioned for him to enter and followed him in, closing the door behind her.

This building was deserted except for the Heretics, but even so it was in sparkling neat condition. Rondel's fetish for orderliness—everywhere but in his mother's house—would not have tolerated dust or signs of decay anywhere in his "Holy City." The fact that a deserted building could exist at all in this Dream without Rondel's constantly thinking about it was amazing enough—but Wayne realized the image could be reinforced by the beliefs of the audience, now that they had free will. If Rondel had once convinced them there was a building here, their own beliefs would maintain it, even if he himself didn't think about it. If all that mutual faith were to waver, though, the building might evaporate like morning mist.

There were more Heretics who had stayed behind here guarding the door. They gave Laura a nod, then looked suspiciously at Wayne's mysterious hooded figure. But Laura ignored their stares, so the guards did not object as the raiding party made its way into the center of the building.

Back on her home territory, Laura walked with even more authority as she led them down a series of corridors to a large central meeting room. There were more women there waiting for them; Wayne estimated the number at a couple of hundred. All of them had apparently joined this underground rebellion against the mad prophet and his cruel regime.

Wayne was struck by the bravery of these women. They didn't know they were in a Dream right now; to the best of their knowledge, this was reality. They were living in a world ruled by a mad genius with magical powers, a man who could make anything come true merely by thinking it. Yet despite the hopeless odds, they found their lives so intolerable that they had to fight back. They had all experienced Rondel's version of Hell, they knew what disobedience would mean, and still they fought it. Looking around at them, Wayne could tell many of them were tired and even more looked scared. But they *all* looked determined. They would no longer willingly submit to the Temple's chamber of horrors in return for a promise of salvation. To Wayne, that was courage far beyond anything he'd ever seen before.

There were a number of startled gasps as the women in the room caught sight of him for the first time. They started whispering among themselves, and one of them was bold enough to blurt out, "He's a man. What's he doing here?"

"I brought him," Laura said. She might have her private doubts, but she was leader of this group and she was not going to let her judgment be questioned. "He says his name is Tim, and he wants to help us."

"You don't trust him, do you?" another woman asked.

"That will depend on what he does. So far he's helped us."

"We don't need any man's help," one woman sneered.

"He's not just *any* man," Laura retorted. "He's im-

132

mune to stun-rifles and he can blast an angel to bits. If he *is* on our side, I'd welcome that sort of help."

She turned to Wayne and said privately, "They're going to need a lot of convincing."

Wayne nodded and stepped forward, wondering what he could say that would not tip his hand, yet would make these women trust him. "I can't tell you much about myself right now," he said, "because I'm under an oath of secrecy. But I can say that I'm as much opposed to the Prophet's reign as you are. I'd like your help as much as Laura would like mine."

"To do what?" someone asked.

"To topple the Prophet from his throne and end the tyranny that oppresses you."

"To what purpose, I wonder?" Laura said. "Maybe all you want is to get rid of the Prophet so you can rule us in his place. We might only be exchanging one master for another."

"I believe that everyone should be free to pursue his or her own destiny," Wayne said. "I already have more power here than anyone could imagine; I don't need more."

"You're full of pretty words and noble sentiments," one woman declared. "But how can we believe you after all we've been through?"

That was the point, Wayne knew. These women had suffered at the hands of men who claimed to be doing it for their own good. There was nothing he could say to counteract that bitter experience—and, until he'd discussed the matter more thoroughly with DeLong and Schulberg, he was reluctant to take any actions that would betray his powers further, lest Rondel become aware of him.

"You'll have to take it on faith," he said softly.

"Faith!" Laura snorted. "The Prophet uses that word a lot."

"There's nothing wrong with faith," Wayne said. "The Prophet has just taken a good thing and twisted it to his own perverted tastes. If you hate all apples

133

because the first one you tasted was mealy, you'll miss a lot in life."

"Including a lot of mealy apples," one woman retorted.

Laura waited for the general laughter to die down, then spoke up in Wayne's defense. "It is a fact that Tim helped us get away from the Temple when we were trapped by the Prophet's guards. It's also a fact that he destroyed an angel when we were about to be discovered."

"How did he destroy an angel?" someone asked in awe.

One of the Heretics who'd been along on the raid answered, "He pointed his finger at it and lightning came out."

There was silence for a long moment. Then Wayne could hear someone whisper, way in the back, "He's one of the Wizards."

"Nonsense," someone else said. "The Prophet destroyed them all when he took over Urba."

"Who else but a Wizard could do those things?" the first woman responded.

All eyes turned to Wayne. The Dreamer didn't know what to say.

"What about it?" Laura prodded. "Are you a Wizard, Tim?"

"Would it make a difference to you if I were?"

"The Wizards were evil, too," someone remarked. "The Prophet destroyed them, but then he became even worse than they were."

"But perhaps there were good Wizards and bad Wizards," Wayne said. "Maybe the good ones were in hiding from the bad ones, waiting for the proper moment to strike."

"You ask us to believe a lot of things," Laura said.

"I'm not asking you to believe anything. All I ask is that I not be condemned without a chance to prove my intentions."

"Our position is tenuous," Laura told him. "In most cases, survival demands that we judge someone guilty until he can prove his innocence. The fact that you've

134

helped us so far is in your favor. It's the only reason we've let you stay this long. But you're still very much on trial."

"I'll keep that in mind. Thank you."

Another woman in the front row of seats, who appeared to have almost as much authority as Laura, stood up and looked him over appraisingly. "Just how do you propose to help us?" she asked.

"I'm not sure yet," Wayne said honestly. "It will all depend on your situation here. Do you mind if I ask you a few questions? I've been . . . out of touch with events in Urba for some time, and just recently came back. Exactly what has happened in the city since the Wizards were destroyed?"

Laura delivered most of the history lecture, with her occasional lapses filled in by other women. The Dream had started out pretty much as planned, up until the first intermission. Then things changed abruptly. The tribal chieftain Rondel had been playing was suddenly struck by divine revelation, and his powers increased accordingly. The Wizards were erased from the city almost as though they had never existed, and the angels descended to keep watch over this new flock. Everyone had begun their existence outside the city, and were warned that, if they wanted to avoid eternal damnation, they would have to be saved by being admitted into Urba. People flocked to the gates, and were given the standard demonstrations of Hell that made believers out of them. Men who volunteered could join the Prophet's guards and become Christian soldiers. The women were segregated and sent to the Temple, where they were treated as Wayne had already seen. From time to time, the Prophet himself would come out and make public exhortations, but most of the time he left administration to his guards and to the angels. At the public exhortations he reinforced the images of Heaven and Hell in everyone's mind and publicly chastised those sinners who had disobeyed his various injunctions.

The Heretics were all escapees from the Temple,

women who'd been abused beyond their ability to tolerate it and who were determined to fight back, even if it did mean eternal damnation. They'd escaped one at a time, at first, and eventually found one another hiding in the city. At that point they banded together for their own protection, to oppose the Prophet's rule more forcefully, and to help free other women trapped inside the Temple. Occasionally one or more would be caught, and an example would be made of them at the next exhortation. Still, their numbers had been growing steadily, thanks to raids like the one just completed. Such raids were hazardous, though—not just because the Temple area had a lot of guards, but also because that was where the Prophet himself lived.

"Are you sure?" Wayne asked, his interest piqued.

"Quite sure," Laura nodded. "He lives in the rooms beneath the ground floor level, where no one else is permitted to enter. I tried to go down there once, but I couldn't. There was some invisible force that stopped me—and then alarms went off, and I had to get away before being caught."

Wayne considered what he'd heard. The Temple had been, in the old scenario, the Central Computer Complex that ran the entire city, with its memory core in the basement; it was only logical that Rondel would keep its function intact and turn it into his own headquarters for running the city. Even though it was the power of his mind that maintained this entire world, he had to have it centralized somewhere; the Temple, as the hub of the city's activity, would be the ideal spot.

Wayne could also well believe that Rondel's public appearances were infrequent. He was expending tremendous quantities of mental energy to maintain this world. Even though, with free will, the other inhabitants would do some of the maintenance themselves simply by believing in what they'd previously been told, the images would all have to be reinforced every once in awhile. For Rondel to do that and still manifest his own presence would be more than even his genius could cope with. When he concentrated on taking a physical form, other parts of this world, particularly at the periphery, would have to weaken. Plus, there was the fact that Ernie White said Rondel was burning himself out. He would have to limit his activities.

Somehow that made Wayne feel a little better. Rondel was strong, but he wasn't invincible.

"So now that you know the situation, what do you intend to do about it?" Laura asked, jarring Wayne out of his reverie.

"That's not my decision alone to make," he replied slowly. "I must confer with others and make our plans accordingly. I think I know enough, now, to give them a good idea of what's going on."

"How will you confer with these others?" someone asked.

"I'll have to leave you for a while. But I promise I'll come back."

Laura shook her head. "We can't permit that. You know too much about us, and you know where we're hiding. We can't let you go and tell anyone else." At her unspoken command, several of her followers blocked the doorway so Wayne couldn't escape.

Wayne had to smile at the futility of their efforts. "I'm afraid you don't have much choice in the matter," he said. "But I do promise that I'll still help you every way I can."

With that, he wrapped himself majestically in his long cloak and began to spin. The room whirled rapidly around him as he let his body dissipate in a cloud of black smoke that eventually thinned out, leaving no trace of him behind.

An impressive exit, he thought, *even if I do say so myself.*

He was almost ready to leave the Dream and return to the outside world. But before he reported back to DeLong and Schulberg, there was one further thing he had to check out. Laura had said Rondel lived in the Temple basement. Wayne would have to see for himself exactly what that was like, and what Rondel was up to.

He was an invisible wraith as he left the building where the Heretics hid out from the Prophet's forces. His sudden departure was bound to stir their animosity and suspicion, but there was little he could do about that now. He simply did not have time to play the game by their rules; he had a whole world to save.

In his intangible form he could travel quickly back to the Temple, moving straight through buildings and walls as though they weren't there, rather than traveling the circuitous escape route Laura had been forced to take. He went directly to the door where, according to Rondel's preliminary sketches, the entrance to the subterranean computer complex was hidden.

The door was a simple one, just plain wood with an ordinary knob. There were no special decorations, no signs to mark its importance; there were neither angels nor guards standing duty outside to ensure that no one disturbed the occupant. Yet Wayne *knew* this was the proper place—and for some reason, the lack of protection here seemed particularly ominous.

He could feel something wrong even as he approached the doorway. The air felt thicker, somehow, as though the Dream around him was coagulating into a solid lump. Wayne paused. He was invisible and intangible, but there were other ways one Dreamer could detect another within a Dream that had nothing to do with the normal senses. Wayne had done his best so far to stay out of Rondel's way—and apart from a few minor miracles to help the Heretics, he'd tried to avoid calling attention to himself. Now he would be entering Rondel's lair, and he would have to be doubly careful; the slightest mistake could tip the other man off that there was an intruder in this Dream.

He came slowly to the door and bumped against it. The obstacle was not the door itself; that was only a convenient visual image created by Rondel, and as such could be uncreated or ignored. No, there was something more fundamental stopping Wayne from passing through, some hard invisible surface that barred the way. Wayne rebounded quickly, then tried again, more slowly, to ooze his way through that barrier.

And still there was no passage. No matter how small Wayne tried to make himself, no matter how finely he spread his consciousness, there were no holes in this defense to let him through. In all his experience as a Dreamer, he could never recall having encountered anything like this.

He was not even given a chance to think about it. Without warning, the whole world tore loose around him. Alarms began blaring and lights started flashing, alerting Rondel's guards that someone was attempting to intrude on the Prophet's private sanctuary. Wayne was not at all worried about them; no matter how hard they looked, the guards would never be able to find him. But, at the same time, something else happened that frightened him enormously.

The Dream itself grabbed him. The very fabric of this reality reached out and folded itself around his mind, squeezing him in a giant fist. He panicked and fought against it for a second, but his efforts only encouraged the Dream to wrap itself more tightly around him. The entire world was spinning. The city was distorted, buildings stretching like warm putty, streets melting and flowing like rivers, voices wailing in and out like sirens. Shapes that had once seemed sharp and clear now looked like an impressionist painting close up—daubed and smeared and unrecognizeable as anything real. Wayne felt as though his mind were going to explode from the pressure.

There was only one escape. With a speed he'd never dared try before, he faded himself out of the Dream and back to the cold, steady world of reality.

CHAPTER 11

WAYNE SAT UP with a start and bumped his head on the low ceiling of the dimly lit cubicle. The Dreamcap was like a circle of fire on his scalp, and he reached up quickly to rip it off his head. In those first few seconds, as awareness filtered back into his mind, he sat panting furiously, his hands trembling with the shock of whatever it was he'd encountered.

Outside the cubicle, he could hear Ernie White letting loose a string of obscenities in a louder voice than he'd thought the engineer was capable of. There was the sound of movement, and Bill DeLong's voice asking what was happening. White didn't answer, though; he just kept swearing as he tried to make some sense of the situation.

As Wayne became aware of the world around him and his breathing returned to normal, he found he was drenched in sweat. His clothes were a heavy, soggy mass clinging to his flesh and his eyes were stinging from the perspiration that had dripped into them. He raised his right forearm to his face to wipe it off, but the gesture was futile—the arm was every bit as sweat-soaked as the rest of him.

That very attempt at movement made him groan. His sitting up and taking the cap from his head had been reflexive gestures, a response to the horror from which he'd awakened. But now that his body'd had time to assert its condition to his mind, he found that every muscle was tight, as though he'd spent a couple of hours in strenuous exercise. He leaned backward onto the couch again, lying limply and trying to will away the feeling of exhaustion. His scalp was still burning with a million prickles from the places where the netting of the Dreamcap had touched it, and there was a low throbbing at the back of his skull that threatened to become a migraine.

The sounds of his exertions brought Bill DeLong rushing to the entrance of the cubicle. "Wayne, are you all right?"

Wayne tried to speak, but his voice came out more as a harsh croak. "No, I'm not. I want to dig a hole, crawl into it and not be disturbed again for at least two years. Help me out of here, will you, I'm all worn out."

The cubicle was too small for DeLong to come in and help him up, but but the program coordinator reached one arm in to give Wayne some leverage. Wayne grabbed hold of it and pulled himself up into a sitting position once more. After a moment he tried to stand, but his legs gave out from under him and he collapsed to the floor on his knees.

DeLong grabbed his arm as he fell and half-dragged Wayne out of the cubicle into the outer room, where he could help him up. Putting Wayne's arm around his shoulders, DeLong supported him as they walked over to a swivel chair where Wayne deposited his body with a grateful sigh.

As DeLong went to the cooler to get Wayne a cup of cold water, Ernie White came out of the control booth. "What in hell happened there?" the engineer asked. "I thought the board went crazy before, but it really exploded for a moment."

"Don't know," Wayne said. He took the cup of water DeLong handed him and drank it greedily, then devoured a second as well. "I've never experienced anything quite like that before."

"It must have been hell," White nodded. "Your dial and Vince's were fluctuating like mad, and we didn't think you'd be coming out that quickly."

"How long was I in there?"

"Only four minutes."

"You're kidding!" Despite the fact that he knew time

had been greatly accelerated in that Dream, Wayne was shocked. Rondel had speeded things up to an extent he wouldn't have thought possible. No wonder he was tired and sweaty. During most dreams, the brain sends out signals to the body, commanding it to act out the events in the dream. Most of the time those signals are blocked; occasionally, as in the case of sleepwalkers or people who gnash their teeth in their sleep, the blocking is ineffective. But the muscles can still undergo considerable strain, as anyone who's awakened from a nightmare could attest.

In this case, with time accelerated as rapidly as it was, Wayne's muscles were really getting a workout. His brain and body were working at top speed to keep up the rapid pace—and the same would be true for everyone else plugged into the Dream.

"I wouldn't kid about something like this," White said, shaking his head. "From almost the second you went in there, you were burning energy about as fast as Vince."

Wayne closed his eyes and concentrated simply on breathing. The panting he'd had to do when he first awoke was less severe now, but he still felt like talking only a little and taking deep breaths. There didn't seem to be enough air in the universe to satisfy his lungs.

DeLong noticed the problem. "Careful. Don't end up hyperventilating."

Wayne nodded and said, "Where's Mort?"

"Making some phone calls, checking up on a theory. As soon as you went under, I called Vince's home, thinking maybe his mother could explain what was wrong with him. There wasn't any answer, which was very odd; she's an invalid, and can't leave the house. I rang long enough that, even if she was asleep, she should have woken up and answered."

"Maybe she's tuned into a Dream."

DeLong shook his head. "She can't. Vince explained it to me once. Her doctors have refused to let her Dream in her condition. Vince doesn't even have a cap in the house. I mentioned all this to Mort, and that made him remember something about the call Vince got during that first intermission. When Mort answered the phone and talked to the guy, there were noises in the background like a paging system calling for Dr. Somebody-or-other. The call may have come from a hospital."

Wayne's mind leaped ahead to the conclusion. "Then you think something's happened to Vince's mother?"

"That's what Mort's checking on now. He's calling all the hospitals in the area to find out if Mrs. Rondel was admitted this evening."

The memory of Mrs. Rondel closed a circuit in Wayne's mind. "That ties in to something. Throughout the Dream, all through Urba, there was a very strong smell that was familiar, but I couldn't identify it. It's Mrs. Rondel's violet perfume. I caught a whiff of it when I took Vince home last night. It's pretty nauseating stuff—and it's all through the Dream."

"What exactly is happening in there?"

Wayne took a deep breath. "It's bad. Vince has set himself up as some sort of messiah. He's changed Urba to the Holy City and he's trying to shove his religious beliefs down everyone's throat. He's giving them hellfire and damnation, with real hellfire."

DeLong sat down on the edge of a desk. "God!"

"Exactly."

"What about the feedback?" White asked.

"You were right, it does seem to be free will. The people in that Dream move and think on their own. They believe Urba is the reality and they act accordingly, but they do make their own decisions. Everybody's acting out his own script on Vince's stage."

"And since Vince can change the stage around, he's still got the upper hand," DeLong mused.

Mort Schulberg burst into the room. "She's dead," he said. "A neighbor found . . ." He spotted Wayne and stopped what he was about to say. "Back so soon?"

"Just go on with what you were saying," DeLong prodded.

"She must have had a stroke or something. She tried to call a neighbor, who came in and found her lying on the floor beside her bed. They called an ambulance and took her to St. Joseph's, but she was dead on arrival. So they called Vince here to let him know."

DeLong buried his face in his right hand. "And that set loose the nightmare," he said quietly.

Wayne thought back on the events of last night, about Rondel's slavish devotion to his mother. Not only did the Masterdreamer wait on her hand and foot, but also allowed her to rule his life. It was at her prodding that he gave a large percentage of his salary to the church, leaving the two of them barely enough to survive on. Rondel had even allowed his mother to interfere in his relationship with Janet—something inconceivable to Wayne. For a man in his thirties to be so fixated was a symptom of serious mental disturbance. When he learned that she was no longer around . . .

"He's going to kill himself," Wayne said with sudden intuition, "and he wants to take everyone with him. He can't stand life anymore; he feels guilty for not being there when his mother died, and he's angry at the world for taking her from him. He knows he'll burn himself out if he continues this way, and he doesn't care. He's trying to even all the scores by killing himself and dragging all the others down, too."

DeLong gave him a weary smile. "Maybe. I don't know. I just wish I'd paid more attention to those psychology courses in college."

"I thought writers were supposed to know every-thing about how people behave."

"I have a few colleagues who think they do. Actually, the only people we know everything about—if we're lucky—are the characters we create ourselves because, like you Dreamers, we can play god with them. Real people are much more convoluted than we could hope to explain. I gave up looking for easy answers to people's behavior years ago—no profit in it. Still, we might as well take your idea as a working hypothesis; it's as good as anything else I've heard this evening."

"But that still doesn't explain the feedback," White argued.

DeLong scratched his head. "Have we ruled out the possibility that it happened accidentally?"

"I don't know. I don't know anything anymore. If you'd asked me this morning, I'd have said it couldn't happen at all—but from what Wayne says, having this be an accident would be too coincidental. I'd have to guess that Vince somehow reached out and pulled the audience in with him before they could resist."

"But why?" Schulberg asked. "If he wanted them to have bad nightmares, it would have been easier for him to keep control of everything himself. Why would he *want* to give them free will?"

DeLong took a deep breath. "Let's see what we know about Vince," he said slowly. "We've all gotten the standard preaching, right?"

"He never really had time to get around to me," Wayne said. "But I saw a lot of it in action in that Dream."

"I think you'd better tell us exactly what went on in there," DeLong said.

Quickly, Wayne gave them a synopsis of what had happened while he was in the Dream. He gave particular emphasis to the tortures of the women in the Temple, and saw that the others were as horrified by the idea as he was. He also mentioned that, because the people did have free will, there was the group of Heretics who opposed Rondel's rule—but that they stood no chance against his total power in the Dream.

Schulberg was at the point of hysteria by the time Wayne had finished, but DeLong was silent for a moment. "Janet told me once," he said at last, "that Vince's mother had given him the belief that all women were sluts and hussies, that none of them were good enough for him. Think of it from her point of view—she didn't want any woman taking her son away from her because she needed him too badly. So she made him hate all other women. Janet fought it for a while, but even she couldn't get through that barrier.

"So now Mrs. Rondel is dead, and all other women have survived. It would be pretty rankling if he thought all the bad women are still alive and well, while his own sainted mother died. By degrading them, hurting them, humiliating them, he thus reaffirms his own mother's worth."

DeLong stopped and shrugged. "Well, it's a theory, at least."

"My guide in the Temple mentioned that the only woman who'd ever been worthwhile was the 'Holy Mother.' I thought he was talking about the Virgin Mary—but maybe that was the way Vince set up his own mother," Wayne said. "It would explain why he kept the air smelling of her perfume."

"But why give the people free will?" Schulberg repeated. "It doesn't make sense."

"Again, we'll have to consider Vince's religious beliefs," DeLong said. "The way he explained it to me, God gives everyone a choice. Only those who choose freely to be 'saved' are worthy of redemption. He's at least staying true to his principles by giving them the free will to make the choice, rather than imposing salvation on them. At the same time, he's loaded the dice wildly in his favor, like any good propagandist. After experiencing that Hell, a person would have to be crazy not to want to stay out of it. I'll bet Vince probably even thinks he's doing people a favor; by influencing their free choice in the matter, he really thinks he's saving their immortal souls."

"That's the kind of favor I can do without," Ernie White muttered.

Schulberg looked at the other three men. "All right, so we've psychoanalyzed Vince and we know why he's doing all this. The question is, what can *we* do to stop him? We've got Forsch coming here tomorrow from the FCC. If word of this gets out, he'll close down the station permanently."

"Worse than that," Delong said. "There are plenty of

people who distrust the entire Dream industry. They could use this as an excuse to shut everything down."

"I don't think there's any way we can prevent people from knowing about it," Wayne said. "Even if we stopped Vince this second, we couldn't go into all those minds and erase what they've already experienced—and some of it is pretty horrifying."

"Let's tick off the alternatives," DeLong said. "One: take the simplest case first. We could do nothing, just let Vince go on the way he is. What would happen?"

"A lot of the homecaps are probably scheduled to turn off in two hours when the Dream was supposed to be over," White said. "But at the rate Vince's burning energy, he can't last much more than another hour. Maybe an hour and a half, maximum, so we can't count on automatic switch-off doing any good. Whatever happens will be over by then."

"And what happens if Vince dies during the Dream?" DeLong turned to Wayne, the only expert in the room.

Wayne shook his head. "It looks to me like he's bent on taking all those people with him. There were repeated references to 'Judgment Day.' I think Vince actually intends to carry that out. Maybe before he goes he'll sound the Last Trump and bring about the end of the world. Maybe he'll judge everybody there and condemn the unlucky ones to his Hell. The problem is, everyone in the Dream will believe it. If they believe strongly enough that they've really died, I suppose it could even kill them in real life as well."

"Just what we need," Schulberg said, rolling his eyes heavenward.

DeLong made a sweeping motion with his hand. "Alternative number one, deleted. Alternative number two: we simply shut off the broadcast, fade it out in everyone's mind."

"I don't think we can," Ernie White said. "From what Wayne says, this Dream now exists in those people's minds independent of our broadcast. That's what the feedback means. Even if we fade it out, *they'll* go right on believing it. That universe has become real for them, and they'll continue to exist in it."

"But there won't be anyone else in it with them," Schulberg argued. "We'll have cut the link they all had in common."

Wayne was shaking his head. "But they'll have the memories of those other people being there. In essence, each person will become a Masterdreamer, following his own individual script through that same universe."

Schulberg considered that. "What you're saying is that it would become just an ordinary old dream, the kind people used to have all the time on their own before the Dreamcaps were invented."

Wayne spread his hands. "Maybe. But we're talking in terms of the worst possible case. Dreamcaps impress their images on the brain far more clearly than the brain could do by itself at random—that's why people always remember our Dreams the next morning. We've built our false reality so firmly in the audience's mind that unless we take great care to fade it out, it could become a permanent fixture."

"Is that so terrible? Lots of people have their own fantasy worlds. . . ."

"But they don't consider them real," Wayne insisted. "The people in this Dream are convinced it's reality. You remember the old advice about how dangerous it is to wake a sleepwalker. If they were broken off from the Dream and then awakened, they might not accept the normal world as reality. Not all of them would have that problem, of course, but even a handful of people going insane because of our broadcast would be enough to cause us trouble."

"Look at the trouble we got in with Spiegelman," DeLong added. "All he did was drop in a little harmless political philosophy. Vince has impressed on people's minds the literal reality of his own religious beliefs. How many people of other faiths do you think might be tuned in right now? How many of them are likely to consider this an attempt to convert them to Vince's religion? Even if no one goes crazy, the proselytizing alone would shut us down."

"Vay is mir," Schulberg muttered.

Delong sighed and folded his hands before him. "Alternative number two, then, leads to possible psychological dysfunction in some unstable individuals, and probable complaints of propagandizing to the FCC. Better than number one, perhaps, but not very. That leaves us with alternative number three: someone goes in and changes the Dream into something acceptable."

" 'Someone' meaning me?" Wayne asked.

" 'Someone' meaning you," DeLong nodded somberly. "We couldn't get anyone else in here and briefed on the situation in time. Besides, you've already been in there; you know the territory and the ground rules."

Wayne closed his eyes and tried to fight the fatigue washing over him. He had now Dreamed two nights in a row; that sort of thing took a lot out of a person. He remembered the hideous *thing* that had happened to him as he came out of the Dream this last time; he still had no explanation for that, and the mere thought of it started his hand shaking. On top of that, he had not the faintest idea how he was going to pry Rondel out of that Dream.

He wanted to mention all these factors—but he didn't, because he knew DeLong was right. He had to be the one to go in there. There was no other choice.

So, instead of protesting, he simply sighed and said, "I'm not at all sure I'll be able to do anything."

"Why not? You'll have a Dreamcap too, you'll be just as omnipotent as Vince is."

"That's an oversimplification. Vince won't just hand everything over to me the instant he sees me coming; he'll fight for it every step of the way. He knows that what he's doing is wrong, and if he gives up in the middle he'll never be given another chance. A naked power grab will get me nothing."

"Can't you just change the whole city to something else, something without all the symbolism Vince has given it?" Schulberg asked.

"Sure, nothing easier. I can make it into a Kansas prairie or a South Sea island paradise. And the instant Vince sees what I've done, he can change it right back again. Or maybe he'll decide to send a storm through there, killing everyone in its path. If I stop the storm, maybe he'll become a giant, squashing everyone underfoot. For every action I take, Vince can always have a countermove—and remember, he's always been a stronger Dreamer than I am."

"There are ways to weaken him," White said. "Even if we don't cut him off altogether, I can weaken the broadcast amplification from his helmet and increase the power to yours. That should make things a little more equal."

"It would be some help, yes," Wayne admitted. "But remember, I'm working under a limitation he doesn't have. I want to keep those people in the audience intact, while he doesn't care if he destroys them. In some ways, I think he *wants* to destroy them. With two people fighting over something, the one who wants to destroy it always has the advantage, because he doesn't have to worry about the weapons he uses.

"At best—at *very* best—I might battle him to a draw. But I doubt even that. Remember, he's bent on suicide—I'm not. He can throw every iota of his mind at me, without holding anything back, without any reservations. Without that fear of personal death, he'd become a berserker—and because I *do* have a sense of self-preservation, I wouldn't be able to commit quite as much of my mind to the fight."

"There's another factor to be considered, too," DeLong added. "A fight like Wayne described would be hell on the audience. Even if Wayne won, they'd probably come out of the Dream shell-shocked. Can you imagine being in a war between two gods battling for control of your mind and soul? I'd rather not even think about it."

The program coordinator drummed his fingers on the tabletop for a moment. "All right, for the time being that rules out a direct assault. That leaves us only indirect tactics to use on Vince."

"What do you mean?" Wayne asked.

"Vince went to the trouble of giving the audience free will, and I think we ought to try using that as a weapon against him."

"But the people in the audience don't have the advantage of a broadcast amplifier behind them," White pointed out. "They won't have enough strength to challenge Vince."

"Not individually, no. But if Wayne can win them over to his side, make them use their free will to *choose* his way over Vince's, he'll have seventy thousand allies against Vince. If Wayne can get the audience on his side, there'll be nothing Vince can do against a mob like that."

"You're talking in beautiful generalities, Bill, but exactly how am I supposed to accomplish this?" Wayne asked.

"You've already got some allies there—the Heretics."

"I'm not sure they'll trust me—particularly after I disappeared on them like that."

"They'll trust you. They can't afford not to, they need all the help they can get. They're already half-convinced you're one of the Wizards who used to rule there; if you come out and admit it, it'll give them some hope to rally behind. Apologize for disappearing; say you had to go off to confer, converse and otherwise hobnob with your brother Wizards. Tell them you're now prepared to lead an all-out fight against the Prophet."

"But there's only a couple of hundred Heretics," Wayne pointed out. "That's a far cry from seventy thousand."

"You just use them to start with, to spread the word, as it were. The only reason most of the people in the Dream are going along with Vince's game is because he seems to have the power to back up what he says. He can make Hell look very real to them, so of course they'll be on his side. But if it looks like his power is slipping, more and more people will start to defect. Never underestimate the human desire to be on the winning side.

"Instead of challenging Vince as Dreamer-to-Dreamer, you work to undermine his confidence. Instead of a big, world-shaking showdown, you concentrate on smaller things. You make sure that all his attempts to destroy the Heretics fail. Maybe a couple of his angels fall out of the sky for no apparent reason. Maybe he tries a few demonstration miracles and nothing happens. You go through the streets preaching freedom of religion, and none of his guards can stop you. I guarantee, the people will start swinging over to you. Most of them are only following Vince because he has the power. If they think you have a chance too, they'll prefer your openness."

Wayne was still unsure. "I'm not exactly a fiery evangelist. Even in a Dream, I don't think I'm capable of brilliant speeches to inspire people's loyalty."

"Hmm." DeLong was silent for a moment. "Well, if you can't be brilliant, the next best thing is to be romantic. A dashing, mysterious figure is just as sure to capture their imaginations."

"What exactly did you have in mind?"

"You were off to a good start with this Wizard you created—the long, dark robes, the strange powers, the air of mystery. Elaborate on that, milk it for all it's worth. It has the added advantage that Vince won't know exactly what's happening. If you go in there as Wayne Corrigan, he'll know immediately what you're up to and try to stop you. But he won't be sure what to make of this mysterious Wizard. Since he's given the people in the Dream free will, he can't be sure it isn't one of them with an unusually strong broadcasting ability. The more confusion you hand him, the better for you."

He paused again. "But the name 'Tim' will have to go. Whoever heard of a wizard named Tim? You need something with more authority to it. You have to be a masked avenger, meting out justice and opposing tyranny. You need a name to inspire confidence, to show the people you have their interests at heart, that you want to keep them safe. . . ."

"Like Zorro or the Scarlet Pimpernel?" Wayne said sardonically.

"Um, they're a little too flashy. Something a bit more somber and serious, in this case. Aha!" He slammed a palm down on the tabletop. "I've got it: the Guardian. That has all sorts of good connotations. You're there to guard people, keep them safe, protect them from evil, fight the wrongdoer. . . ."

Wayne stared at the program coordinator with unabashed amazement. "I don't believe it. You can turn *anything* into the plot of some hack novel."

DeLong spread his hands apart in mock humility. "Some of us are blessed with strange talents." Then he became serious again. "Everything I've given you this far, though, is still just window dressing. We want to wear down Vince's mind and increase the opposition to the point where you can take over the Dream yourself safely and somehow coax the people back into this world. Maybe, once you're in control, you'll have to tell them all that it's only a Dream.

"But regardless of that, there's going to come a point at which you'll have to challenge Vince for supremacy in there. That can't be changed. You'll be fighting a deadline of sorts, because you don't want to wait until he declares Judgment Day—but at the same time, you're the only one who can decide when Vince is weakened enough to let you move in on him. If you tip your hand too soon . . ."

Wayne didn't need DeLong's warning to drive that point home to him. He was already well aware of what could happen if he miscalculated. The fact was balanced precariously on one side of the scales; on the other was the knowledge of what could happen if he did nothing at all.

"It kind of makes me wish I'd been a plumber." Wayne rose to his feet and braced himself against the chair and table until he felt steadier. His body was still wobbly, and he knew it would take a major effort just to cross the room back to his cubicle. He asked White to get him several more cups of water, drinking them greedily to replace the fluids his body had sweated away during his previous brief Dream session. He tried to clear his mind and not think of what lay ahead of him inside that Dream.

The room seemed much too warm. He peeled off his still-soggy shirt and trousers. Each moment was slow and deliberate. "I guess I'm ready," he said at last.

White and DeLong insisted on helping him back to his cubicle, and Schulberg followed behind them, clucking mindless advice into Wayne's ear. Wayne eased himself into his dim little room and lay back reluctantly on the padded couch. He picked up the Dreamcap and stared at it, as though it were a monster that might turn and bite him at any second.

He remembered the horror of his final moments in the Dream, caught in the grip of . . . *whatever* it was. In his retelling of his story, he hadn't mentioned that to the others, simply because he had neither words nor explanation. He had never experienced anything like that before, and he never wanted to again—yet it could be waiting there for him, right on the other side of consciousness.

You don't have to do this, he told himself. *It's not your fault Vince went crazy. There's no law that says you have to clean up after his mistakes. You're so weak you can barely stand. No one will think less of you if you say you can't do it.*

But there were seventy thousand people out there, and Vince seemed determined to kill them. If any of them did die, how could he possibly face himself again with the knowledge that he'd passed up the chance to help them?

The Dreamcap felt like a crown of thorns as he slipped it expertly onto his scalp. The last thing he saw before reality slipped back into Dream was DeLong standing in the doorway of the cubicle, whispering, "Good luck, Wayne."

CHAPTER 12

HE ENTERED THE Dream stiffly, his mind braced for another attack by whatever force had grabbed him before. But everything was quiet and peaceful—no upheavals, nothing out of the ordinary. The city of Urba spread out quietly below him, its citizens going about their normal business of praying for their souls. There was no indication of the titanic struggle he had undergone just a short while ago.

He relaxed after a few moments and oriented himself once more. On the surface, nothing had changed since he left the Dream, but he couldn't be certain of that. He'd spent at least half an hour outside, and that was quite a long period here in the Dream, where Rondel had accelerated the action considerably.

His first step was to relocate the Heretics and regain their confidence. He looked for them in the deserted building where he'd last seen them, and found they'd left. This didn't surprise him; a group like theirs would have to be on the move constantly to evade Rondel's guards. It cost him a few extra moments while he quickly tracked through all the tall towers of Urba before he found them again.

They were hiding in the upper stories of one tower, with one-way glass giving them a clear view of the city stretched out below them. He took great pains to materialize around a corner, out of their sight. Once again he was the tall, mysterious robed figure with his face obscured by the cowl of his robe. Satisfied with his appearance, he stepped around the corner and into the women's view.

There was a series of startled gasps at his dramatic entrance. Laura, who'd had her back turned toward him, spun quickly to see what the matter was—and by the expression on her face, Wayne could guess she was far from happy to see him. "You again," she said.

"I promised I'd return."

"You promised you'd help us, too, and we've seen precious little evidence of that. There were times we could have used some help, but you weren't there. I don't think it's worth our while to depend on someone who just appears and disappears so unreliably."

"My absence couldn't be helped," Wayne said, letting his voice become deeper, more authoritative. "I am an emissary from others who cannot come here themselves. I had to discuss and argue the situation with them to determine how I might best help you. That has now been determined, and I'll be here to help you as long as you need me."

Laura stood with her hands on her hips, a disbelieving look on her face. "And what do you plan to do for us, Tim?"

"My name's not really Tim," Wayne said. "That was just a convenience of the moment. You may call me the Guardian."

"Whoever you are, that doesn't answer my question."

"I have come to destroy the cruel and oppressive reign of the Prophet. I have come to rouse the general populace to combat his evil, to build them into an army to overcome his forces of corruption and to establish a society where people are free to believe and act as they choose." His own fervor surprised him. *Bill's melodramatic style must be contagious*, he thought.

Laura, though, was less impressed. "Noble words," she sneered, "but I've yet to see any results."

She's right, Wayne thought. *So far I have been long on promises and short on delivery*. He nodded and said aloud, "Very well, it's time for a demonstration. Would you care to come with me down to the street?"

"Alone?"

"If you're worried about your safety, you may bring

as many of your people as you like. The more of you who watch me in action, the easier it'll be to convince you of my true intentions."

Laura asked for volunteers, and ended up with fifteen other women willing to accompany her down to the street to watch Wayne's demonstration.

Out in the main part of the Holy City, the Heretics kept well back into the shadows of an alleyway where they'd have a good view of what went on. Wayne, however, strode purposefully into the street, in plain sight of everyone passing by. In his dark robes, he stood out from the crowd of men who wore light-colored garments.

"Good people of Urba!" Wayne began. He did not have to raise his voice; he made sure the sound of it carried quite well to everyone in sight. He gave it the resonant quality that people usually associated with doomsayers and prophets. "You are living under the harsh oppression of a cruel tyrant. The Prophet you serve has enslaved you all; he has used your fear to subjugate you to his iron will."

The men around him stopped dead in their tracks, stunned with disbelief. Who was this person who dared to blaspheme against the Prophet? Hadn't he accepted God when he entered the Holy City, like everyone else? Hadn't he seen the fires of Hell for himself? Didn't he know the punishment that awaited anyone who showed less than proper homage to God and His prophet?

Wayne let the questions simmer in their minds for a moment before he continued. "I am the Guardian, and I have come to help you overthrow this tyrant and live like free men once more. Look, and I shall demonstrate my powers!"

He raised his right arm upward, and a crackling bolt of lightning descended from heaven, striking his arm and making his whole body glow so brightly with electricity that the men around him had to shield their eyes to keep from being blinded. Slowly the crowd around him grew as men from other streets came over

157

to see what was happening. Wayne let the crackling sound build until it drowned out all other noises.

When he could see they'd had enough, Wayne lowered his arm once more and the lightning stopped. "The Guardian has powers to challenge this false prophet," he declared. "I will use them in your name, to keep you safe from his tyranny."

"No one can stand against the Prophet," someone yelled back. "His powers come from God Himself."

"Anyone can stand against the Prophet, if he truly believes in liberty and justice. Your so-called prophet offers only darkness and death; I offer you the choice of light and life. Those who accept, and follow the Guardian, will suffer no harm from the Prophet."

It was at this point that one of the angels flying overhead chose to intervene. This blasphemy had gone on long enough; it was time to put a stop to it. The angel swooped like a bird of prey, emitting a high-pitched shriek calculated to deafen the sternest enemy. Its hands curled forward into sharp talons, ready to grasp Wayne and shred him into tiny bits.

Wayne stood his ground calmly and watched the angel descend. When it was only a few meters over his head, he raised his arm again and pointed at the figure. As he'd done before when he was helping the Heretics escape from the Temple, he made the angel explode into a shower of colorful, harmless sparks.

The audience's astonishment was almost tangible. This was the first time any of them had ever seen the Prophet's power defied successfully, and it unnerved them. They looked at Wayne with new respect, but still no one made a move toward him. They were not ready to switch allegiance and become his followers. Not yet. The fear of the Prophet was still too strong.

He supposed it was to be expected. Social critics had been complaining about public apathy for as long as Wayne could remember. The people would be led if he could persuade them he had the power to beat Rondel—but it would take more than one miracle to do the trick.

"I ask now that you remember me," he said simply.

"I ask that you remember the Guardian and the cause of freedom. I ask that you remember this sign, and know it as my handiwork." Using the first two fingers of his right hand, he drew a pair of parallel wavy lines in the air. The passage of his fingers made the air glow red for several seconds, clearly revealing the pattern. People gasped as they saw the fiery marks. The sign faded, but the memory was clearly etched in the minds of all the witnesses.

"I ask only your support when the time comes," Wayne continued, lowering his voice so that every listener had to strain to hear him. "Remember, when you see my symbol, that I fight in your name, for your freedom."

He turned and started to leave the intersection when suddenly a group of onlookers parted to admit a squad of the Prophet's troops. Five of the silver-clad soldiers walked arrogantly into the center of the intersection, their stun-rifles drawn. "What's going on here?" snarled the leader.

"I was preaching blasphemy and rebellion," Wayne said calmly.

The leader leered at him. His rifle was aimed squarely at Wayne's chest. "Think you're smart, eh? We'll see how well you hold up at the next exhortation. Come along with us."

"I don't think I will."

Wayne's quiet refusal to play the game properly was starting to make the squad leader edgy. By all rights, this sinner should have been frightened out of his wits; instead, he stood there, boldly defying the Prophet's authority. Nervously the man hitched up his pants and said, "We'll see about that."

He took a step toward Wayne, but before he could come any closer a purple fog swirled into the area. No one saw it coming; one moment the air was clear, the next it was almost impossible to see. The citizens yelled in panic, but they were afraid to run anywhere because they couldn't tell where they were going.

Then the fog vanished as abruptly as it had come.

The citizens of Urba looked around them, startled, and suddenly burst out laughing.

There, in the middle of the street, stood the Temple guards, just as they had before the fog rolled in—except that the fog had mysteriously disintegrated their uniforms and weapons, leaving them stark naked in the middle of the street. In addition, branded into the right cheek of each guard's posterior, were the parallel wavy lines that were the symbol of the Guardian.

The Guardian himself had disappeared from the street. He was now in the alley where Laura and her Heretics had been watching his display. Wayne looked at the rebel leader. "Well?"

Laura smiled at him for the first time. "Let's go back to the hideout," she said. "I think we can make a deal."

When the incident was related to the other Heretics, they warmed to Wayne considerably. His very presence gave them a morale boost they sorely needed. Up until now they'd been forced on the defensive, making a few small forays against the Temple but mostly just trying to hide and remain free of Rondel's clutches. Now, at last, they had someone who had the power to take the initiative, who could act with seeming impunity against the tyrant. Going on the offensive made them feel useful for the first time in longer than they could remember.

"We've struck the first blow," Wayne told them, "but remember, it is only a first blow. The Prophet has not yet stirred personally. His powers are at least as great as mine. In order to fight him and win, we must have the people of the city on our side."

One woman in the back stood up angrily. "Those are the same men who tortured us in the Temple. I refuse to have anything to do with them."

Wayne sighed. This would be a little more tangled than he'd imagined. "I understand your feelings completely. You were all brutalized and humiliated in there, and there is no way of excusing the men who did it. But we're fighting a bigger war, now, and we'll need everyone's help if we're going to win."

"Marsha's right," said another woman, standing beside the first. "I won't cooperate with animals."

"There's an animal side to everyone, man and woman," Wayne argued. "The Prophet, for his own twisted, perverted reasons, has encouraged the animal side of men to be unchained, to be let loose on the helpless women in the Temple. But those same men, once they're freed from the Prophet's influence, will be ashamed of what they did in there. . . ."

"That's no consolation," the first woman, Marsha, said coldly.

Wayne paused and took a deep breath. "No. No, I don't suppose it is. There is nothing anyone can say or do to make up for the horrors you and others faced in there. But remember, our goal is to stop the Prophet and make sure such abuses don't happen again. At least, I *assume* that's what you want, correct?"

Marsha said nothing, so Laura filled in the gap. "That's what we *all* want," she said.

"Well, if we're going to defeat the Prophet," Wayne went on, "we'll need the cooperation of everybody in the city. My powers alone, great as they are, are not enough to topple him if other people still support him. Even with the help of you Heretics—even with the help of all the women in Urba—it might not be enough. We need the support of the men, too. That's a simple fact. Granted, there's no retribution possible to make up for the hideous treatment you've received. But if we're going to keep these abuses from happening in the future, we'll need the support of the entire populace. If you can't forgive them—and I'm not asking you to—at least try to forget the injustices for the time being while we work for the greater good of everybody."

Silence greeted his remarks. Marsha and the other woman who had risen to speak looked at him for a long moment and then sat down. They did not necessarily agree with what he said, but at least they were willing, for the moment, to raise no new objections. Laura looked over her people and saw general acceptance, with minor reservations, through the crowd. "I think you can count on our support for the time being," she said, turning back to Wayne. "What can we do for you?"

Wayne noticed, with a certain degree of satisfaction, the way she phrased her offer. No longer was she demanding to know what he could do to help her. Her wording implied that, because of his superior powers, he was the one to take the lead; she and her Heretics would be in a supporting position.

If this fragile alliance was to hold together, he had to make sure they never felt he was treating them as inferiors. "We have to undermine the Prophet's power over people. We have to show them, over and over again, that they have nothing to fear by speaking up against him. The only way we can do that is by example. We must all go to various parts of the city and preach against his rule, show people we're not afraid to defy him."

"That's easy for you to say," Laura told him. "But the rest of us don't have any magical powers to protect us from his angels and his guards. What are we supposed to do when they come to stop us?"

That was a problem. Wayne thought for a moment. "I'll give each of you a small device to protect you," he said at last. "Whenever you find yourself in trouble from the Prophet's forces, all you'll have to do is press the button and they won't be able to harm you."

"How can we be sure of that?" one woman asked.

"You have the word of the Guardian," Wayne said. The actual situation would be more complicated than that, but it would have been hard to explain to them. He couldn't give them something that would really protect them from anything Rondel could throw at them. What his devices would do was alert him to the presence of trouble. He could be anywhere in this Dream instantly, if he wanted, and he should be able to offer protection invisibly if it was required, to make the devices look as though they worked.

Some of the Heretics still looked unsure, so Laura stepped forward. "Your word is good enough for me," she said, and several of the other women began nodding their consent.

"What are you going to do about the Temple?" another woman asked.

This was the subject Wayne had been avoiding so far. The activities in the Temple were obviously of key concern to the Heretics as well as to him; the longer he let those tortures go on, the worse would be the psychological effect on the women involved. He would have to find some way of neutralizing the activities there, quickly.

Yet at the same time, he was reluctant to go near there. The last time he had gone to the Temple, he'd encountered that *thing* in the doorway to the bottom levels, and the memory still scared him. Then too, the Temple was the center of Rondel's activity, and that was where Wayne would run the greatest risk of discovery. As DeLong had pointed out, he'd have to face Rondel in a showdown sooner or later, but he was not ready yet. His power was not nearly consolidated enough to win such a battle.

"That is the most dangerous place, of course," he said aloud slowly. "We'll have to shut it down, but we'll have to move carefully. . . ."

He was interrupted by the sudden tolling of bells and blaring of trumpets. He looked around, startled, and saw out the window that the sky was glowing and filled with angels. He felt his heart rise to his throat. *Not Judgment Day already!* he thought. *There's still too much to prepare.*

But the Heretics, although as startled as he was by the sudden noise, took the event much more in stride. It was obviously something they were familiar with, which gave him the courage to ask, "What's happening?"

"It's one of the Prophet's exhortations," Laura said. "Everyone's supposed to go to the Temple Square to

163

hear him preach. He tells us all how sinful we've been, and he makes a public example of the particularly sinful. He even lets the women out of the Temple to attend the services."

She frowned as a thought crossed her mind. "He'll probably use this opportunity to torture Judy and Maria, the two women who were captured in our last raid on the Temple. Damn, I wish I could help them!"

"We will," Wayne said quietly. Even though it meant coming face-to-face with Rondel, this was a chance he couldn't pass up. Most, if not all, of the people in the Dream would be assembled together in one place; he might never have a better chance to affect the entire audience simultaneously. If he took enough precautions, he should be able to disguise himself well enough to fool Rondel.

Briefly he outlined his tentative plan to the Heretics and they accepted it avidly. They were all eager for action, and Wayne was promising them the chance for their first serious blow against Rondel's regime.

Wayne, Laura and some of the other Heretic leaders went down to the street level on the first elevator; the rest of the Heretics would come in small groups until they were all ready. It would take a little time for the crowd to gather in the Temple Square, which would give the rebels the opportunity to position themselves properly.

Wayne went off by himself. This stunt was one he'd have to do alone, and it would have to be done exactly right. He could have a major psychological effect on both the audience and Rondel if he pulled it off correctly—but if he made a mistake, Rondel would spot him instantly and the whole event could blow up in his face. It was a calculated risk, but the prize seemed worthwhile.

As people began pouring into the square, they filled the broad grassy area in front of the Temple, crowding together obediently to hear the Prophet's speech. As Wayne watched, he began to realize just how many people were represented by the number seventy thousand. The magnitude of his task nearly overwhelmed him, but he forced that consideration from his mind, cleared it of everything but the job he knew he had to do.

A dais had been set up at the front entrance of the Temple. Several people stood on the platform, including a central figure glowing with internal light; that could only be Rondel, though Wayne was too far away yet to see him clearly. Off to one side, in chains, was a group of men and women, including the two former Heretics—obviously today's object lesson. Wayne wondered what the men had done to earn Rondel's displeasure. Not that it mattered; if they were against Rondel, they would probably make worthy recruits for his revolution.

He materialized a massive wooden staff in one hand and began making his way through the crowd. He did not need to push; there was something about his presence that made people stand out of his way, no matter how crowded they were. They all noticed him in passing, and some of them whispered to their neighbors. Apparently, word of his demonstration a short while before had spread rapidly through the Holy City.

As he came closer to the front of the crowd, he was able to get a better view of the platform. The people on the dais around Rondel must be his higher functionaries and civil servants. Rondel would hardly need anyone like that to administer his world, but the perfectionist in him would probably insist on such minor touches to make things seem more realistic.

In particular, there was a woman standing close beside Rondel, in clothing better than he would expect of one of the Temple women. Considering Rondel's views on the opposite sex, Wayne was surprised that any woman would be that exalted. He wondered whether Rondel had chosen to reincarnate an image of his mother—and then he remembered the soldier at the Temple mentioning something about a High Priestess.

Curious, he improved his vision until he could see the figure more clearly—and when he recognized who it was, he could barely stifle a gasp.

The person standing on the dais beside the Prophet was Janet Meyers.

CHAPTER 13

AT FIRST, WAYNE was dumbfounded. What was Janet doing here? How had she gotten into this Dream? Had Bill and Ernie sent her in to help him?

Even as he thought of that, he knew it was wrong. At the rate time was flowing in this Dream, it couldn't be more than a minute or two since he'd reentered it himself; they wouldn't have had time to get Janet prepared and send her in, even if she'd come to the studio the instant Wayne went under. And they certainly hadn't been expecting her. DeLong had said when Wayne first arrived at the studio that he was the only Dreamer they'd been able to contact.

His mind racing in confusion, Wayne would have liked nothing better than a chance to leave the square and sit down to think this out. But that wasn't possible now. The Guardian had been spotted walking to the front of the crowd, and the Guardian must never be seen retreating from the Prophet. That would indicate fear, and it would undo all he had accomplished so far.

Reluctantly, then, Wayne continued to press forward through the growing crowd until he was near the front rows. Rondel, occupied with other matters, did not notice him until he'd made it almost to the dais—but once he spotted Wayne, he gave him his full attention. The Guardian, with his dark robes and impressive build, stood out easily in this mob. Depending on how much attention he'd been paying to the happenings in the Holy City, Rondel might already have heard some of the Guardian's exploits; at any rate, he recognized instantly that the figure approaching him was not one of the ordinary audience members, and deserved special attention.

As Wayne moved through the mob, more and more of them had fallen silent, watching him and wondering what would happen. When the Prophet, too, turned his eye to the mysterious figure, everybody in the square fell silent. Wayne was suddenly reminded of the gunfight on a lonely street in a Western, with the townspeople watching nervously through the windows on either side. There was no place for them to hide in this showdown, though; they simply had to stand around and hope no stray lightning bolts were thrown their way.

Wayne could feel the heat of Rondel's glare, but he refused to be hurried. He continued to move at a slow, dignified pace toward the front. He was even tempted to slow down the time scale of the Dream, to make his march seem even longer, but he knew that would give him away instantly. He had to settle for what he could get. He picked a spot, an open place just in front of the dais, and walked resolutely toward it. When he reached it, he stopped and stared calmly into Rondel's face.

Rondel was burning. The other Dreamer made a strong attempt to make the Guardian's robes disappear, but Wayne maintained them. In this battle, he had more strength than Rondel did, because Rondel was using most of his energy to maintain the city around them; Wayne could channel his effort into concealing his identity.

Tiring at last of the silent battle of wills, Rondel spoke. "Who are you, fiend?"

"I am the Guardian." Wayne didn't have to raise his voice to make sure everyone in the square heard him.

"You're a fraud. There is no guardian."

"I am here. Judge for yourself."

"Why have you come?"

"You know why. You have violated these people's souls. They must be set free."

"I have given them the Word!" Rondel bellowed, his

voice thundering through the city. "The Word is God, the Word is law."

"The word is bullshit," Wayne said.

Rondel's eyes burned with the very fires of Hell. He gestured dramatically, and from out of the clear blue sky a massive lightning bolt shot down to disintegrate the challenger. Wayne raised his hand and casually flicked the bolt away, as he might brush at an annoying fly.

Rondel's anger merely increased. "I have saved these people from their sins. . . ."

"You've enslaved them to the harsh tyranny of your twisted prejudices. You've forced them to bend to your iron law."

"I am no tyrant," Rondel said. "I myself am the humblest servant of God."

"You serve a god of cruelty and hatred, not a god of love. You force people to commit perversions in the name of piety. There are many beliefs, many concepts of God that do not agree with yours. You've robbed these people of the right to follow those."

Rondel redoubled his efforts to remove Wayne's robes, and again Wayne was able to maintain them. "Who are you?" the Masterdreamer bellowed again.

Wayne was struck with a sudden, brilliant idea. In a small voice that only Rondel would hear, he said, "I'm your conscience, Vince."

Of all the possible answers, that was the one for which Rondel was least prepared. "What?"

"You can't fight me, because I'm a part of you. You created me because a part of you is appalled at what you're doing. You know these people have no more free will than a man at gunpoint does. You know God wants people to choose His way freely, because they love Him, not because they're afraid of you. Release them, let them go back to their own lives."

"They came to the city of their own accord."

"You can't fool your conscience. You know what you've done to them."

"Go away. Leave me alone."

"You can't get rid of your conscience, either. I'll always be here, always be with you. You know you're doing something wrong, violating the laws of man and God. I am the voice of your shame, of your guilt, of your doubt. You will never be rid of me."

"YOU LIE!" The very buildings trembled at the sound of that roar.

"Take a look at yourself in the Mirror of Truth." Wayne lifted a hand and created a looking glass in front of Rondel that the Masterdreamer could not help but look into. The image it showed was his own, but Wayne tastefully supplied the addition of small goat horns coming from the forehead and a satanic gleam about the features.

"You are Satan himself, the master liar!" With a gesture, Rondel caused the mirror to shatter, and Wayne didn't bother to defend his creation. He'd made the point adequately.

"You must abandon this foolishness," Wayne continued for the general audience. "I will not allow your tyranny to continue. Everything you try will fail. The people you sought to enslave will rise against you. Men and women will be free to worship as they like, free from the narrow restrictions of your petty theology."

"I will destroy you!" Rondel swore.

"You may try," Wayne replied calmly. "But before you do, dare to gaze on the face of your enemy."

With that, he pushed back the cowl of his robes and revealed himself to Rondel and the entire crowd. There were gasps as people recognized the image Wayne was projecting. His face was Rondel's face, but innocent, more cherubic, with a small halo glowing behind his head. Rondel's eyes widened with fear, and the lashings of his hatred increased tremendously. Wayne could feel himself in the eye of a mental maelstrom, but he himself remained calm. He knew there was nothing Rondel could do to him personally, so he just let the force of the other's personality batter away around him.

The very fabric of reality wavered, flickering on and

off like a child playing with a lightswitch. At the edges of the city, the buildings began melting like putty in the sun, and the sky glowed with the burning red of Rondel's fury. The people in the square, not knowing what was happening, began to panic, running and screaming in all directions while the two combatants held firm in their positions.

Have I managed to do it this quickly? Wayne wondered. *Have I weakened him enough to step in and take it over?*

But even as he thought that, Rondel regained control of himself and the Dream. The Masterdreamer was a man who would impose his own will at all costs, and was not about to let some anomaly defeat him. Reality stabilized once more, the sky was blue again and objects returned to their normally solid selves. The Prophet was once again in control of the Holy City. At his command, people stopped their outward flight, and a semblance of order returned.

Rondel looked to his guards, as though he himself didn't deign to deal with this interloper. "Seize him!" he commanded. "We'll show the people exactly what the penalty is for defying the will of God."

Wayne merely smiled and raised his staff to the skies. A cloud of dense purple fog suddenly blanketed the square, making vision impossible. More confusion. Wayne took advantage of the fog to break the chains of the captives on the dais who were about to be punished for their imagined sins. With the speed of teleportation, he transported them safely to the Heretics' hideout. Meanwhile, at the edges of the crowd, the Heretics had been waiting for their cue. They now raced over to where the Temple women had been standing and tried to drag as many away from the area as they could under cover of this mysterious darkness.

The fog lasted only a few brief moments, until Rondel cleared it away again with a single thought. But the panic in the crowd could not be stopped so easily a second time, and he found his audience deserting him. His guards found themselves under attack by the fiercely determined Heretics. And the mysterious Guardian had completely disappeared.

But branded into the wooden platform of the dais were two parallel wavy lines, symbol of the Guardian.

Despite his triumph in the Temple Square, Wayne's thoughts were far from happy. Janet's appearance in this Dream had shocked him, and he needed someplace to be alone for a few moments, a chance to gather his wits and deal with the situation. There was nowhere in all of Urba that fit such a description; all of it was subtly infused with Rondel's presence. In desperation, Wayne left this reality altogether, surrounding himself with a small bubble of his own personal being where he could relax and ponder this confusing turn of events.

His first thought was that Rondel had decided to create an image of Janet, out of love, to follow him to his death. Wayne desperately wanted to believe that, because it would mean that this Janet was not real, any more than the city itself was real. She could then be dismissed as an imaginary wraith, and would end unheeded when the Dream itself died.

But the inner core of him knew that was wishful thinking. Rondel had seventy thousand people in this Dream to draw on; he didn't need to invent other images, and they would merely draw more of his power unnecessarily. He had to maintain this entire universe —why would he bother with a superfluous encumbrance, even one as wonderful as Janet, to complicate the process?

Besides, thinking back on his conversation with Janet as he'd driven her home earlier that evening, Wayne remembered her saying she'd be tuning in to Rondel's broadcast. She admired his work, she'd said, and she tried to experience it as often as possible. Rondel didn't need to create a false Janet, Wayne knew—that was the real one beside him on the dais, though what role she served here Wayne could hardly guess.

He pondered the implications of that. Janet would be

exactly like everyone else in this Dream, convinced it was the only reality. She would remember nothing about a man named Wayne Corrigan. Whatever the fate of the people in this Dream, she would share it equally.

Suddenly Wayne felt very tired. Up until now this had been an intellectual game, played for impersonal stakes. He'd met a handful of people in this Dream briefly; most he didn't know at all. The number seventy thousand was impressive, particularly when they were all crowded into the Temple Square—but it was only a number. It was easy to think of them as poker chips in a large pot, and his only worry was how to snatch them away without Rondel catching him.

Janet's presence changed all that. She was someone he knew, someone he cared about very much. If he made any mistakes and allowed Rondel to win, Janet might die or be mentally scarred for the rest of her life. He thought of her as she'd been in the Dream with him yesterday, full of poise and confidence. Knowing all that could be destroyed by a careless move on his part was an awesome responsibility.

I'm tired, he thought. *I shouldn't be having to do this. I don't have either the strength or the ability to stand up to Rondel. Maybe I should quit and hope they can find someone else.*

But he knew that was hopeless. There simply was no one else, and there wasn't enough time even if there were. He alone was responsible for rescuing these people; he alone could save Janet from this fate.

An idea occurred to him. Perhaps he need not be completely alone in this fight. Janet was a Dreamer by profession, a damned good one—and, like everyone else in this Dream, she had free will. If he could go to her and restore her memory of the real world, she could help him in his crusade. Her knowledge of how to manipulate Dreams, combined with his, would make a force that Rondel couldn't fight. She didn't have the broadcast power of the studio behind her, just the tiny signal from her home receiver, but she was expert at some techniques Wayne could hardly touch. With her talents and his broadcast power, they'd make a formidable team.

There were dangers associated with this idea, of course. Janet wouldn't recognize him as Wayne Corrigan, nor would she readily believe that what seemed so very real to her was only a figment of her imagination. Then too, the fact that she was on the dais indicated she held some special position within Rondel's administration. If Wayne told her too much of the story and she didn't believe him, she might betray him to Rondel, and his only advantage—surprise—would be lost.

He weighed both sides of the argument carefully, but eventually the pro side won. He knew his own limitations only too well and, when it came to the final showdown, he knew Rondel would fight like a madman to preserve his maniacal vision. Wayne needed all the help he could get, and Janet was the best ally he could ever have hoped for. He resolved to talk to her at once.

He made himself invisible once more and dissolved the private bubble around himself, venturing into Rondel's universe again. He had no specific idea where Janet would be—and even as powerful as he was, it would still take some time to find one individual in a city of seventy thousand. He ventured a guess that she would be in or around the Temple area, since that was the center of Rondel's administration, so he concentrated his search there.

He breezed quickly through the more public rooms, where men were mutilating themselves or torturing defenseless women. He didn't want to face those crimes again, and he was pretty sure Janet would not be there. Her place of honor beside Rondel on the dais indicated she held a special position that was unlikely to bring her out among the common crowd.

The upper floor of the Temple, Wayne's guide had said, was where the High Priestess tended the shrine of the Holy Mother. As soon as he remembered that, Wayne zoomed up there, darting right through "solid" walls until he reached the place he was seeking.

It was a large room, like a Gothic cathedral with high pointed arches. Enormous stained glass windows filtered multicolored sunlight into the room, which was otherwise lit only by the glow of thousands of candles. Against one wall was an altar covered with white satin cloth; it stood beneath a larger-than-life-sized statue of a woman. Wayne recognized her as Rondel's mother—not the fat, pallid slug of a woman Wayne had glimpsed briefly in his one encounter with her, but rather the young, attractive woman from the photos in her bedroom and Rondel's office. This was the image Rondel had kept of her, even though the years had been less than kind. This was what he'd seen when he looked at her, wallowing in that bed of filth. *Some illusions die hard,* Wayne thought.

Rondel and Janet were before the altar. Rondel was standing, but he had forced Janet to kneel. "What kind of tricks are you trying to pull?" he bellowed. "You conjured that thing up, didn't you?"

Janet was on the verge of tears. "I don't know what you're talking about. I don't know how to conjure anything."

"Sure you do—you more than anyone else here." Rondel was trembling with rage. "Oh, I should have listened to her, she was so right about you. Deceitful, ungrateful little bitch, that's what you are. . . ."

"I swear, I don't know what you're talking about." But her protestation did no good; Rondel slapped her, knocking her off balance onto the ground.

As Wayne had feared, Rondel was clearly reasoning that only another Dreamer could have performed tricks like that. Janet was the only other Dreamer Rondel definitely knew was in this Dream, and so she had to bear the brunt of his suspicions. She had broken off their love affair, which he might logically view as a betrayal—so of course he would expect her to betray him again.

"I took you out of the crowd the instant I saw you," Rondel ranted on. "I set you up as High Priestess, above the others, hoping you would prove your worth.

But all you proved was that my mother was right: you're a no-good, treacherous whore. But I won't let you destroy me, I won't let you tear down what I've worked for. I have more power here than you do. You'll burn in Hell forever if you don't give in."

"Vince, please, I don't know what you're talking about."

Wayne decided this treatment had gone far enough. With part of his mind, he reached out to the boundaries of Urba and caused a massive earthquake, toppling a couple of empty buildings and demolishing a section of the outer wall. It was not major damage, and no one would be hurt, but he hoped it would distract Rondel enough to make him go look at the scene in person.

Rondel paused in his diatribe, sensing the earthquake as a direct attack on the fringes of his consciousness. He glared at Janet's cowering form. "That couldn't be you," he said. "You're not strong enough. But just wait. I haven't finished with you yet."

He stormed out of the room, leaving Janet sobbing on the hard stone floor. As soon as he was gone, Wayne materialized again in his Guardian robes and walked over to where Janet knelt. She was crying so hard that she didn't even notice his presence until he touched her shoulder in an attempt to comfort her.

She gasped and looked up, expecting to see Rondel again, and pulled suddenly away when she saw who it was. Her eyes were red and brimming over with tears, and now a new look had been added to them—fear. "You!" she whispered. "Get away from me. Leave me alone!"

"I mean you no harm," Wayne said gently, trying to defuse her fear. "I only want to talk to you for a bit."

"I won't listen," she said, cupping her hands over her ears. "You've caused me enough trouble, you've made the Prophet damn me to Hell. I won't be unfaithful to him."

"He'll hurt you no matter what you do—you and everyone else in Urba." It didn't matter that she'd covered her ears; he made sure his words went right through her hands, into her mind.

"Help! Guards, somebody, help!"

"No one will hear you, and the door is sealed. We're alone here together, just the two of us."

Janet dashed to the door anyway, and found he was right—it was sealed shut, and the knob wouldn't turn. After a couple of frantic attempts to open it, she turned around to face him. She was bravely trying to regain her composure. "All right, I guess I have to listen to you. But I want no part of your fight against the Prophet."

"Not even if I'm fighting for your own safety, and the safety of everyone in Urba?"

"We don't need your protection. God will protect us. The Prophet says so."

"The Prophet is mad, and the only god he serves is his own twisted ego. All he gives people is pain and suffering."

"He gives us salvation," Janet said, mouthing her phrases like a well-trained parrot. "He gives us hope that our souls will be redeemed on Judgment Day."

"Redemption for what? So you won't burn in Hell? Look around you. If Heaven is supposed to be like this so-called Holy City, you're in Hell already."

Janet was on the point of sobbing again. "What choice do we have?"

Wayne hated to see her crying, and softened his tone immediately. "That's why I've come here—to give people a choice. What's your name?"

"Huh?" Janet was startled by the sudden change of topic.

"Please bear with me. Just say your name."

"Janet."

"Janet what?"

She looked at him in puzzlement for a moment, then knit her brow as she tried to recall. "Meyers," she said at last. "Janet Meyers." She said it as though it were a major breakthrough—and, in a way, it was.

Considering how hard it was for her to remember something as basic as her name, Wayne knew he could never count on her to remember other things by

177

herself—not in the short period of time he had. He'd have to goad her memory along. "That's right," he said. "Your name is Janet Meyers. Do you want to know why the Prophet accused you of 'conjuring' me?"

"No one may question the Prophet's motives."

"He accused you," Wayne went on, "because he knows the truth about you, the truth he's made you forget."

Janet looked at him defiantly. "What is this so-called truth?"

"That you are a born Wizard, with magical abilities to rival his own."

"That's ridiculous. I don't know any magic."

"Why do you think he selected you, out of thousands of women, to be High Priestess?" When Janet didn't answer, he continued, "Because he knows how potentially powerful you are, and he wants to keep an eye on you."

"And how do you come to know all these secret things?"

"Because I'm a Wizard too, the same as you are. I control powers beyond your comprehension; I can perform impossible feats."

"You're mad," Janet said.

"Perhaps a few simple tricks will convince you."

Wayne shrank himself until he was only half his former height, then expanded until his head brushed the ceiling. Returning to his normal size, he turned himself upside down and floated that way in midair before her. Detaching his left arm, he twirled it like a majorette's baton before joining it once more to his shoulder. He altered the arrangement of his face so that his eyes came between his mouth and his nose. Then, correcting his features once more, he turned back right side up and stood on the floor facing her.

Janet's eyes had widened and her lower lip was trembling as she watched him go through his paces. Her mouth opened and closed a few times, but no sounds came out. She backed up against the wall and clutched at it, as though needing its firmness to reassure her of reality.

"I'm sorry if I shocked you," Wayne said softly, "but words alone couldn't convince you. I had to do something."

"You certainly did something," Janet answered hoarsely.

"Will you let me explain the situation to you? Are you willing to suspend some small part of your disbelief?"

"You leave me little choice." Her voice was still shaky, but her face indicated she was bringing herself more under control.

Wayne sat irreverently on the altar and motioned for her to sit beside him. She chose, instead, to sit on the floor, facing him. His demonstration was still a little too fresh in her mind for her to be at ease with him.

He built his story slowly, trying to keep it within the framework of this universe as she knew it. He told her that Rondel had destroyed the evil Wizards, but that the good Wizards went into hiding. Janet had been one of the good Wizards, but Rondel—unable to destroy her—had stolen from her all memory of her past life, and of the powers she could command. The Prophet had now become as corrupt as the Wizards he'd destroyed, and Wayne—on behalf of the good Wizards—was trying to save the people of the city from the Prophet's mad reign.

She was the key, he told her. He needed her help. She must struggle to remember her life before coming to Urba, to remember the powers at her command. Then she must join with him to defeat the Prophet—otherwise everyone in Urba was doomed.

Janet listened without interruption. It was clear from her face that there was a war going on in her soul. His story sounded like a fairy tale, and it was hard to believe him; yet she could hardly deny the performance he had so recently given, the demonstration of remarkable powers.

When he was finished, she was silent for a time. She avoided looking directly at him, preferring to stare at the floor by her feet. "You're saying that unless I help you betray the Prophet and his God, evil will triumph in Urba."

"It's possible. I'm trying to prevent the worst of it, and I'm prepared to do it alone, but your help would be of immense value. It might even be the deciding factor."

"Yet everything I know, everything I experience, tells me the Prophet is right, and I must obey him if I want to prevent myself from being eternally damned."

"How much do you know of your life? What's the earliest memory you can recall?"

Janet hesitated. "I . . . I was in a field with some other people when the voice of the Prophet came to us and told us to come to Urba if we wished to be saved."

"But you remember nothing of your childhood, nothing of your life before that?"

"No," Janet said quietly.

"Then how do you know I'm not right?"

"I . . . I don't. But if you're wrong, if the Prophet is right, then betraying him would damn me to Hell forever."

Her unwillingness to accept what he told her was infuriating. Wayne had to remind himself that, given everything she knew, she was really behaving in a rational manner. "All right, then. I can't and I won't force you to do anything against your will. All I ask is two things. First, promise you won't tell the Prophet about my talk with you."

Janet rose and turned away from him. "He thinks I created you. He'll continue to blame me for the things you do. How can you ask me to suffer your punishments for you?"

"Believe me, Janet, I wouldn't if there were any other way. There are seventy thousand people involved here. For their sakes, if not for mine, this conversation must be kept secret."

"All right," she said. Her voice was barely audible.

"Second, I'd like you to think about what I've said. I'm not asking you to believe it all instantly—just don't disbelieve it. Search your memory, see if you can recall anything about your life before coming to Urba. The more you can remember, the more you'll see I'm right."

Janet just nodded, without saying a word.

"Thank you," Wayne said. "I'll leave you alone now."

"Wait a minute." She turned to face him again. "If I'm a Wizard, as you say, then I should be able to do tricks like you did, right?"

"You should—but until you regain your memory, I don't think you'll know how."

She closed her eyes tightly and strained very hard to do something, yet when she opened her eyes again nothing in the room had changed. "Did anything happen?" she asked.

"Not that I noticed. What were you trying to do?"

"I . . . I tried to make myself as tall as the ceiling."

Wayne shook his head. "You must regain your memory first, and the techniques will come. I'm sorry, but don't give up hope. Keep practicing, keep trying to remember. In the meantime, I must go. The door will open freely again after I'm gone."

Wayne faded out of the room. He was annoyed at himself for not being able to convince her and worried that, despite her promise, she might betray his presence to Rondel if she was placed under enough pressure. Even so, he was glad he'd taken the risk. Perhaps he'd planted a seed that might yet sprout. Even a reluctant ally like Janet would be some help when the big showdown came.

CHAPTER 14

WHEN HE RETURNED to the Heretics' hideout, Wayne found them abuzz with enthusiasm. The chaos he'd created at the exhortation had enabled them to snatch nearly a hundred women from slavery in the Temple before the guards were able to rally and herd the rest back inside. Though some of the rescued women were too timid to take part in the revolution against the Prophet's rule, most of them were quite willing to strike a blow at their oppressor. As before, the most difficult part was getting them to accept the fact that the real enemy was Rondel, not the ordinary men who'd engaged in the debauchery he encouraged. Wayne would have to accept the fact that, for the remainder of this Dream at least, the affected women would have very little liking for men. His major concern was that the dislike would hold over into their waking lives as well.

He distributed, to as many women as wanted to participate, small devices that looked like TV remote control boxes. Each box had on it a single red button. The women were to go out into the city and begin preaching against Rondel's rule. They were to stress the fact that there were many different systems of belief, and that people should be free to choose among them. They were also to preach that women were the equals of men, and that the tortures within the Temple must stop. He gave them permission to say that the Guardian would look with extreme disfavor on anyone who abused a woman against her will, whether the Prophet encouraged it or not.

When any of the women encountered trouble—as they were sure to do, preaching directly against the Prophet's tenets—either from the angels or from the soldiery, all they had to do was press the button on their remote control box and the trouble would not be able to hurt them. Though they'd originally been less than enthusiastic about this, they had now seen ample demonstration of the Guardian's powers to believe in his devices. The rumor that he was one of the old Wizards was a help; it was widely known that the Wizards had held mystical powers, and these mysterious boxes were just another marvel they could accept with little explanation.

In short time, the Heretics were scattered all over the Holy City, preaching the gospel of freedom to any man who would listen and sometimes even buttonholing a few who didn't want to listen. They had no miracles to dispense, these streetcorner preachers—but the very fact that they spoke so openly against the Prophet, without any fear of his wrath or the wrath of God, was a miracle in itself. People have always been fascinated by the perverse and, since there was very little for anyone to do on the streets of the Holy City except pray, many people stopped to listen.

At first, Rondel's forces did pose a threat. One of the Heretics would only be able to speak for a short time before an angel would zero in on her. The instant the button was pushed on one of the devices, Wayne would travel invisibly to the spot and protect the woman involved from harassment. Sometimes he would cause the angel to explode in a shower of harmless fireworks; sometimes he would change the angel into a harmless rubber mannequin and let it fall to the ground and lie in a silly heap; or sometimes he would merely surround the target with an invisible, impenetrable shield that left the angel banging helplessly against clear air like a fly against a window. People's awe of these celestial messengers began to diminish, until eventually they became little more than laughingstocks, and no one could see an angel without smiling secretly to himself.

Rondel's guards didn't fare much better. When attacks by the angels against the Heretics did not work, the guards were called out on more occasions. Whenever they tried to seize one of the women, though, they broke into fits of uncontrollable itching. If they tried to shoot a rebel, they found their stun-rifles turned to water pistols spraying their victims with gently scented cologne. Sometimes, just for amusement, Wayne would unravel the seams of their silver uniforms and let them stand naked before the public. And always, wherever his mischief occurred, there were the double wavy lines of the Guardian to signify his part in the encounter.

His aim was not merely to defeat Rondel's forces; while that would gain him some support, it would also leave martyrs to the other side. Defeat, he knew, could be even more noble than victory. His purpose, instead, was to humiliate the enemy, to strip them of all dignity and make their very presence a parody of what it had been before. If Wayne could get the general public to laugh at Rondel's forces and ridicule his ideas, he would be well on the way to winning them to his cause.

At first, the guards carried out their duties despite the peculiar hazards they now faced. But the Heretics were all over the city and the guards couldn't be everywhere, nor could they continue to put up with the barrage of ridicule they received. Their morale dropped, and their members began to defect. After awhile they were so few in number that the Heretics could preach openly in the streets and not have to worry about opposition at all.

The symbol of the double wavy lines Wayne had created began appearing everywhere—even in places where he and the Heretics had never reached. This bemused Wayne at first, until he stopped to think about it. Those lines were easily duplicated and totally anonymous. They represented a perfect safety valve for all the normal people who'd chafed under Rondel's tight rules but were afraid to openly defy the Prophet. Scrawling the lines was a way of thumbing one's nose at authority—and yet if the person was questioned, he could deny his guilt, saying the Guardian had done it. Without realizing it, Wayne was fulfilling a need in this society by giving people a safe way of venting their hostility.

The adoption of the lines by the masses also had an accelerating effect. The more often those lines appeared, the more it would seem as though the Guardian was everywhere all the time, and the more potent a figure he became. Given time, Wayne was sure, he could rival Kilroy as a mythical figure.

But the Guardian's most important area of concentration was to stop the heinous activities inside the Temple. His conversation with Janet had been a calculated risk, and he dared not try using that much of his power again so close to Rondel's nerve center. On the other hand, he had to put a stop to those horrid functions before they permanently damaged the psyches of the people involved. Fortunately, he was able to think of little things he could do that would have major effects.

Rondel's torture machines kept breaking down, no matter how often he repaired them. Wayne developed a sneezing powder that only affected men, and set it through the entire building; soon, even the most pious of men were sneezing too hard to abuse anyone. When the Prophet had fans installed to blow the powder away, Wayne sent a horde of flies in to distract the men. After Rondel eradicated the flies with a cloud of pesticide, Wayne gave the men a rash that kept them busy scratching themselves. Soon the Temple gained a reputation as a place to be avoided. The Guardian never once claimed credit for that, but everyone in the city knew who was responsible. The effective end of the Temple as a house of torture made the Heretics redouble their efforts on Wayne's behalf.

Rondel's control was being eroded by attacks from a thousand different fronts. The scheme of granting free will to the audience now seemed to have backfired. Rondel couldn't be everywhere to discipline everyone at once, and the automatic forces he had set in motion were breaking down. The less control he had, the more people were willing to take advantage of their newfound freedom. The situation soon reached a point where Wayne began to doubt whether Rondel could reestablish his dictatorship, even if he wanted to.

The curious part was that Rondel didn't seem to want to. The Guardian and the Heretics repeatedly preached against the Prophet's views, and no steps were taken. The angels were systematically destroyed, and no steps were taken. The Prophet's elite force of guards suffered increasing defections from their ranks, and no steps were taken. The Temple attendance fell off until the women kept there had nothing to do but sit around and talk to one another, and no effective steps were taken. Rondel did not come forward to condemn the increasing lawlessness, or to exhort people to return to the ways of God. He didn't try to repair any vandalism caused by the rebels or increase his forces to deal with the problem. After a few halfhearted attempts to keep the Temple operating, he didn't even challenge Wayne there.

This sudden withdrawal worried Wayne immensely. Rondel was the true god of this Dream, it was his imagination that sustained it in all its glory—yet he was letting it be demolished almost without a fight. He would do little things like the fans and pesticide within the Temple, but they were trivial compared to what he had within his power. He could have conjured up an army of a million musclemen, reinforced by battalions of flying angels—yet the actions he *did* take amounted to putting Band Aids on a severed limb. His creation was slowly bleeding to death while he stood by, seemingly impotent.

Wayne wrestled with the implications of this problem for a long time. Ernie White had said he'd be decreasing Rondel's broadcast power while boosting Wayne's as much as possible. Added to that was the fact that Rondel had been burning up his own energy at a prodigious rate just to maintain this universe against the collective wills of seventy thousand people.

The strain would have to be taking its toll. Perhaps Rondel was weakening so much that it was all he could do to keep up the facade. Perhaps he could mount no effective action because he simply didn't have the strength. Perhaps Wayne could simply take over the Dream now and try to end it happily with everyone going back peacefully to his or her own bed.

But still Wayne hesitated. There was also the chance that this was a feint, an attempt by Rondel to draw him out beyond the safety point. Once he committed himself, Wayne knew, the fight would begin in earnest. Rondel might know that, too. Wayne had too much respect for the other man's abilities to take that lightly. Rondel had earned his star reputation fairly; even in a weakened condition, he would be a formidable adversary.

Wayne had never fought for control of a Dream before; to the best of his knowledge, it was a totally unprecedented situation. He didn't know what to expect, but he knew that Rondel would have him at a disadvantage. Wayne was responsible for the safety and well-being of seventy thousand people, while Rondel had only his own twisted goals to achieve. There were just too many factors; how could anyone possibly compute the odds of winning?

Wayne waited. He continued his guerrilla activities, hoping to wear down Rondel so that the final confrontation, when it came, would be as insignificant a contest as he could make it.

Catastrophe struck without warning. One moment Wayne was lecturing on the principles of religious freedom to a group of perhaps two hundred men, and the next, all hell broke loose. The ground shook with the power of a mighty earthquake, and large cracks appeared in the streets. Buildings split and toppled to the ground. Flames sprang up from the cracks in the earth, igniting the fallen structures and setting the world afire. A hurricane wind swept through the city, howling with the torment of a million lost souls and fanning the flames to blast-furnace intensity. At the same time, loud trumpets could be heard blaring even over the howls of the wind, signaling a cataclysmic fanfare. The overpowering stench of sulfur swirled in great yellow clouds that enveloped the shattered city.

The people panicked, running wildly in all directions and screaming at the top of their voices, even though it was impossible to be heard over the noise of the wind and the trumpets. They ran even though there was no safe direction to go; anywhere they went, there were falling buildings, fires or cracks opening in the ground. The Guardian and his promises of freedom were forgotten in an instant; this was the Apocalypse the Prophet had warned them of, and now all their penitence would be too late.

Caught off balance, Wayne needed a few moments of calm thought before he could quiet the raging storm around him. With a deliberate act of will, he forced the earth to be still again, quenched the fires and righted the fallen buildings. He fought against the wind, but found he could do nothing; it tore through the city with all the fury and anger of Rondel's anguished soul. Slowly, painfully, Wayne built up a series of baffles to keep the winds at bay, gradually pushing them inward, toward the center of the city—the Temple, where he knew Rondel would be waiting for him.

This was a challenge, issued in a way only a Dreamer could understand. Rondel was saying, "I know you're there. Come and get me. Stop me if you can, or I'll destroy everything." The battle could be put off no longer. Now came the test of strength, to see which Dreamer's will was the greater.

There was no further advantage to subtlety. Wayne increased his size to ten stories as he marched through the city, a colossus en route to Armageddon. He totally ignored the audience scrambling like insects around his feet; for the moment they were only an inconvenience on his way to the combat. He would be fighting for their sakes, but he couldn't divert any of his attention to them right now.

Wayne came to the Temple and found a large wall around it. He realized that most of the women in the audience would still be trapped inside there; he had to get them away from Rondel's clutches before he did anything else. He reached for the wall, to knock it down, and some invisible force pushed his hand away. He pressed against it, and the force grew stronger. Rondel knew the value of the hostages he held, and he was going to make Wayne fight for them.

Taking his mind away from all his other supportive functions, Wayne lashed out at the Temple. The barrier gave way before his onslaught, and he quickly picked up the building and set it down safely outside the wall Rondel had built. But in doing so, he left himself mentally off balance, and Rondel was quick to take advantage of that. Wayne suddenly found himself pushed entirely out of the universe, into a gray space where nothing but himself existed.

"We meet again." It was not a voice, actually, but a sensation that pervaded the grayness. "Now we'll see who you really are."

Wayne found his mind under attack. He was bombarded with bright images everywhere he focused, dazzling him, distracting him, breaking his concentration. He tried to fight, tried to pull a cover around himself or at least return to the former world of the Holy City. But Rondel's will was too strong, too overpowering. With the flashing brilliance all around him, he could find no way to hide himself from Rondel's probing intellect.

"Corrigan." Rondel's tone was one of both surprise and contempt. "I thought they'd send someone better than that."

The words stung at his own sense of inferiority, but Wayne fought the feeling down. *Don't let it get to you,* he told himself. *You're as powerful as he is, now. He can't keep this up much longer.*

And even as he thought that, the grayness around him dissolved and he was back in the world with the rest of the audience once more. But the Holy City was no longer in existence; all that remained was the Temple, standing proudly in the middle of a vast, barren plain that stretched endlessly to the horizon in all directions. The entire audience, men and women, was gathered together, seventy thousand people standing confused and frightened on the hard, dusty ground.

Between the crowd and the Temple was a tall pedestal. Rondel stood atop it, a larger-than-life figure gazing down with implacable hatred at the milling throng below him. "Woe unto you, sinners," he announced in deep, somber tones that rolled over the audience like waves of thunder. "The Day of Judgment has arrived, and now you will reap the rewards of your evil ways. Hear the words of God, and feel His divine wrath. Tremble and quake that you did not freely give Him your love before."

Wayne enlarged himself once more, putting himself on another pedestal some distance removed. "I am the Guardian," he said. "I say, don't listen to this false prophet, this purveyor of hatred and despair. Listen to your hearts and minds. Listen to the inner voice of your soul. Each of you knows about God; you learned when you were children. Remember when your parents took you to services for the first time. Remember the words, remember the songs, remember the spirit in your heart. Hold onto these things. Don't let this false prophet steal them from you."

But Rondel was bellowing just as loudly. "You all have been wicked, you all deserve to die. Only the Holy Mother, of all people, deserves the blessing of eternal life. The rest of you will burn forever in the fires of Hell. You will know the agony of everlasting torment, and rue the day you ever listened to that blasphemer."

Along with his speech, Rondel started the hellfire sweeping through the crowd again. Some people screamed, others cowered, still more dropped to their knees and tried to pray for last-minute absolution. Wayne raised his hand and rain poured from the sky, dousing the hellfire with a hiss of steam.

But the hysteria that had taken over the crowd could not be stopped so easily. He had tried to make an appeal to their rational minds, to bring back childhood memories hoping it would make people remember their real lives. But an appeal to the memory would not be enough—not when Rondel was bombarding their minds with images, distracting them from rational thought.

Dreaming was, primarily, a visual medium. Wayne realized that, if he was going to get his point across, he would have to use the language of images himself. But what images could counter the apocalyptic propaganda Rondel was spewing forth from his own pedestal?

"The Prophet tells you there is only one form of truth," Wayne announced to the trembling multitudes. "But there are many paths to salvation, and that false prophet would lead you along a treacherous one. Listen to some other prophets telling you about their paths:"

Wayne waved his hand, and more pedestals appeared. On the first stood a tall, solemn recreation of Jesus Christ, in his robes of pure white with long, flowing brown hair and beard. His face held a kind expression, his eyes were filled with love for the people below him. He spoke in a soft, soothing tone, as Wayne put into his mouth as much as he himself could remember of the beatitudes and the sermon on the mount.

On the pedestal next to Jesus was the pope. He was dressed in his full ceremonial regalia, looking properly solemn. He crossed himself and then began to recite the mass in Latin—or as much of it as Wayne could remember from his childhood trips to the church.

On the other side of the Pope, on his own pedestal, stood Moses. Wayne created him as a blend of the Michelangelo Moses and the Charlton Heston image from de Mille's *Ten Commandments*. The face was lined with care and compassion, and the long white beard added majesty to the performance. He carried the two stone tablets in his right arm and gesticulated with his left while he recited the commandments and told people of the land of milk and honey.

The people became quiet as they beheld these figures, all talking at once, all uttering platitudes that the audience had been raised with since birth. Wayne could see recognition on some faces, reverence on others. His strategy was working.

Rondel could see that, too. "These are tricks of the Devil, intended to lure you away from the path of righteousness. They shall be destroyed, as shall you all!"

He hurled a lightning bolt toward the other pedestals. The Guardian stood where he was, and did not interfere directly; instead, he had the Christ figure knock the lightning aside. Jesus looked over at the raging figure of Rondel with sad eyes and said, "Would you strike me down again, Judas?"

The loyalties of the crowd wavered. Some of them began moving over toward the pedestals Wayne had created, to grow closer to the childhood symbols of their faith. Wayne decided to broaden the spectrum still further.

He'd heard somewhere that there was a taboo in Islam against portraying Mohammed, but this was no time for ideological purity. He created the Moslem Prophet as a tall, bearded man with Arab robes and a burnoose. Wayne had no knowledge of the Koran whatsoever, so he just had Mohammed repeat the phrase, "There is no god but Allah" over and over.

Next to Mohammed, on another pedestal, sat Buddha in his posture of perfect serenity. Buddha did not say anything, but an aura of overwhelming tranquility radiated from him into the crowd.

Wayne was totally at a loss of how to represent Hinduism until he remembered seeing a statue of a dancing multilimbed goddess. He doubted she represented the central concepts of the Indian religion—but he also doubted there were many Hindus in the audience, anyway. He brought the statue to life, on a pedestal next to Buddha's, and let her dance in that peculiar Asian style, surprisingly seductive for so bizarre a creature.

"All these, and more, represent the paths to truth,"

Wayne told the crowd. "You all have your own images, your own beliefs. Bring them to life, let me see them. Show your own brand of truth to the entire world."

And, to his pleased surprise, the people took his advice. Other pedestals began popping up, ones that Wayne did not create—nor, he was sure, did Rondel create them. Over there was Joseph Smith, and not too far away was a black figure who Wayne supposed was Elijah Mohammed. A woman preached over there; was it Mary Baker Eddy or Aimée Semple McPherson? Wayne couldn't tell, and he didn't really care. The important thing was not who it was, but that she was there at all. The people were doing it themselves. They were re-creating their own religious symbolism, turning to the prophets they themselves believed in to combat the terror they felt at Rondel's apocalypse.

Wayne could feel reality dissolving around him. The Dream was beginning to flicker like a candle in a breeze. And still more pedestals appeared with their holy figures atop them: Martin Luther, and his namesake, Martin Luther King, Jr.; the Virgin Mary; Fitzgerald Baker; Billy Graham; several black preachers Wayne couldn't recognize. A figure in Tibetan robes might have been the Dalai Lama; there was even a woman preaching atheism. More and more, like mushrooms, the pedestals sprouted as people turned to their own familiar faiths in this time of crisis.

As Wayne gazed over the crowd, pleased that his initiative had gone so well, he was startled to see some of the people disappear. One moment they were there, and the next they had utterly vanished from the Dream. His first assumption was that Rondel had launched another offensive of some kind, but then he realized the truth: those people were no longer part of the Dream. Re-creating their faith had brought back to them the memories of their real lives—and with the knowledge that this was just a Dream, they woke themselves up from it of their own accord. They were leaving the battlefield, and were beyond Rondel's

193

control—which was fine as far as Wayne was concerned.

Rondel realized this, too, and his fury reached new peaks as people began popping out of the Dream not just one at a time, but in groups of ten, or even twenty. He was losing his hold on them. Wayne was winning. That was a situation he could not tolerate.

The Masterdreamer cut loose with a blast of mental energy stronger than Wayne had expected. The attack was wordless, a silent rage that caught Wayne unprepared. He was suddenly drowning in a seething sea of Rondel's hatred.

"Vin! Vinnie!" A sharp female voice, vaguely familiar, cut through the air. The waves of anger stopped as abruptly as they'd begun, to be replaced by equal amounts of confusion. Rondel and Wayne both looked around to see where the voice had come from.

Above their heads, suspended in space, was a four-poster bed with scraps of lace as a canopy. On the bed was the gross form of Mrs. Rondel, with her white hair and her fat, painted face. She looked down over the side, directly at Rondel, and shook a thick finger accusingly.

"You've done bad, Vinnie. Don't you remember my telling you never to hurt people? You've sinned, Vinnie, sinned very bad. Remember that naughty kitten of yours, the one who scratched me? Do you remember what I did with it?"

Rondel's lower lip was trembling. "You flushed it down the toilet," he said, so softly Wayne could barely hear him.

"Do you want me to do it to you, too? Do you want me to take the bad Vinnie and flush him down the toilet?"

Wayne was almost as stunned by this apparition's appearance as Rondel was. He had not thought to create this image, and he knew Rondel hadn't. Who else could there be with knowledge of the situation—and knowledge of Rondel's psychology—to perform such an impersonation?

The answer was obvious the second he thought of it.

Janet! She had probably been thinking over what Wayne had told her, and this final confrontation jarred her memories loose. She knew Rondel—and his mother —far better than Wayne ever had. She knew the man's weak points, his fears and his frustrations. Operating only with a home Dreamcap, Janet didn't have the power to make major changes in the universe all by herself—but she had enough strength to create this one illusion.

Her impersonation was clearly pushing Rondel past the breaking point. The man was trembling—and, more importantly, the universe all around him seemed to be disintegrating. The sky cracked in a thousand mirror shards. The horizon crept ever closer as he couldn't maintain its distance. The ground on which people stood began to fade slowly into nothingness. Wayne prepared to bolster it himself if Rondel dropped it altogether, rather than let the rest of the audience fall into empty space.

People were disappearing in large groups. Pedestals had multiplied beyond counting, and now there were easily a hundred or more prophets, messiahs and saints preaching their messages simultaneously to the waiting throngs. Fifty, a hundred people at a time would suddenly wink out of their existence as they awoke from this nightmare to the security of their own beds. Wayne hated to think of all the complaints that would be lodged tomorrow against Dramatic Dreams—he was only thankful that so many people were able to get away safely.

"NO!" Rondel's scream reverberated through the shrinking universe. "She's dead! You're a lie! It's all a lie!"

As he cried out, he unleashed a bolt of mental energy directly at the image of his mother. Janet, unable to defend herself against such a naked surge of power, exploded into dust. But Rondel, without even waiting to see the result of his barrage, turned and fled the scene of his defeat. He ran off into the Temple, through the main doors which closed solidly behind him.

Wayne ignored him; Janet was his main concern now. Instantly he was over at the spot where he'd last seen her, sifting his consciousness through the strange fabric of pseudoreality. "Janet? Are you all right? Where are you?"

"Wayne?" The thought was feeble, but it was there.

"I'm right here." Wayne poured some of his own personal energy into the area, hoping to build up Janet's strength again. His efforts had the desired effect; after a few moments she rematerialized—as herself, this time, rather than as Mrs. Rondel. She had never seemed more beautiful.

She looked up into his face, almost as though she'd never seen him before. "Wayne? It *is* you. When my memory came back and I realized this was a Dream, I knew the Guardian had to be one of the other Dreamers —but I still didn't know which one it was. But somehow . . . I was *hoping* it would be you. Can you believe that?"

"I'm not sure I dare, but I'd certainly like to." He looked more deeply into her eyes and then, on impulse, leaned forward to kiss her. It was a gesture that meant nothing; after all, this was only a Dream, it wasn't really happening. But it meant a lot more than nothing, too. Janet put herself into the kiss, just as though this was real life. When they finally pulled themselves apart, she looked at him with an almost bashful smile.

"It's only a Dream, right?" she said modestly. "Anything can happen in Dreams."

His heart sank a bit. Did that mean she didn't really mean it, that she was still not willing to consider him in the real world? But before he had time to think about it, she asked, "What happened? Why is Vince doing all this?"

"He got word during the first intermission that his mother died."

"Oh my God!"

"Yeah. It sent him round the bend, and this is the result."

Wayne glanced around. There were very few people

196

left, just a few stragglers who were slow to get the message—or maybe they were just heavy sleepers. Even most of the pedestals were gone by now; when the last of a particular prophet's believers disappeared, there was no one left to sustain his presence in the Dream, so he disappeared as well.

"I think we saved them, though," Wayne said wearily. "Most of the people are gone, and the rest seem to be going at their own speed."

But Janet's expression was still one of shock. "I didn't know," she said. "I didn't know she was dead. If I knew I'd have done something else, used another image. What happened to him? Where is Vince?"

"He ran off into the Temple. He knows he's beaten; I don't think he'll come out again. The job is just about finished. I'll stick around until everyone leaves. . . ."

"The job's *not* finished," Janet insisted. "Saving the audience was only half of it. We've got to get Vince out of here, too."

Wayne stared at her in disbelief. "There's no problem getting Vince out," he said. "All Ernie has to do is cut the power to his cap."

"You don't understand," Janet said, shaking her head. "All that'll do is take Vince out the broadcast circuit. His problem is more serious than that. I didn't know his mother had died; I just wanted a strong image to use, and it turned out too strong. I pushed him too far. By taking refuge in the Temple, he's folded in on himself. The Temple is the center of his personality. If we just abandon him there and cut off the Dream, he'll come out of this as a catatonic."

"I don't really give a damn. He's just put the lives of seventy thousand people in jeopardy. Not only that, this guy Forsch will probably shut down the entire station because of this, putting both of us out of work. I'm tired and I'm angry, and frankly I don't care if Vince is a vegetable for the rest of his life. He deserves it."

"Nobody deserves *that,* especially not someone with a mind like Vince's. For all his faults—and I know

197

more of them than you do—he was a Dreamer, a man who created universes greater than himself. I can't see throwing a mind like that away forever. How would you like it if your mind was boxed in like that, unable to Dream?"

"That's not the point," Wayne said defensively. "I didn't go crazy and try to kill seventy thousand people. I don't owe him anything."

Janet stared at him for a long moment. "You're right," she said at last. "You've already fought your battle, and won it. Whatever happens, I think tonight will be a landmark in the history of Dreaming, and you'll be famous for what you did.

"But I can't leave Vince like that. Maybe my conjuring up his mother pushed him over the edge. Maybe there's still a touch of guilt in me for breaking off our affair. I left him. I quit. Maybe, in some slight way, I contributed to his breakdown in the first place. But I have to at least try to help him."

"What if he doesn't want your help?"

"I don't think he knows *what* he wants, at this point."

"He'll fight you every step of the way," Wayne argued. "You've just got a receiver on, you're no match for him. He'll destroy you if you go in there."

"You can come with me if you want to, use your power to protect me. That's up to you. But I'm going in there, Wayne. It's just something I have to do."

Wayne looked around, confused. There were only half a dozen people left in the Dream, apart from Janet and him—and as he watched, even they vanished into nothingness. He and Janet were now alone, standing on a barren plain in front of the Temple where Rondel had disappeared. There was not even a faint breeze to stir the dust on the ground.

It wasn't fair, he thought. Everything had gone so well until now. He'd won, he'd saved the audience from the fate Rondel had planned for them. He should be able to wake up and go home, and worry tomorrow about what the FCC would say. He was tired, he shouldn't have to worry about any more work.

But Janet needed him. For reasons of her own— guilt, loyalty or perhaps the last vestiges of a dead love—she had to try to help Rondel. They both knew she couldn't do it alone, but she was willing to try if Wayne refused to help her. But he loved her. How could he abandon her when she faced a challenge like this?

Janet was staring at him. When he remained silent, paralyzed by indecision, she finally turned and flew off toward the door of the Temple.

"Janet, wait!" he called after her, but it was too late—she'd already disappeared inside.

Making up his mind at last, Wayne flew after her. He paused at the entrance to the Temple and looked inside. He could see nothing but darkness in there. He remembered the terrible sensation the last time he'd tried to invade Rondel's privacy, and shuddered. He didn't want to face that again. But he might not have a choice.

With a deep sense of foreboding, Wayne entered the Temple.

CHAPTER 15

HE WAS IN total darkness, a womblike lack of sensation all around him. He might as well be in a sensory deprivation tank. There were no sights, sounds, tastes or smells. He wondered idly if this was what being in a coma felt like.

"Vince? Janet?" he called. The silence was not broken by his voice; it absorbed the sounds instead. There was no reply. For lack of anything better to do, Wayne began walking—even though there was no floor to walk on and no direction in which to go.

Then suddenly the world around him was lit up with the brightness of a child's daytime. The scene was an amusement park. There were carousels and roller coasters, clowns selling enormous balloons and food stands selling peanuts and cotton candy. But all around him were bars; he was in a cage that prevented him from reaching all the fun. He squeezed through the bars, trying to get past this obstacle, when suddenly a giant hand picked him up and raised him into the air. He found himself confronting the enormous face of the young Mrs. Rondel. "It's naughty," she said in a booming voice that echoed against his eardrums. "It's sinful. You mustn't give in to the temptations of Satan."

Then she opened her mouth wide and popped Wayne inside, swallowing him whole. The darkness covered him once more. Wayne continued walking forward until he again found himself in daylight. This time he was in a jungle, with lush vegetation intertwining all around him. The air was hot and stuffy, so damp it made breathing difficult. As he looked around, he could see that the jungle was only in his immediate vicinity, which was on top of a hill; to either side of him, the ground sloped sharply down into a series of pits. There were women in the pits. Wayne recognized some of them as movie stars and fashion models; there were others he didn't know at all, but presumably Rondel did. Some of the women were dressed seductively, others were completely naked.

The women were moaning with passion, their bodies swaying sensuously in some imaginary breeze. Their arms reached upward to him, offering their quite obvious charms. The moaning grew louder, until it was nearly a chant. He took a step downward when suddenly the jungle around him came to life. The long, slender vines grew rapidly, twining themselves around his legs, around his thighs, inward across his groin and around his abdomen. The vines squeezed at his testicles, all the while exuding a strong fragrance of cheap violet perfume.

He broke free of the vines' grip and ran through the jungle, pushing away at the vegetation that constantly reached for him. His feet squished through mucous-mud, but he continued onward. At length the jungle gave up and let him go.

He came to a dark tunnel and walked through it. Images flashed all around him like a surrealistic slide show. The images may have held some significance for Rondel, but to Wayne they were just unrecognized people and objects: a man who might have been Rondel's father appeared frequently, along with other figures who may have been relatives, teachers, friends. There were favorite toys, pets, remembered bits of scenery, a quick flash of a sandcastle by the ocean. There were books, and scenes from movies and TV shows, jumbled indiscriminately with images from church meetings and religious observances. Wayne walked resolutely on, determined to get past these surface memories.

Then he was through the tunnel and in a woman's bedroom. As he stood there, Janet came into the room, totally nude. A confused series of thoughts ran through

201

Wayne's mind, and he was about to call out to her when he realized that this was not the real Janet— merely a memory of her in Rondel's mind. Still, it was frighteningly realistic as Janet came up to him and slid her arms around him, pressing her naked body tightly against his. This was too close to some of his own fantasies for Wayne's comfort.

"Stay away from that harlot!" came Mrs. Rondel's voice. "She'll drag you down to Hell. She's not good enough for you."

A whip cracked, catching the image of Janet on the back and making her retreat. Wayne turned and saw Mrs. Rondel, a glowing figure seated on a golden throne, with choruses of angels on either side. She smiled at him, and the warm glow spread from her to him. Tossing the whip casually away, she reached down for him and picked him up, seating him like a little boy on Santa's lap. She was naked, now, and she hugged him to her bosom between her massive breasts, until Wayne thought he was going to smother.

He pushed against her, and she became a giant marshmallow that enfolded him. Like a victim struggling to escape from quicksand he pushed against the gooey mess until he found a breathing hole, and then he pulled his way slowly up out of the mire onto more solid ground.

He was in a place that bore a slight resemblance to Rondel's living room; but where the present version was cluttered with squalor, this room was neat and tidy, with beautiful objects on the shelves and an aura of magic in the air. Wayne was the height of a little boy, with the figures of Mrs. Rondel and the man Wayne presumed was her husband smiling down at him.

Then six men in black entered the room. They picked up Mr. Rondel and carried him out the door as though he were a coffin. He was still smiling as he vanished from view.

With his disappearance, things changed suddenly. A whirlwind hit the room, which immediately lost its magical aura. Objects lost their beauty; the room cracked like a broken mirror and fell to pieces around him. Mrs. Rondel blew up like a balloon in a Thanksgiving parade, hovering over him with an inane cherubic smile. Then he, too, was caught in the whirlwind; it picked him up and carried him away to another place, where it deposited him just as abruptly as it had lifted him.

He was standing on an open plain, with a high wind whipping the dust around him. The only other feature was a large cross in the distance. As he walked toward it, it grew larger, and he could see the living figure of Jesus still on it. Jesus dripped bright red blood in enormous drops that fell to the ground at the base of the cross, forming a small lake.

Jesus looked directly at him, the pain of his suffering mixed with holy compassion. "What can I do for you, my son?" he asked quietly. When Wayne did not reply, Jesus continued, "Absolution? What was your sin?"

And then Christ's face contorted in horror. "No. Not that. Not even I can forgive you for that. Let it be on your head alone. I renounce you forever. You will never enter my Father's kingdom, you will never attain His mercy." And with that condemnation, Jesus pulled his cross out of the ground, set it on his back, turned away and walked slowly off, carrying his painful burden.

Then the wind whipped up to gale force, blowing sand and dust so thick Wayne could not see. He walked ahead blindly through the storm, wondering again what he was doing here and what he expected to accomplish. All he'd done so far was see a lot of things about Rondel's mind that he didn't like very much; there was no indication that Rondel had been helped, or even that he *could* be helped.

He came to a chapel that glowed with the light of a thousand candles. Everything was quiet and peaceful here, but there was nothing for Wayne to do. He walked to the door at the far end of the chapel, his footsteps echoing hollowly through the vaulted room.

As he reached for the door handle, he heard a voice say, "Go away, Corrigan. I don't want you here. Leave me alone."

"I came for Janet. She wants to help you."

"Leave her to me. Go away."

Wayne didn't answer. He opened the door and stepped through.

Suddenly he was falling down a bottomless chasm with a cold wind whipping by him. The walls of the chasm sparkled with a myriad of twinkling lights, and Wayne couldn't begin to guess what they represented. He tried to stop the fall, and found he couldn't. Here inside Rondel's mind, the other man had ultimate control of everything that happened. That frightened him a little.

Wayne hit the ground with a hard bump. He was in a maze, now, a maze with glass walls. Through the walls he could see the maze twisting its convoluted way off into the distance, with no indication of what would be the proper path. He called out for Janet, and thought he heard a reply far off in the distance. There was nothing else to do but move in that direction, so he started on his way.

There was no easy path through the maze. The route before him twisted, turned and forked so often he lost count. He frequently hit on blind alleys, and was forced to retrace his steps and try a new way—and even that was tricky, because the path behind him had a habit of altering itself once he'd passed over it.

He stopped in one dead end, and was nearly hit by a heavy weight that dropped to the floor just beside his feet. Wayne calmly stepped over it and continued on as normal. A short while later he was narrowly missed by a sharply pointed grating that slid into place behind him, blocking his escape route. The air was filled with strange noises, like the sounds of birds being strangled, and his nostrils were occasionally assaulted with whiffs of dead, decaying flesh. The air alternated hot or cold at random. Wayne walked on.

The maze began spiraling inward, like a nautilus

shell, and the walls became less transparent, more mirrored. Wayne quickened his pace, sensing that he was approaching a crucial junction. As the spiral became tighter and tighter, the ground under him started moving, speeding him along the way, accelerating the motion inward. By the end he was in a headlong rush, and couldn't have stopped if he wanted to.

In the very center of the maze, he ran smack into a mirror, so hard that he fell backward onto the ground. Around him, all the walls closed in until he was surrounded by mirrors. Everywhere he looked was a different image of himself sitting on the ground, staring back at him, mocking him.

Wayne Corrigan stared back at him with deepset, black-rimmed eyes. Wayne Corrigan the failure, Wayne Corrigan the incompetent, Wayne Corrigan the perpetual loser, Wayne Corrigan the second-rate Dreamer, the man destined to spend the rest of his life as a hack, never knowing the true greatness that others would achieve by stepping over his fallen career. The Wayne Corrigan in those mirrors would spend his life mired in mediocrity, while people with lesser talents constantly made it to the top ahead of him.

"No," he said aloud quietly, to himself as well as to the image in the mirrors. "You are not a true reflection. I beat the best here in the Dream, and I can do it again. I will not accept second place. Not ever again."

He rose to his feet again and shook his fist at the mirror image. "Never again, do you hear? I'm anybody's equal!"

He struck out with his balled fist and punched a hole in the mirror. All around him, the failure images shattered in a million shards and fell with utter silence to the ground. Beyond was more of the blackness. He strode into it, stepping over the pieces of the failure-Wayne as he did so.

There was a shriek in the air, and Wayne knew it was Janet—the real Janet. He looked around, trying to see where the cry had come from, and thought he saw her kneeling figure off in the distance. But as he ran toward her, he found himself entangled in a forest of mirrors again, each one showing not his own reflection, but an image of Janet. She was collapsed on the ground, sobbing loudly, but there were so many images of her it was impossible for him to locate the real one.

He swung his arms wildly around him as he ran, shattering the mirrors on all sides of him. The broken glass cut into him, lining his arms with bleeding slashes, but he ran on, oblivious to the pain. Somewhere out there, Janet needed him; that was enough to spur him on.

Then he found her, like Alice in Wonderland surrounded by a rapidly growing lake of her own tears. Kneeling beside her, he put his arms around her and said, "It's all right now. I'm here with you."

She leaned against him, trying desperately to talk through her tears. "Oh Wayne, it was hor—horrible," she sobbed. "There were the mirrors, and—and I looked, and—I'm ugly and I'm untalented and I deserve the way he treated me. I'm not fit for anybody."

"Is *that* what he told you?"

"It's what I saw in the mirrors. It's what I've always known. That's why I became a Dreamer, to escape. . . ."

Wayne stood up, pulling her to her feet as well. She buried her head against his chest, but he put his right hand under her chin and lifted her head until she was looking straight at him.

"Look at my eyes, Janet," he said slowly. "Look at your reflection in there. Do you see any ugliness, any sign of imperfection?"

She hesitated, blinking back tears. "No," she said at last.

Wayne held her tighter to him. "Of course not, because there isn't any. The ugliness came from Vince. He put it there, magnifying any tiny self-doubts you had to distract you, to keep you from finding him in this funhouse of a mind he has. We've got to show him he's wrong, that he won't be able to stop us."

The tears had stopped, and she smiled at him. " 'We'? You really want to help me, then?"

"I've got to," Wayne said, remembering his own experiences with those mirrors. "I've got to show him—and myself—that I can beat him on any battlefield he chooses, even the stronghold of his own mind."

The world around them shook ominously, but nothing further happened. After a few moments, Wayne let go of Janet and said, "Let's go."

"Do you know the way?"

"No, but does it matter? He's in here somewhere, hiding. All we have to do is keep turning over the junk in the attic, and eventually we'll find him."

They walked on together. Rondel's mind flung scores of memories at them, some crystal clear, others tangled and overgrown with private symbolism. Some of the memories were sharp, with pointed edges; others were eroded from constant use. Some were happy, some sad, some horrifying, some peaceful, but the two Dreamers refused to be distracted and continued on.

At one point, Janet said, "Don't look, Wayne!"

Wayne obediently turned his head, but asked, "Why not?"

Her answer was slow in coming. "It's a memory of . . . of me and Vince together. It's not one I'm proud of. I don't want you ever to think of me that way—not after tonight."

Wayne did as he was told, taking encouragement from her words. Whether she realized it or not, she was committing herself to a relationship.

When she'd guided him past that juncture, they continued on as before. Sometimes they found themselves facing high crystal walls, and the only way to proceed was to climb over them. For one of them alone it might have been difficult; together, each was able to help the other scale the obstacle, and they proceeded deeper into the mind of Vince Rondel.

At last they came to a room that each knew instinctively was the center of this universe. The walls of the chamber were draped with midnight black velvet. Around the perimeter was a vast collection of waxworks. Each of the figures was Vince Rondel in another guise: Rondel the cowboy, Rondel the astronaut, Rondel the policeman, Rondel the big game hunter, Rondel the fairy tale prince—every Dream role he'd ever played was represented here, a lifetime of make-believe staring silently at the two intruders.

And in the center of the room, like a modern sculpture, was an enormous stainless steel egg suspended in space. Its hard shiny shell glinted a challenge at them. This was the final barrier. They had traced the mazes and weathered the memories, and now the essence of Vince Rondel lay encapsulated before them.

"Any suggestions?" Wayne asked.

"We'll have to break in there," Janet said. "We'll have to pry him out, or else everything we've gone through so far has been for nothing."

"That won't be necessary," said a voice. Wayne and Janet looked around, startled, and saw that one of the waxworks had come to life. Vince Rondel walked toward them, dressed as precisely as ever, with suit and tie and manicured fingernails. He was smiling sheepishly, but he made no threatening gestures as he approached.

"You found me," he continued. "I put up a good fight, but you managed to track me down."

"We did?" Wayne asked suspiciously.

"That's right. I'm ready to leave with you now. Why don't we all go together?" Rondel put his arms around the both of them and started to steer them away.

"What about that?" Janet asked, pointing back at the large steel egg.

"Oh, that's nothing. You wanted to find me and here I am. We can go any time you're ready."

"Just a minute," Wayne said. "Why did you do what you did tonight? Why did you try to hurt all those people?"

Rondel hesitated. "Well, you see . . . my mother died. She and I were very close, and . . . well, I kind of went off the deep end. Grief can do that to a person. You don't know how sorry I am, really. I know I'll have to be punished; what I did was terribly wrong. But it's understandable, isn't it? When a person's mother dies, he *should* be pretty broken up, don't you think?"

"I think," Wayne said, "that I want to have a look inside that egg."

"Really, it's nothing, I swear it," Rondel said. "Why should I lie to you? I've just told you the full reason for everything. I'm not trying to escape punishment; I know I'll be suspended for what I did, maybe even kicked out of the business altogether. Have a heart; what more could you want from me?"

"We want to see what's inside that thing," Janet said coldly.

"What business is it of yours, anyway?" Rondel's expression darkened; there was a return of the mad gleam in his eyes. "What right do you have to come trampling through my mind, overturning all my emotions, rummaging through my private memories? You have no business butting in where I don't want you. Get out. GET OUT!"

Wayne and Janet exchanged glances. There must be something pretty important inside that egg for Rondel to defend it this vigorously.

"It's for your own good, Vince," Janet said.

But Rondel wasn't listening. Around the perimeter of the room, the waxwork figures began moving slowly, converging on the trio. "That's what they always say—'it's for your own good.' But it isn't. It's always for *their* own good. Nobody knows what's good for me. It's her own good, that's all she thinks about. But not anymore. I've got it all now, and nobody's going to take it away from me. I won't let her take it away. I won't let you in there. I won't!"

His grip on their shoulders tightened. The waxwork figures all leaped at them at once, blurring into one vast image. Rondel pushed Wayne and Janet together, squeezing them as though trying to form them into one being. His physical manifestation faded out completely, but he was still there as a suffocating, all-enveloping presence. Wayne struggled to escape, and realized he

209

couldn't. With a sudden flash of insight he knew what was happening.

This was the mysterious force he'd encountered before when he tried to enter the Temple's forbidden area. It was not some casual element in a Dream, to be manipulated at will—it was Rondel's very life essence defending itself against unwelcome intrusion. Wayne remembered the terrifying pressure he'd encountered before, and panicked for a moment. He knew, in the deepest part of himself, that Rondel could literally kill him by squeezing his mind into nothingness. He knew, too, that there was a way out, the way he'd taken before—to leave the Dream entirely, return to the safe reality of the broadcast studio.

But if he did that, he'd lose. Everything he'd fought for in terms of his own self-esteem would be destroyed. He'd never be able to come back here again, never be able to fight a rematch. This was the final battle, once and for all.

There was also Janet to consider. She had never experienced this before, she wouldn't know what to make of it. Her presence here was powered only by the weak signal from her home Dreamcap. What if she couldn't pull herself free of Rondel's grip? What if the Masterdreamer dragged her down into the abyss of his madness along with him? Wayne couldn't let that happen—not now, after he'd finally gotten the flame to start.

For a moment he gave in to the crushing strength around him, preferring to use his energies to fight his internal panic. Only when he'd steadied his own mind did he reach out again through the suffocating pressure Rondel was applying, searching for a trace of Janet. He touched her, and slowly, laboriously, pulled the little kernel of her mind closer to his own. She was frightened, she was as panicky as he himself had been an instant ago. He tried to let his own thoughts cool and soothe her, protect her from the worst of the pressure that was slowly squeezing the life out of them.

We've got to fight him, he told her mind. *We've got to*

do it together. He's stronger than either of us individually, but together we can make it.

She tried, but it was no good. They were still two individuals in close proximity. And still the pressure mounted, Rondel squeezing at their minds, their souls, until they were about to burst.

Open to me, Janet, Wayne thought. *It's the only way.*

To illustrate, he dropped his barriers to her. He let down the walls and showed her the love he felt—as well as the hates, the depressions, his own self-doubts, the late-at-night feelings he'd never divulged to anyone before. He spread his soul before her, knowing that only by her acceptance could they succeed against Rondel's force.

She resisted a little more—and then broke all at once, with a rush of emotions that nearly overwhelmed him. Wayne saw the insecurities she'd gotten from being the homely younger sister of a campus prom queen, the loneliness, the pressure to excel in school, the escapes into fantasy that led to her becoming a Dreamer, the succession of hopeless love affairs with men who were bound to abuse her and reinforce her bad self-image. But there was more. He saw himself through her eyes, and saw a spark of hope grow where none had been before. He fastened onto that, pulled her into himself, made her the *yin* to his *yang* so that, for one brief, dramatic moment they were one entity, united with a single drive for survival.

The heat from their union was a blazing inferno. It cut like a torch through the vise Rondel was applying, clearing a path so easily it was as though the other didn't even exist. Not only did they escape from the hideous, crushing confines, but the force of their united minds cracked right through the hard, shiny shell of the stainless steel egg in front of them, releasing its contents for their inspection.

It was over in a fraction of a second. For just that instant their souls touched in a way they'd never experienced before, and then they were back to being the way they were—two different people, each individuual, each with a separate life. But not completely separate. Never again.

Wayne's senses were reeling from the impact of that union, but a sense of self-preservation made him turn toward Rondel's hard shell which had now cracked open. He was facing the inner core of Rondel's being, the secret force that had driven the madman into an insane attempt to kill seventy thousand people. What kind of dragon or ogre or hideous deformed monster would he have to confront when it came out of its protective coating?

Sitting there on the ground was a little boy, no older than six or seven, wearing little blue sleepers with a pattern of airplanes flying across the chest. He was crying.

The image was so ludicrous, so contrary to what he'd expected, that Wayne almost burst into hysterical laughter. He managed, just barely, to control himself, and walked over to stand beside the child. "What's the matter?" he asked.

The boy didn't look at him. "I killed her."

"Killed who?"

"My mommy. I killed her dead."

Wayne hesitated. Was that true? Had Rondel murdered his mother? But in that case, wouldn't the police have come by the studio to investigate, rather than just a call from the hospital? "I heard she died of a stroke," he said.

The boy shook his head vigorously. "I killed her. I prayed her to death."

Janet came over to where they were standing. She, too, appeared shaken by her recent experience, but she was determined to help. "You can't pray someone to death, Vinnie."

The boy looked up at her. His lower lip was out, pouting. "Yes I can. God answers all prayers, that's what she always said. I wanted her to die. I prayed to God, I prayed and prayed and prayed so hard He finally listened. He came and took her because I asked—and now He's going to punish me."

"Why did you want her dead?" Wayne asked.

The Rondel-child looked at him, his face contorted into a hideous mask of hatred. "I killed her. She wouldn't let me alone, she wouldn't let me play. She was always on me, always pushing me, always telling me not to do something. Vinnie, don't do this. Vinnie, don't do that. Vinnie's a bad boy, must punish bad Vinnie. Honor thy father and thy mother. Kill her. Always holding me, can't let me breathe. Push, push back. But I can't. Honor thy father and thy mother. I want to go out and play, but I can't. It's bad, they're all bad. Can't play. Honor thy mother. She won't let me go. I want to go, she won't let me. Honor thy mother. Let me breathe, please let me breathe. No. Bad Vinnie. Honor thy mother. No. Let me out. Please, let me out. God, please kill her. Please, God, please, oh please, please, please. Honor thy mother. Bad Vinnie. Please God, please kill her, make her dead, let me out, let me out, please, God, please." The boy collapsed into tears again.

Wayne was stunned by the vehement outburst, but Janet was more prepared to cope. Kneeling beside the weeping boy, she said, "It wasn't your prayers that made her dead, Vinnie. God takes everyone in His own time. He just decided now was the time to take your mother. Your prayers had nothing to do with it."

"But God always answers prayers," the boy sniffed. "She told me so."

"Yes," Janet said. "And I'll bet she also told you that sometimes the answer is 'No.'"

"He answered my prayers, and now I'll be punished," the boy insisted.

"How long were you praying for her to die?" Wayne asked.

"Years. Years and years and years and . . ."

"If God was going to kill her in answer to your prayers, He would have done it a long time ago. He was telling you 'No' all those years. But tonight it was just time for Him to take her. He didn't do it because of your prayers, He did it because it was her time to die."

213

"But I wanted her dead. I was bad. He'll punish me for that."

"Not if you ask Him for forgiveness," Janet said. "His mercy is infinite. If you pray to Him now, it will all be all right. Come on, I'll pray with you, we'll pray together." She cupped his tiny, trembling hands in hers. "Our Father . . . come on, say it with me, Vinnie. Our Father, Who art in Heaven . . ."

By the time they had gone through the Lord's Prayer, the boy was much calmer. He looked up at Janet and Wayne, and even managed a faint smile for them. Janet smiled back and tousled his hair. The boy yawned and lay back on the ground. He stuck a thumb in his mouth, curled into a fetal position and went peacefully to sleep.

Wayne breathed a slight sigh of relief. "I didn't know you were that religious," he whispered.

"I'm not—but Vince is," she replied. "I had to say things that would calm him, whether I believed them or not."

She looked back at the sleeping boy. "The problem's out in the open now. I don't think we cured it, but at least the doctors will know where to focus their attention. We've done all we can do in here."

She looked at Wayne for a brief instant, and quickly looked away. The memory of their personality merger was still too raw and recent. There was so much for both of them to assimilate. Neither wanted to talk about it.

Wayne nodded. "Then we'd better leave, before we wake him up again. I'll see you back in the real world."

Wayne waited until Janet had faded out of the Dream completely, so he knew she was safe. Now he was alone. He gave one last look at the child who had caused all the misery, now sleeping like a peaceful angel. Then, without regret, he faded himself out of the Dream and back into his real body.

CHAPTER 16

HE WAS NOT prepared for what he found when he woke. His body was a solid mass of throbbing pain from head to toe, particularly down the left side. He was awash in a sea of his own sweat, and the top of his scalp where the Dreamcap had rested felt embedded in lava. He tried to move, and found he couldn't. Even opening his eyes proved too great an effort. There were sounds and voices around him, but they all seemed terribly far away, as though at the wrong end of some auditory telescope. There was excitement, people moving quickly, and he could feel himself being lifted and carried somewhere, but that was the total extent of his awareness.

Funny, he thought, his intellect totally detached from his body. *In the Dream I was a god, I could do anything. Now, in real life, I can't do anything.*

He could feel himself being carried some more, and then he was moving rapidly in some sort of vehicle, but his mind became too fuzzy to recall more than that. Reality faded out just like the Dream had, and Wayne slid easily into a more natural, more wholesome sort of sleep.

He drifted in and out of consciousness dozens of times. Sometimes, though he never lifted his eyelids, he could tell there was light around him, and he heard the indistinct sounds of voices far away; at other times there was only darkness, and his bed was bathed in silence.

When he finally woke completely, there was a light-headed feeling to his brain that he couldn't seem to get rid of. Physically, his body seemed much better. The muscles were very stiff, but they did obey when he tried to stretch them. After some effort, he found he could open his eyes again, though he couldn't force them to focus properly. Everything had a blurry quality, like a nearsighted man's view without his glasses.

He was in a hospital room; there was no mistaking the institutional feel of the place. Everything around him was crisp and clean and smelled of disinfectant. There were baskets and vases full of flowers on the small table across from his bed and on the floor around the room's perimeter.

He must have been wired to some telemetry device, because a nurse poked her head in the door almost the instant he looked around. He gave her a feeble grin; she smiled back at him, then went to notify the doctors.

Within just a couple of minutes, a team of people arrived to look him over. They checked his pulse, respiration, eye dilation, neural reflexes, blood pressure, temperature and other functions. In between tests, he tried to ask them some questions. His tongue felt funny, like a lump of lead in his mouth, and he had trouble pronouncing some of the words, but he managed somehow to make himself understood. From the terse answers they gave, he pieced together something of what had happened.

His own brain activity had been greatly increased during the Dream, and coming out again had caused a slight overload of the neural circuits. The result was similar to a very mild stroke, and he'd been unconscious for the past three days. He might have to undergo some sessions of speech and motor rehabilitation, but the doctors all assured him that within several months, at the most, he would be as healthy as ever.

Just this minor activity completely exhausted him, and he fell back to sleep right after the doctors left. When next he woke, he was told he had a visitor.

The man who entered was short, with graying, closecut hair and a small mustache. He wore a conservative suit, tortoiseshell glasses, and an unreadable expression. Wayne had never seen him before, but could tell at a glance that the man would be a fantastic poker player; the face and eyes gave no indication of what was going on in the mind behind them.

"How do you do, Mr. Corrigan," the man said. "I'm Gerald Forsch."

"I've heard of you," Wayne said slowly, annoyed that his speech was still slurred.

"I imagine you have. First of all, I'd like to apologize for having to bother you while you're still so weak, but I have other business in Washington that's been put off for a couple of days, and I have to get back to it. We'll have more time to talk later, when you're fully recovered from your ordeal, but I did want to chat with you briefly now, to get some quick impressions of what happened. Would you mind talking to me—completely off the record?"

"I guess not. I don't have any other appointments."

"If I may say so, that was a magnificent thing you did, rescuing all those people from the Dream. You have the government's thanks, for whatever that's worth—and more importantly, you have the thanks of the people you saved. These flowers are all from them, and I'm told there are so many more the hospital refused to bring them all in. The story of what happened has been on the national news for the past few days. You've become something of a hero."

Wayne could think of no response that wasn't either flip or cynical, so he said nothing.

After a momentary silence, Forsch continued, "The accounts of what happened in the Dream are, of necessity, vague and confusing. Could you give me a rundown of what happened, as you saw it? Just a thumbnail sketch; I know you're ill. There'll be time for a more complete report later. I just have to know something for my own report."

Wayne summarized the events in the Dream as briefly as he could. Forsch listened attentively, making a few notes to himself occasionally. When Wayne had finished, the government man stared at his notepad for a few seconds before speaking again.

"I know that something of a reputation preceded me out here," he said. "I've made statements in the past that have been critical of the Dream broadcast industry, and they weren't calculated to win me any friends. The Spiegelman affair, and now the Rondel business, have emphasized the dangers inherent within your industry.

"I'm not an ogre, Mr. Corrigan. It's not my intention to come charging into Dreaming like Carry Nation into a saloon, swinging an axe and bringing the entire structure down. But I do have a legitimate concern for the public's safety. When you went into Rondel's Dream, you were trying to protect the audience as best you could, and you worked in the best way you knew how. That's all I'm trying to do. I'd like you to help me."

"I won't condemn the industry," Wayne said defiantly. "It means too much to me."

"I'm not trying to condemn it, necessarily," Forsch sighed. "But it has to be answerable to someone for what it does. We can't afford to have some other Dreamer go crazy and kill his audience before we can stop him. I'm a politician, I know the art of compromise. I'm willing to listen to reasonable solutions, as long as the public is protected.

"As I see it," he went on, "the problem lies in the fact that there's no way to know what a Dreamer will do before he does it. The ideal solution would be to tape Dreams and inspect them before broadcast—but we both know that's impossible. The experts tell me the technology to do that is still ten years away. In the meantime, a Dream has to be live, and the Dreamer has absolute power over what happens in it. In politics, we have a maxim about the corrupting influence that can have on somebody. As long as the Dreamer is in total control, the possibility remains that he may abuse his power."

"But if the Dreamer isn't in full control," Wayne argued, "you can't have a structured Dream. It wouldn't have any entertainment value, and you'd defeat the entire purpose."

"Do you have any suggestions?"

Wayne thought for a moment. "There are only two ways I can think of to limit a Dreamer's power. Either you limit the broadcast strength—which cuts down on the potential audience—or else make sure he isn't the only Dreamer in there."

"You mean have two Dreamers in there together, like when you and Rondel were both sharing power."

"Hopefully not like *that*. But yes, having two Dreamers in tandem does work. I've done it lots of times, so have most of us. It takes more manpower and a lot more coordination, but it can be done."

Forsch mused on the idea. "Two Dreamers in tandem, neither in total control, each able to check the other in case of accident. The odds against both of them cracking up at once are pretty high—and even if they did, they probably wouldn't both want to go in the same direction." He nodded. "Yes, it has distinct possibilities. I'll have to think about it and talk it over with some other people. I'll get back to you on it in a couple of weeks. If any other ideas come to you, just give me a call. Mort Schulberg has my Washington number. In the meantime, let me offer again my congratulations for a job well done."

After he'd gone, Wayne tried to put the meeting out of his mind so he could go back to sleep. He was perpetually tired, and a year-long nap would not have been out of order. He barely closed his eyes, however, when the nurse came in to ask whether he wanted to see two more visitors—Bill DeLong and Janet Meyers. Even as tired as he was, Wayne was delighted to see them.

"How's the hero?" DeLong asked as he escorted Janet into the room.

"Dreadful," Wayne said. "If I ever want to be a hero again, talk me out of it." He became a little more serious. "How's Vince?"

"He's worse off than you are, if that's any consolation," Janet said. "In fact, he's in the room just a couple of doors down. He's so weak he can hardly move or speak, and so high-strung that the slightest thing will send him into crying jags. Like you, he sweated off a lot of weight. The doctors say he may never fully recover from the shock to his system—and he'll never be able to Dream again, even if his license weren't revoked."

Janet didn't have to underline that last statement. That, more than anything else, would be Rondel's real punishment. A Dreamer lived to create his own realities and express them through Dreams. It became a reason for his very existence. To shut him off, to forbid him to Dream, was like chopping the wings off an eagle and telling it to hop for the rest of its life, never to know the freedom of the skies again. For a Dreamer of Rondel's caliber, not to Dream was to be sentenced to a worse Hell than Rondel himself could have imagined.

He changed the subject. "How's the studio?"

"Quiet," DeLong said. "The whole thing's been shut down."

"Everything?"

"And not just us," Janet said. "The whole Dream industry, all across the country. All shut down, just like that. Didn't Forsch tell you?"

"No, he didn't mention that," Wayne said.

DeLong gave a chuckle. "Yeah. He was probably afraid that, sick as you were, you'd hop off your bed to strangle him. I'm afraid our boy Vince has caused a national uproar. Lawsuits are rolling in, particularly from women—and from what you told me, they're all justified. But I don't know where the money's going to come from. Dramatic Dreams will probably have to fold. Everyone's afraid, no one knows quite what to do. And in the meantime, we've got an entire industry in suspension. Everybody's out of work until Forsch and his friends decide how they want us to go."

Wayne told them about the conversation he'd had with the man from the FCC, including his suggestion that Dreams be done in tandem from now on and Forsch's positive response.

DeLong was not as optimistic. "Well, it's easy enough for him to say—but knowing the government, it'll be another six months at least before we get an official opinion from them. In the meantime, with no more Dreams to write, I'll have to earn some honest money for a change."

He looked at Wayne cagily. "You're the one positive thing the industry has going for it—a genuine hero. You've been in all the papers and all the newscasts. People love you almost as much as they hate Vince. Tell you what. Don't sell the rights to your story to anyone else. Let me ghost it for you and we'll both make a fortune."

"It's a deal," Wayne laughed. The two men shook on it, and then DeLong excused himself, leaving Wayne alone with Janet.

For a long time they were both afraid to speak, or even to look directly at one another. Finally Wayne asked, "How are you doing?"

"Pretty good," Janet said. "I was a bit shaken when I woke up, but I didn't have to put out nearly as much energy as you did. I'm fine now."

"Good." And then, before he could stop himself, he blurted out, "I meant it all, Janet. Everything I showed you. There was nothing fake there. It was all real."

"I know." Her voice was so soft he could barely hear it. "You couldn't have faked what I saw in there—anymore than I could have faked what you saw. We've both been through something pretty spectacular."

"For two people who know so many intimate details about one another, we're being awfully shy, aren't we?"

Janet shrugged, and gave him a half-smile. "I don't know what the custom is from this point."

"I love you, Janet."

"I . . . I love you too, Wayne." She reached down and put her hand on his for a moment, then just as suddenly turned away. "But that all seems so much beside the point, now. We're both out of a job, the whole Dreaming industry may be dead. How can two Dreamers

221

live without Dreaming? What kind of future will there be for people like us?"

"It'll be whatever kind of future we make it." Four days ago, this news might have depressed him as badly as it was now depressing her. But after what he'd gone through in the Dream, after what he'd seen of himself and his abilities, the future held no unsolvable terrors. He had confidence in himself, now—enough to know that *he* would be the ultimate shaper of his dreams in real life as well.

"I know the outlook is bad right now," he continued, "but it won't stay this way. No one can stop technology once it arrives; they can only slow it down. Things will start up in another six months or so. The public wants Dreaming as much as we do. We'll just have to prove to them we can do it more safely than we did it before.

"Why do you think I suggested tandem Dreams to Forsch? It was so I could get a chance to work with you some more. We're a team now. We proved it, there in the Dream. Together, you and I, there's no obstacle we can't overcome."

He reached out and took her hand again, pulling her toward him. She bent over him and they kissed . . . and all thoughts of the future were lost in an everlasting present.

GREAT ADVENTURES IN READING

NEW FROM FAWCETT CREST